Janet Edmond ... ... was
educated at Portsmouth High School. She
moved to Oxfordshire in 1967 and taught English and History in three of the county's compre-
hensive schools, becoming Head of English in
one of them. With the publication of her first
two historical romances, she decided writing
was more fun and now writes full-time. A
breeder, exhibitor and judge of pedigree dogs,
her Cotswold home is run for the benefit of the
Alaskan Malamutes and German Spitz that are
her speciality and her *History and Management
of the Alaskan Malamute* has been described as
the definitive work on that breed.

SMALL EDMONDS

JANET EDMONDS

Dog's Body

To Carol —

Happy reading

Janet Edmonds

FONTANA/Collins

First published in Great Britain by
William Collins Sons & Co. Ltd 1988

First published in Fontana Paperbacks 1989

Copyright © Janet Edmonds 1988

'Highnoons' is the author's own registered kennel affix

Phototypeset by Input Typesetting Ltd, London
Made and Printed in Great Britain by
William Collins Sons & Co. Ltd, Glasgow

Chapter One

Linus Rintoul sat and stared at Elias Ashmole and Elias Ashmole stared back, as he always did. It was, Linus thought, a face worthy of consideration. There was a determination about the mouth and chin which the outward indications of good living had failed to blur, yet the determination and strength of character that had forced the University to build a museum to house his collection or forfeit the chance of owning that collection, had not affected the man's fundamental humanity, a humanity that was reflected in his eyes. Elias Ashmole was someone Linus Rintoul would have liked to meet.

A woman came in and his attention was drawn away from the portrait. He studied her appreciatively. He could look at Elias whenever he wanted to. Beautiful women were rare. This one was tall, he noted with some regret, being only of middle height himself. She was also exceedingly elegant. There was nothing flamboyant about her appearance. It was understated and well-groomed and in some indefinable way it left the onlooker under no misapprehensions about the state of her bank balance – or her husband's. He found himself looking at her shoes. What was it his mother had always said? His wife, too? 'You can always tell a lady by her shoes.' If that was a valid criterion, then this was undoubtedly a lady, whatever that might be these days. The ankles above the shoes were pretty good, too, and the legs they belonged to seemed to go a long way up. He found himself willing her to turn round so that he could confirm his first impression but she seemed more interested in Hester Tradescant in her demure Puritan collar.

She passed Elias with scarcely a glance and stood before the more unusual portrait of Hester's son, John, bearded in a clean-shaven age, but then she redeemed herself in Linus's estimation by returning to Elias. As she left the Founder's Room, she glanced at its only other occupant, the man sitting on the circular, leather-covered seat behind her. She smiled fleetingly at him, as one smiles at strangers with whom one has the fragile bond of a briefly shared interest. The dark hair swept gracefully back in a smooth chignon reminiscent of a ballet dancer framed a face that was all Linus had thought it was – and more. His first impression had been one of sheer beauty. The thing that struck him now was that it wasn't a modern sort of beauty. It was a medieval face. It was a face that would have looked entirely at home in a Leonardo. He rather thought it conjured up one particular sitter but she was gone before he could decide which. Ah well, what did it matter? There would certainly be a rich husband in the background and even if there wasn't, she would want to look a bit further than the likes of Linus Rintoul.

He had no right to be here, of course. It was about time he inspected that halal slaughter-house. He grimaced to himself. It was legal but that didn't mean he liked it. Maybe, once upon a time, it had been the most humane way to slaughter livestock. It almost certainly had been, along with kosher slaughter, but it wasn't any more and he didn't like it for that reason. Still, while the law allowed it, all he could do was see to it that it was carried out correctly. He was neither squeamish nor religious and he could see no reason why religion rather than humanity should dictate the way a cow died – or anything else. He didn't care two hoots what happened to the carcase once the animal was dead, it was the manner of its death that was important and ritual slaughter offended him. Tomorrow. He'd do it tomorrow. He'd spent so much of the afternoon here already that he might as well stay a bit longer. At least the place was nearly empty. When it was like this, he could almost believe it was his. Catherine the Great must have felt like this in her Hermitage with only her mice for company. He smiled to himself. Delusions of grandeur, that's what's wrong with you, my lad, he told himself.

He turned to the other portrait of John Tradescant, the one that showed him leaning on his shovel, enjoyment apparent in every feature. They must have been quite a family, these Tradescants. Like magpies they had foraged all over the known world, bringing their eclectic treasure trove back to their nest before passing it on to Elias. The contents of their collection interested Linus not at all. What fascinated him was the faces.

'Excuse me.' A melodious voice behind him broke into his thoughts. The woman had returned and was addressing him. Linus stood up. As he had suspected, she was slightly taller than he but perhaps it was her high heels. Without them they would have been on the same level, perhaps. 'This is a confusing place,' she went on. 'I'm looking for Powhatan's mantle. I promised a friend in the States I'd go and see it but I can't find it anywhere.'

Linus nodded towards the doorway beside John Tradescant and his shovel. 'Through there,' he said. 'The Tradescant collection's in that little room. You can't miss the mantle: it's straight in front of you.'

She thanked him and he watched her cover the short distance to the exhibit she sought. He sighed. The voice matched everything else. Melodious, well-bred, slightly husky and entirely self-confident. He watched her study the mantle and then read the explanatory label that effectively dismissed most of the legends surrounding it. She looked at the mantle again and then cast a cursory glance around the rest of the collection. When she came out again, she wrinkled her nose.

'I expected it to be all coloured beads and leather fringes,' she said.

'Wrong sort of Indian, I think,' Linus told her. 'Wrong century, too, in all probability.'

'Is this your field?' she asked, her head managing to indicate every picture in the room.

Linus chuckled. 'Hardly. No, I just like the faces. Look

at them,' he went on, taking her arm and leading her over to John, forgetting that they were strangers. 'Look at him. He collected all those odds and ends in there. Look at his mother. Does she look like a woman who traipsed all over the world with her husband and children, encouraging them all to dig things up, bargain in the market-place, bring everything home? No railways, no trucks, no planes. No effective defences against cholera, typhoid, plague or anything else. Yet she went and her son carried on where his father left off and if his face is anything to go by, he enjoyed every minute of it. What sort of a man do you think he must have been to allow himself to be painted with his shirt open and his sleeves rolled up, leaning on a shovel?'

She nodded. 'I see what you mean. Unusual – and you're right: his mother looks as if the furthest she ever went was down the lane to church.'

Linus led her to the adjacent wall. 'And these two. Look at them. Charles II made it possible for the Tradescants to do what they did and his brother here helped Elias. Look at those faces. Both from the same litter. The similarities are obvious but look at the differences. There's nothing of the Merry Monarch in Charles's face, you know. It's the face of a world-weary cynic but a shrewd one, one who knows how to use the world to his own ends. James here is a very different case. Discontented, sour, mean-spirited. No wonder he had to go.'

The woman studied the two faces and then turned to Linus, smiling. 'Do you know, I've walked round museums and art galleries all round the world and all I've seen has been rows of faces. I've never seen the character behind them before. I'll never look at a portrait that way again.' She looked at him curiously. 'You've been in this room for a long time this afternoon. What's its particular attraction?'

Linus shrugged dismissively. He felt a bit of a fool trying to explain to this extraordinarily beautiful woman what brought him here. 'It's partly the people – Ashmole and the Tradescants,' he said. 'They're people I wish I could

8

have known. They'd have been interesting company. But it's more than that. Three hundred years ago, they were beavering about, putting together a peculiar assortment of curiosities (none of which I find particularly exciting, I must admit). It isn't even a very large assortment – at least, not by today's standards though it represents a mammoth achievement in seventeenth-century terms. What fascinates me is not just that that assortment is still here, but that the foresight of one man – Elias, here – made it the foundation of a great museum and, above all, a museum that the public could enjoy. That, for my money, puts Elias Ashmole in a class of his own. It's not just the size it's all grown to, it's the originality of thought. Millionaires do it all the time nowadays but he was the one who thought of it first. Anyone not born in the purple who enjoys great paintings and sculpture, furniture and ceramics but can't afford them owes him quite a debt. He's the man who started the ball rolling.'

She laughed. 'When I came in, I thought you were some studious academic who would resent being interrupted. You're really quite human.'

Linus felt it might be wiser not to inquire whether this observation was entirely complimentary. One thing was certain: the ice was broken. Maybe the time had come to step into the water, even if he risked being frozen.

'I'm human enough to feel hungry from time to time,' he said. 'I don't suppose you'd join me for tea across the road?'

The smile told him that the water was distinctly warm. 'I'd love to,' she said.

Linus took her arm and led her through the French bronzes, down the stairs and out on to the steps in the autumn sunshine. 'By the way, I'm Linus Rintoul,' he told her.

'Clarissa Pensilva,' she said and he groaned inwardly. Clarissa! Couldn't she be a Margaret or a Susan or a Jane? His wife used to take the *Tatler*. She liked to kid herself she knew the people who recurred on its pages. They had names like Clarissa and Henrietta and Charlotte and they sat on the stairs at hunt balls with men called Piers and Peregrine. He sometimes wondered if she had married him because he was called Linus Rintoul and not John Brown. Or maybe she had thought that the ambitious wife of a young vet might, with a bit of careful husband-shoving, end up on one of those staircases herself. She'd have done better to pick a husband by his ambition instead of going for one whose name would have looked good in the *Tatler*, he thought bitterly. They had been divorced a long time but many memories still rankled.

He shepherded Clarissa across the road to St Pancras's sister, the Randolph, and into another world. He didn't come here very often and didn't want to, but when he did, he enjoyed it. The hushed, over-furnished comfort of a Victorian hotel where service and presentation still mattered was a welcome change, an oasis of bourgeoisie in a desert of McDonalds and pizza parlours and Golden Eggs. He ate at all these other places often enough: they were quick and clean and the food filled you up but they weren't strong on atmosphere and sometimes atmosphere mattered. This was one of those times.

He helped Clarissa out of her coat and noticed, when she removed her gloves, that she wore no wedding-ring. His spirits lifted two or three notches and he indicated the jade-green edifice soaring ceilingwards in the centre of the lounge.

'Do you want to sit on it or look at it?' he asked.

'Sit on it,' she said without hesitation. 'It's so much easier to talk on those curved seats than side by side on a sofa.'

He was pleased and not only because of the hint of conversational intimacy. One of the joys of the Randolph, in his opinion, was its traditional English afternoon tea. Another was this quite extraordinary example of Victorian opulence. It was an insult to call it a seat, an understatement to call it furniture. A huge mahogany-framed concave-sided triangle, each side upholstered and button-backed, was surmounted by three identical, decently-draped but

10

unmistakably nubile nymphs who should have been carved from marble but weren't. At each of the three angles, above the heads of those sitting below, rose a double-branched lamp, its upturned globe illuminating its nearest maiden.

He ordered tea. 'You're not local?' he asked.

'No. London. You are, I take it?'

'I work here. I grew up in Bristol.'

She smiled. 'That explains the burr. What do you do?'

'I'm a vet,' he told her. It was true and put that briefly, it always seemed less off-putting than saying he was a sort of government busybody, which was how some people regarded his job.

She looked at him with renewed interest and again he had the feeling that he could identify her face if only the recollection would come out of the shadows. 'You don't look like one,' she said.

'What does a vet look like?'

She thought about that. 'I don't know. I've never met one with quite such well-cut clothes before – or so neat a beard. I like it,' she added inconsequentially.

'Just my own little vanity,' he said. 'I promise you, the green wellies and the overalls, not to mention the Barbours, are all in the boot of the car. You've met a number of vets?'

A hint of something that might almost have been evasiveness flickered briefly in her eyes. 'Not really. One bumps into them from time to time, you know, just as one bumps into accountants. You look more like an accountant, as a matter of fact.'

'And what do you do?' He glanced down at her hand. 'You're not married?'

'No, I'm not. I run a little business – that's why I live in London.'

'It's presumably why you know what accountants look like,' he commented. 'Let me guess. You run a small fashion house. What do they call them these days? A boutique.'

'Not at all. I'm a sort of clearing-house. I facilitate import-export arrangements.'

11

'I always thought they were run by crooks!' he exclaimed involuntarily and hastened to make amends for so ill-judged a remark. 'I'm sorry. That was uncalled for. If it's any comfort, you don't look the least like a crook.'

She didn't seem unduly annoyed. 'Good,' she replied. 'Mind you, I don't think my business would thrive if I did. And you – are you married?'

Linus was happy to accept the change of subject. 'Not any more. Not for some years.'

'Do you mind?'

'Not really. I've got used to being on my own and I can always find plenty to do. That was one of the problems: I was never there.'

Clarissa laid a hand on his arm and there was the hint of a smile on her lips. 'I don't imagine you're obliged to be on your own if you don't want to be,' she said. 'You're an attractive man.'

Whether it was the half-smile or the hand that triggered his memory, Linus was never quite sure, but suddenly he knew her face. The similarity to one of Leonardo's sitters was no fanciful imagining. Clarissa Pensilva was the *Lady with an Ermine*. He felt a twinge of disappointment, almost of distaste. The beautiful features were very slightly sharp, there was a hint of that reserve which is closer to secrecy than to modesty in her eyes and her soft, white, beautifully manicured hand rested gently on his arm in an utterly feminine gesture that faintly whispered the paw of Leonardo's stoat.

He mentally shook himself. He spent too much time looking at pictures, reading into them things that weren't there and now it was spilling over into the real world. He smiled at her. 'Flattery will get you everywhere,' he said, knowing it sounded fatuous and longing for the ability to be witty. 'Does that mean I can ask you to have lunch with me tomorrow without risking a rebuff?'

Before she had time to answer, one of the hotel's smartly coated porters came over and coughed discreetly behind his glove. 'Miss Pensilva?'

Clarissa nodded.

He handed her a slip of paper. 'There was a call for you. The receptionist took a message.'

She thanked him and glanced at the piece of paper before slipping it into her bag.

'I hadn't realized you were staying here,' Linus said. 'You should have said. I could so easily have taken you somewhere else.'

'But I like the Randolph,' she protested. 'I was perfectly happy to be brought here. If I hadn't been, I should have said so – and, yes, Linus, I'd love to have lunch with you.'

'Half past twelve? I'll pick you up here.'

She shook her head. 'I've a busy morning in front of me. Could we make it one o'clock?'

'One o'clock it is, then.' He got to his feet. 'Till tomorrow,' he said. 'I look forward to it.'

He paid the bill and made his way to the back street where he had managed to find a space to park his car, a lightness in his step that certainly hadn't been there when he had entered the Ashmolean earlier.

Linus Rintoul was no admirer of the celibate state but he was no spring chicken, either. He had watched acquaintances drop their middle-aged wives in favour of bright young things, secretaries or newly appointed colleagues, and wondered with more than a touch of envy how they did it. He had a sneaking feeling that if he tried to chat up one of the girls in Government Buildings, she'd dismiss him as a dirty old man. As for those rejected middle-aged wives, the catalogue of complaints that was their substitute for conversation was enough to send any man into a monastery.

He knew that what he had been looking for was a woman like Clarissa: mature – he guessed her age to be somewhere between twenty-eight and thirty – poised, elegant, intelligent and with the self-confidence bred of independence. Such women must exist but they seldom came the way of a mere Veterinary Officer. She had said he was an attractive man but that was a compliment he took with a large pinch of salt. If it were true, he would not still be single. As a vet, he was something of an eccentric and he couldn't deny this was an image he had tended to work at, especially since his divorce. He had nurtured the small, neatly-trimmed beard and eschewed the shapeless flannels and well-worn sports jackets adopted by most of his profession. His love of fine art was his great indulgence and he supposed was his greatest source of joy since he had been on his own. Most people regarded it as another facet of his eccentricity and he was perfectly content for them to do so.

Now, quite unexpectedly, Clarissa Pensilva had walked into his life. Don't exaggerate, he warned himself. All she's done so far is brush up against it. She was here on business and knew no one. That was why she had been prepared to accept his invitation instead of offering the usual excuses of washing her hair or having promised a friend whatever it was women promised their friends. Excuses Linus had heard so often that he had come to regard them as the inevitable consequence of any invitation he uttered. The fact that Clarissa had used none of them made him feel good – better than the fact warranted. They would have lunch and perhaps, if she was going to be in Oxford for a few more days, he might be able to persuade her to have dinner with him. Possibly a show. If that went well, if he didn't blow it with some tactless remark, well, London wasn't impossibly far off, was it? You're jumping ahead again, he reminded himself. You haven't even had lunch together yet. She may find you a total bore.

Where could he take her? He'd made up his mind to tackle the halal slaughterhouse tomorrow and if he put it off again, he would despise himself for evading his responsibilities when they became irksome. He also had some paperwork to catch up on. Lunch tomorrow could not become an indefinitely extended meal and he didn't want to spend half the available time escorting Clarissa there and back. For the same reason, he must avoid those trendy haute cuisine places that punctuated each course with a long interval. It looked like the Mitre: a cut above the average pub and a straightforward, unpretentious menu. It seemed terribly important to him to strike exactly the right note. Besides, it was well patronized and he'd be very happy to be seen there with someone like Clarissa Pensilva. Any man would, the Leonardo connection notwithstanding. Not that most of them would have noticed it.

He turned his car off the main road, over the bridge and on to Osney Island, concentrating on negotiating the narrow streets without knocking down some footballing youngster waiting for its mother to come home and feed it. He drew up outside his front door and frowned. He wished that similarity to the Leonardo portrait hadn't struck him. It made him recall the one or two instances where she had been a bit secretive. Not that there was any reason why she should be entirely open with a complete stranger. Still, it was there. He wondered why she hadn't said, as he guided her across the road and into the hotel, 'Oh, I'm staying here,' or something like that. Most people would have done, surely? Then there was the compliment which, to his ears, smacked more of flattery than sincerity, but perhaps he was unduly sensitive on the subject. Finally there was that odd and entirely inexplicable feeling that her acquaintance with his profession was greater than she would have him think, though why she should wish to be reticent on the subject was beyond him.

This was ridiculous. An hour in the company of a very attractive woman and he was allowing himself to become this intense. It was a pleasant acquaintance, that was all. Don't read into it more than there is. If you do, you'll blow it. He climbed out of the car and locked it and when his front door closed behind him, he was back in his own world.

Osney Island was a little enclave of nineteenth-century artisans' terraced cottages. When Linus had come here after his wife had left him, it was seedy and rundown, but he had always thought these little houses had a character quite lacking in many more impressive ones. Now they

15

were being snapped up by young left-wing trendies with little spare cash but plenty of ideas, not necessarily original ones. Linus could see little point in putting Madonna-blue walls and coral ceilings in such small rooms. He put style before fashion. Style and comfort. But above all, he put his pictures first and everything in the house was subordinate to them.

The few colleagues and the occasional friend who visited expected to see reproductions of *Sunflowers* or *The Haywain* on the walls – after all, Linus went to all those exhibitions, so you'd expect him only to hang Old Masters, wouldn't you? They couldn't understand that a carefully chosen original by a lesser artist was more satisfying than a mechanical reproduction of something famous. Linus did not 'collect'. He bought what appealed to him and there were as many pictures by modern artists as by those long dead. His criteria were simple: Did he like it? Would he go on looking at it? Could he afford it? There were no furnishing pictures in Linus's house – no pictures chosen to look good with the décor as a whole. The colour of the walls, the placing of the lights, were designed to enhance the pictures and the few comfortable and discreet pieces of furniture had been chosen because they would not distract the eye from what really mattered. Linus felt a warm affection for this little cottage and only here did he ever really relax.

Chapter Two

It was nearly midnight when the phone rang. Linus almost didn't answer it: no one with any consideration for others phoned at this sort of time. The ringing persisted, making him wish he'd unplugged it before he settled down with a book and his cocoa. Doubt began to gnaw at his irritation. What if it was urgent? He picked it up.

'Rintoul here.'

'Dad? I haven't got you out of bed, have I?' His son sounded anxious and impatient.

'Not quite but it's an ungodly hour to be ringing. What's the matter?'

'I'm worried, Dad. I need your advice. Your help, too, probably.'

Linus looked at his watch and resisted the temptation to sigh. 'You'd better come round, then.'

'I can't. Not tonight. Not now.'

'I suppose that means I've got to come out to you. Where are you?'

There was a hesitation at the other end of the line. 'Right now I'm at the John Radcliffe but as soon as I put the phone down, I'm going to the Churchill.'

Any annoyance Linus felt was replaced by alarm at the mention of two of the city's hospitals. 'What's happened, Sean? Have you been in an accident? Is anyone else hurt?'

Sean's laugh was short and forced. 'No, Dad. I know you've always predicted that my old banger will end me up in a ditch, but it's not that. It's to do with a friend who's in some trouble. That's where you can help.'

'Have you thought of trying this friend's parents?' Linus said, his annoyance returning as the alarm subsided. 'They're the ones you need to get hold of, not me.'

'They're already here but they're just ordinary people. They'll have no idea what's involved. In fact, I'd rather they didn't get the chance to talk to you just yet. I don't think it would help. They'd just be terrified.'

'For God's sake, Sean, what's this all about? Have you – or this friend of yours – got involved in the drug scene? If you have, you're bloody fools. That doesn't mean I won't help but you'll get precious little sympathy.'

'No, Dad, it's not that, I promise you. Look, I must go. Can I come round first thing in the morning?'

'I'll be at the office at nine. That's not far from the Churchill if you're going to be spending the night there.'

'Not the office. Too many of the wrong sort of ears. What

17

about the Covered Market? We could have breakfast there. I'll be about ready for a good meal.'

'All right. Let's say eight o'clock. Brown's?' Linus found himself disproportionately relieved to learn that his son's lifelong obsession with food had apparently not been affected by current events, whatever they might prove to be.

'OK – and, Dad: don't worry. There's really no need. At least, not so far as I'm concerned.'

Linus heard the click that cleared the line and replaced his own handset thoughtfully. What was all that about? Not an accident and not drugs, apparently. Presumably it wasn't the police, either, if Sean had been calling from a hospital. What else was there to worry about? What other difficulties might a twenty-year-old student get into that needed his father's advice? More particularly, perhaps, why should that son require his father's advice on behalf of a friend?

Linus finished his cocoa and carried his mug into the kitchen, filling it with cold water to stand till morning. Of course, people often talked about 'a friend' when what they really wanted was to find out something that affected themselves without the listener realizing it. He dismissed that. The bit about the friend's parents had the ring of truth. He turned the flap of the dust-jacket into the page he had been reading and replaced the volume methodically in its place on the shelf. 'A place for everything and everything in its place,' his mother had taught him. As a child it had irritated him. Now it was automatic. It had irritated his wife, too. He looked around the room before turning off the light. It was a principle which had the merit of leaving the house relatively tidy. If his desk at work was anything to go by, tidiness did not come naturally to him.

He undressed and cleaned his teeth, experiencing his usual quiet glow of satisfaction that, at forty-eight, they were all his own. He climbed into bed, set the alarm and turned off the light. If he were meeting Sean at eight, he'd better waste no more time. It looked as if he would need to be wide awake right from tomorrow's start, and that was not his custom.

He soon discovered that, while he had been feeling suitably sleepy before Sean's call, that conversation had effectively destroyed the inclination. Why had Sean been so irritatingly vague, leaving his mind nothing to get to grips with? He supposed it should be some comfort that the boy had actually turned to him. Sean was very attached to his mother and had always blamed Linus for the fact that she left, taking both Sean and Jessica with her. 'You drove her out,' Sean had said once, resentfully, accusingly, unwilling to listen to anything that might moderate his opinion.

Jessica had been older, more comprehending, and now she was married and had children of her own. Sean, several years the younger, was the cleverer of the two and, although he was now at Balliol reading engineering, of all unlikely disciplines for so venerable an institution, Linus doubted if he had seen him more than two or three times – and one of those had been an accidental encounter in Blackwell's.

Pondering his relationship with his son, digressing into thoughts of what might have happened if . . . and the recurring anxiety about what lay behind the phone call, all conspired to drive sleep further and further away until Linus knew there was only one thing to do. Pretend it didn't matter. Go downstairs and have a bowl of cereal followed by a largish brandy and return to bed with a ballpoint and the crossword.

When the alarm smashed through his dreamless sleep, he found the light was still on.

Sean was there when his father arrived and Linus was slightly relieved to see that he was already tucking into a plate of bacon and eggs. More worrying was the boy's appearance. He looked drawn and haggard. He hadn't shaved for a couple of days and Linus suspected that last night wasn't the first he'd slept in those particular clothes if, indeed, he had slept at all in the last twenty-four hours. Looking at him, it seemed unlikely.

Linus ordered his own breakfast and sat down opposite his son.

'Tell me about it,' he said.

'It's my girlfriend,' Sean began, 'Gail, her name is. Gail Thatcham.'

Linus groaned. 'Let me guess. You've got her into trouble.'

Sean flushed angrily. 'Isn't that just like you? Jumping to the nastiest conclusion you can find! Last night it was drugs. This morning it's pregnancy.'

'So far you've told me nothing calculated to allay any fears,' Linus pointed out reasonably. 'All I've had from you has been a midnight call conveying all sorts of vague hints of disaster coupled with an instruction not to worry. Now you produce a girlfriend apparently connected with these non-worrying disasters. What do you expect me to think?'

'I am twenty. There's no reason why I shouldn't have a girlfriend,' Sean said defensively.

'I'm not suggesting there is.' Linus hoped he sounded more patient than he felt. 'Now, if I keep my mouth shut, will you tell me exactly what the problem is? I conclude she isn't in foal.'

'Of course she isn't. We're neither of us that naïve.' His tone was scornful and Linus found himself rather shocked that his son had grown up more than he had realized. 'She's ill, Dad. She felt very low on Saturday and took the day off. She was very depressed and that made her irritable. I suggested she had a couple of aspirins and went to bed but she couldn't settle. On Sunday she was worse, if anything. It looked a bit like 'flu and her throat seemed to hurt. She said it was difficult to swallow. I insisted on getting the doctor. Miserable sod! He didn't want to come out at all, said it could wait till Monday. Anyway, I managed to convince him and when he saw her I think he was quite worried. He gave her some antibiotics and came back in the evening, so he must have been. She wasn't any better. Worse, in fact, and he rang for an ambulance to take her to the John Radcliffe. I went with her – she didn't want to

20

go there without me. Once she was settled there, I went back to college but I was at the JR again first thing on Monday morning, even though I knew they most likely wouldn't let me see her. They'd said the night before that they'd be doing tests most of the day. When I got there, they seemed quite pleased to see me. Apparently Gail had been too feverish to give them the information they needed on their confounded forms and I got the impression she hadn't improved during the night. Anyway, I told them what I could and when I told them where she worked, there was a sort of heavy pause and Sister asked me what I'd said, almost, but not quite, as if she hadn't heard me first time. Then she said, "Excuse me a moment," and I heard her telling a nurse to bleep Dr Gopal. Then she came back and went on as if nothing had happened. I remember her words. She said, "Sorry about that. Something I just remembered," but I had the feeling it was said as much to avoid alarming me as out of politeness.'

Linus interrupted him. 'As a matter of curiosity, where does Gail work?'

Sean looked him straight in the eye. 'Towards Enstone,' he said. 'She's a kennelmaid at the Highnoon Quarantine Kennels.'

'I see. Go on.' Now things were slotting into place. Linus knew why his son had got in touch with him.

'Dr Gopal's an Indian. She asked me if I knew whether Gail had been bitten at any time in the last two months. I knew then what they were thinking. I said I didn't know. All I did know was that she'd certainly been wearing a piece of Elastoplast on her hand a week or so ago but I didn't think anything of it and I didn't ask her about it. She asked me to be more exact: precisely when had I seen it? When I calculated back, she shook her head. She said it was on the outside edges of possibility. I said, "You think it might be rabies, don't you?" I don't think she liked the direct question. She said they didn't know what it was. She said the symptoms almost fitted a number of things but didn't quite fit any of them exactly, but that wasn't necessarily significant because it often happened like that. On the other hand, once they knew where she worked, another possibility presented itself and it *did* fit the symptoms. She said the shortest known incubation period was ten days, so nine was pushing it. Usually it was more like six or seven weeks, by which time the dog would be dead and the kennels would have sent its head to the Ministry. I told her Gail hadn't mentioned a dog dying and I think she would have done: she got very attached to them, you know.'

'The kennelmaids often do,' his father told him. He became increasingly aware that his son was making a very conscious effort to go on talking in as matter-of-fact a voice as he could manage, trying to erase from it the emotion he felt so that Linus should be presented with dispassionate facts.

'She went back into the ward then and she and the Sister had a look at Gail's hands. I could see them through the window in the door of the ward. Then Sister came out and shut herself in her office and I think she was telephoning but I couldn't make out what she was saying. When she emerged, she called a couple of nurses and they wheeled Gail's bed into a little side ward. I asked Dr Gopal what was going on and she hesitated a bit and then said they'd found a puncture mark on her hand and were isolating Gail to be on the safe side. She asked me if I knew whether Gail had kept up her boosters of Diploid vaccine each year.'

'Had she?'

Sean shook his head. 'She'd never had it in the first place. She had tetanus jabs because she reckoned that was quite a real risk but, as she said, there's been no case of rabies in quarantine since 1970, so what was the point?'

Linus snorted. 'Silly girl! As it happens, that's not entirely true, though it's what's usually put out. Even if it were true, it's a remarkably foolish risk to take. It looks as if she didn't report the bite, either. If she had done, she could have had the vaccination then, before the symptoms showed.'

'That's what I wanted to ask you, Dad. Is it true that once there are symptoms, it's too late to do anything?'

Linus hesitated. He would have given almost anything to be able to wipe out the agony from his son's face. 'Yes,' he said. 'I'm afraid it is.'

'Then, if it is rabies, she'll die.'

'Yes.'

'When?'

'It depends. You'd really need to ask the doctors. Not long, though. A matter of two or three days, I think.'

'I saw some film once of Africans with rabies. They'd put them in cages, like wild animals.'

'Rabies attacks the nervous system. Sufferers go into wild convulsions that are potentially very dangerous to anyone near them. But don't worry. They won't cage Gail. Once she gets to that stage, they'll give her barbiturates to quieten the convulsions.' He leant across the table and patted his son's hand. 'Don't despair yet. We're not sure that's what it is.'

'I don't think they're in much doubt about it. They moved her to the Churchill last night. The John Waring ward.'

'Just a precaution,' Linus told him. That was true enough but it wasn't a good omen. 'What we've got to do now is find out which dog it was. I haven't heard of any being reported and I'd have expected it to have died by now. Isn't Highnoon the kennel with all the Pit Bulls?'

'Those things? Yes, but Gail didn't have anything to do with them except when their regular girl was off. The Highnoon specializes in quarantining them. Some kennels do that, Gail says. Specialize in one sort of dog or another, I mean, though most of them don't stick exclusively to one breed. Nasty things.'

'Vicious, you mean? Do you think it might have been one of them that bit her?'

Sean looked surprised. 'Oh no, I didn't mean that. In fact Gail always said they seemed very friendly. It's just that they rip each other apart, given half a chance, and some people enjoy watching it.'

'You can hardly blame the dogs for that,' his father pointed out.

'I suppose not,' Sean said absently. It didn't seem a terribly important point right now. 'What happens next?'

Linus looked at his watch. 'As soon as the office opens, the Health Authority will get on to the Ministry. I've got a slight head start: quarter of an hour in terms of time and I've already got the background facts. First I make a phone call. Then I'll take you to the Churchill and ask my own questions. We've got to find out which dog it was before they make her permanently woozy on barbiturates.'

'She wasn't in a condition to answer questions last night,' Sean said doubtfully.

'She'll have lucid periods,' his father replied. 'That's what's so terrible about rabies: the sufferer knows what's happening to him. I want to know which dog it was, whether she's reported it and what's happened to the dog – if she knows. We'll check it with the kennels later. Now, where's there a phone? I've that call to make. I'll contact the office from the Churchill.'

Linus felt sneakingly guilty that, in the midst of a crisis such as that facing his son – not to mention the Department of Animal Health – he could think about his lunch date with Clarissa. He wasn't going to be able to keep it, of course. It was out of the question. The chances were that what had just come up was going to keep him fully occupied for the time being. He didn't want her to think she'd been stood up, though. That mattered to him terribly. One of the things his wife had hated most was the sudden emergencies of the job: the call in the middle of the night, the interrupted dinner-party. That was why he had, with some regrets, given up private practice in favour of the nine-to-five hours of a civil servant. Even so, it hadn't saved the marriage. He didn't make as much money and she decided it had less prestige, so she had still been dissatisfied.

He called the Randolph and was put through to Clarissa.

He would have to be vague. It was hardly in the public interest to bandy words like 'rabies' around at this stage. He was relieved when she laughed.

'I'm glad you phoned,' she said. 'I was wondering how to contact you. I've got to cry off lunch, too: a business hitch that's likely to take me most of the day to sort out. I'll be free this evening, though, if you've nothing on.'

'Dinner, then. I'll pick you up at half seven, if that suits you. There's a nice little place in the country I think you'll like. We'll go there.'

'I'll look forward to it.' It was the conventional reply but Linus felt considerably heartened by the whole conversation. After all, it was she who had volunteered the suggestion of dinner. That had to be a good sign.

Despite the heavy, last-minute-dash-to-work traffic, they reached the Churchill marginally before nine o'clock and Linus introduced himself to the Administrator. As he had suspected, the man was quite glad not to have to go through all the time-consuming explanations that he had been preparing for.

'I was just going to ring your people,' he said. 'My fingers were crossed that someone in authority got in on the dot. One never knows with civil servants.'

Linus forced himself to smile politely. 'I think you'll find we start promptly. Of course, some Officers won't be there at all: they'll have been at the fatstock sales or out testing cattle since much earlier than nine.' He resented the idea that all Veterinary Officers did was sit at a desk and push paper around in between cups of coffee. 'I'd be obliged if you'd ring Trevarrick, though, and fill him in. He's the Regional Veterinary Officer. Tell him I'm here already and I'll let him know the situation as soon as I've a clearer idea of it myself.'

'The one thing we have to avoid is a public panic,' the Administrator told him. 'We don't want people refusing to come in for essential surgery because they learn there's a rabies case here.'

'I think you'll find we're perfectly well aware of the importance of that,' Linus told him stiffly. Did the man think his department was the only one with a sense of public responsibility? 'I take it there's no doubt?'

'That's what it looks like. Dr Gopal is quite sure. She's dealt with it in India. I gather Gail's boyfriend is your son?'

Linus nodded. 'He'd better be vaccinated to be on the safe side. Where is he?'

'Outside. I've told him the prognosis won't be good if the diagnosis is correct. He's pretty cut up.'

'We'll go down to the ward. I take it your own jabs are up to date?'

'You can bet on it. There are some areas where I don't take risks.'

'Come with me, then. We'll take the boy along with us,' the Administrator said, keeping to himself the suspicion that Linus was not a man to take risks of any sort.

Linus liked Dr Gopal. Any fears he might have had that there would be a language problem were swept away as soon as she opened her mouth. He suspected her English might well prove to be better than his. She was not a young woman and she was briskly efficient but what he liked most about her was the sympathy in her eyes when she spoke to Sean.

In his discussions with his son at breakfast, Linus had imagined that the boy had largely come to terms with what had happened. Now he realized he had been wrong. It wasn't until the doctor vaccinated him that the full significance of the last few days made its impact. Sean, suddenly white and trembling, looked into the doctor's eyes.

'There isn't any hope, is there?' he said.

'I don't think so,' she said gently. 'We have two things to do now: make Gail as comfortable as we can and see to it that no one else becomes infected.'

'Where are her parents?'

'Trying to come to terms with it. I believe they're in the chapel. I expect they'd like to see you but I would suggest you leave it for the time being. The priest is with them.'

'Can I see Gail?'

'Not just yet. Your father needs to see her first.' She turned to Linus. 'You must find out which dog it was. I take it you've no reported deaths yet?'

'Not so far. It's a bit worrying: the dog ought to be dead by now.'

'I suppose it's always possible that she got bitten at the very beginning of its infective stage?'

'In which case it should have died by yesterday. Today at the latest. Still, there's time for that yet.'

A nurse in full protective clothing came out of Gail's room. Even Linus, who was expecting it, found the resemblance to one of the nastier science-fiction films unnerving. Sean took one look at her and buried his face in his hands.

'She's lucid, doctor,' the nurse said. 'Have they got hold of the Ministry yet?'

'The Ministry's here,' Linus told her. 'You'd better find me some clothes.'

Gail was a pretty girl. Far too pretty to be condemned to such a nasty death. 'I'm Sean's father,' he said, uncertain how to initiate a conversation in these circumstances.

She smiled weakly. 'We've left it a bit late to meet, haven't we? Are you the vet from the Ministry?'

'That's right. I'm sorry I have to pester you. Believe me, I'd far rather not but I'm sure you realize there are things we have to know.'

She nodded. 'The dog that bit me, that's your first priority, isn't it? It was Lucky. Mr and Mrs Milton's Golden Retriever that they brought back from Germany with them.'

'Had it shown any signs of being ill?'

'No, none at all – except the epilepsy, of course. That was when I got bitten.'

'Epilepsy? What do you mean?'

'Lucky came in with a history of it. They knew there was a risk, putting a dog with that condition through quarantine because it might have a fit when no one was there, but they couldn't find a home for it in Germany. Who would want to take on an epileptic dog? And they couldn't bear the thought of putting him down so they decided to take the risk. He didn't bite me deliberately, you know. If he had, I'd have reported it but it wasn't like that. He had one of his fits and it was just sheer chance that my hand got in the way. I didn't think anything of it. It was just one of those things. Of course, I disinfected it and put a plaster on it, but that was all.'

'Did he seem to be ill over the next few days?'

'No. A bit depressed, perhaps.' She was finding it hard to breathe now and a nurse stepped forward to wipe some of the saliva from her chin. Linus looked at her eyes. They seemed to be becoming restless and he suspected he didn't have long to find out any more.

'Is that all? Nothing but depression?'

She shook her head from side to side and the nurse shot Linus a warning glance over her mask. Gail seemed to be making a great effort to hold on to her mind. 'Only an upset tummy,' she whispered. 'The day before I was ill. He started vomiting. I left a note in the book for Mrs Jones-Drybeck.'

Linus felt a tap on his shoulder. 'I think you'd better go now,' Dr Gopal told him. 'Is there anything else you need to find out?'

'I don't think so,' he replied cautiously. 'I know which dog we're looking for. I'm sure I shall be able to find out everything else from the kennels. If they can't help, will it be any good coming back here?'

'I'm afraid not. We'll be sedating her now. She'll recognize people and talk to them to a limited extent but she's not going to be able to concentrate on the answers to questions.'

'Poor kid. How long has she got?'

Dr Gopal shrugged. 'A couple of days. Maybe three.'

'I suspect my son will want to stay. Is there any point?'

'If he's going to feel better staying here, then let him. If he goes away against his will, he'll feel guilty after she's dead. He'll have an irrational belief that if he'd stayed with her, it wouldn't have happened.'

Linus nodded. 'You're a wise woman, Doctor.'

'Not wise. Just experienced. Death can do strange things to those that grieve.'

Chapter Three

Linus wasted no time getting back to Government Offices and went straight to Len Trevarrick's office. The Regional Veterinary Officer was clearly relieved to see him.

'There you are. I've been half expecting a phone call. What's the picture?'

'What do you know?'

'Not a great deal. I had a very guarded phone call from the Churchill. Afraid of listening switchboard operators, I suppose. I deduced that they have a patient who may be rabid and that you were there already. Second sight?'

'No – a love-sick son.' Briefly, Linus gave his boss all the information he had gathered and they went through the filed import licences relating to dogs quarantined at the Highnoon.

'Here we are,' Trevarrick said. 'Lucky. Golden Retriever. Male. Three years old. Pet dog. No value. Came through Schiphol to Birmingham. I wonder why they didn't bring it in by sea through Dover?'

'The carrier's fee would have been enormous. It was probably no dearer to send it out from Holland and it would have been a lot quicker. Birmingham airport's less than an hour from Highnoon. Dover must be at least four. Do we tell them?'

'Not yet. We've had no notification of the dog's death. Let's wait for the post-mortem on him or the girl's death, whichever comes first. Then we'll be absolutely sure. In the meantime, the dog needs to be isolated.'

'Have you spoken to the kennels?'

'No. There was nothing they could do until we knew which dog or at least which block. Do you want to take it on?'

'I'd like to be able to follow it through, yes. It's not the sort of opportunity one gets very often.'

'Thank God! You're right, though. It breaks the routine.'

Linus collected protective clothing from the store and put it in the boot of his car. The heavy gauntlets and the visored helmet looked sinister lying next to the green wellies and the flat cap.

He drove carefully out of Oxford on to the bypass and then sped along the dual-carriageway until he could turn on to the A34. As he headed north-west his mind's eye still held the image of his son's stricken face and he found himself cursing the stupidity of the girl who was causing Sean so much distress because she hadn't thought there was a risk. He had to remind himself that Gail was paying the heaviest price of all for her stupidity and that Sean would, eventually, get over the worst of his present grief. At least some good had inadvertently come out of it: Sean had sought his father out for help. That suggested that the breach was not irrevocable. The fragile bond they had established in the last few hours must not be allowed to snap. It was up to him, Linus, the older of the two and the father, to see to it that it was welded into something stronger, something upon which a new and better relationship could be riveted.

He turned off the main road into the country lanes that led to the old airfield where the quarantine kennels was situated. It was an ideal location: well away from settlements so that there was no nuisance from smell and the noise was diminished, though he didn't doubt that on a clear night the sound of dogs barking carried a fair way. It wasn't visible from the road. Quite an asset, that, since no quarantine establishment was architecturally satisfying and this was one of the prettier parts of England. In addition to these natural advantages, Mrs Jones-Drybeck had planted a thick screen of Leyland's Cypress round the perimeter which had now achieved a degree of maturity that must surely muffle still further the noise of two hundred dogs who knew that dinner was on its way.

When he reached the private access road, he pulled over and stopped. Then he got out of the car and stood looking at the landscape around him. He had always been impressed with the security at Highnoon and it was inconceivable that a dog from there might escape but if it did . . . He looked about him and groaned. They'd have one hell of a job. There were plenty of open fields, all right, but beyond them to the north were the woods and deeply dipping valleys of the Tews. Plenty of foxes, too. This was hunting country and if once the disease got into foxes . . . It didn't bear thinking about. Nor did the public uproar when the army of sharpshooters went out to comb the woods and shoot every fox they found, to say nothing of cats, badgers, crows and any stray dogs. It was odd that the public fear of rabies always centred on dogs and yet there was only a one in four chance of catching the disease from a rabid dog whereas it was a virtual certainty if the affected animal was a cat. Still, this was as yet unnecessary worrying. The Highnoon was secure. He climbed back into his car and turned into the private road.

The quarterly inspection of quarantine kennels was not always carried out by the same vet and, although Linus had inspected this one several times, it was far from being his favourite. This was nothing to do with the efficiency with which it was run nor with any lack of cooperation from the owner or her supervising vet. It was just that he couldn't stand Mrs Jones-Drybeck and had to make a conscious effort to be even ordinarily polite to her. One day, when he was serving out his last three months before retirement, he would permit himself the luxury of being rude to her. Even as he made the promise to himself, he knew he wouldn't keep it. It was that sort of promise. Still, it helped to imagine it. He drove through the gates and drew up on the small, neatly tarmacked car park. Opposite was the perfectly hideous red brick box that Mrs Jones-Drybeck had somehow persuaded the planning authorities to let her put up as an 'agricultural dwelling'. He could only conclude she had got away with it because it couldn't be seen from the road. The gate leading to the quarantine complex was padlocked. The door of the office beside it was also locked. He looked at his watch. Lunch-time. He would rather be spending it with Clarissa Pensilva than with Mrs Jones-Drybeck. He walked over to the red brick box and knocked on the door.

Mrs Jones-Drybeck made no effort to seem pleased to see him.

'You!' she said. 'What are you doing here? We're not due for an inspection for a month or more. Besides, we usually have a day's notice.'

It was her voice that Linus most loathed. She had the arrogant accent of one brought up in the British Raj. The sort of voice that proclaimed to the world – a world that had little choice but to listen, since it had the singular stridency of its kind – that no opinion was of any value unless it was the opinion expressed by Mrs Jones-Drybeck. When one heard it over the telephone, one had a mental picture of a Wagnerian Lady Bracknell. The reality was otherwise. Mrs Jones-Drybeck was small and stooped, with the dowager's hump that comes from years of calcium deficiency. He suspected that more gin passed her lips than milk, which was not to say that he ever saw her in the slightest bit inebriated. She could probably drink the average General under the table. Linus had no idea whether she had been brunette in her youth but her hair was a most improbable colour now and its shade deepened from visit to visit. Twenty years ago it had probably made her look younger. Now it simply drew attention to the fact that it no longer fitted the face. He supposed that no one had ever had the courage to tell her to go with time rather than against it. It was strange because she dressed quite well. Her kennel overall, like those of her kennelmaids, was always spotless, but to surmount it with a cluster of unfashionably tight, raven-black curls was somehow faintly ridiculous and he was quite sure that that was not her intention.

'May I come in?' he said. 'Here or the office, it doesn't matter. I need to speak to your vet as well. Can you reach him?'

'If you'd given us notice, he would – naturally – have been here. As it is, I've no idea whether he's available or not. He could very well be out on call.'

'Perhaps you'd ring him and find out?'

'You'd better come in,' she said grudgingly and led him into the kitchen. 'Coffee?' she asked.

'Thank you. That would be most welcome.' He looked about him, trying not to appear inquisitive. It was a perfectly ordinary room, as neat and tidy as everything about the kennels. He perched on a stool at what he supposed was called a breakfast bar and accepted the mug of coffee. She pushed a biscuit tin over to him.

'Help yourself,' she said. 'I'll go and ring James.'

She went out of the room and Linus noticed that there was a perfectly good wall-phone in the kitchen. He wondered why she hadn't used that and would dearly have loved to have picked it up and listened in.

'You're in luck,' she said when she came back. 'He was at home. Says he'll be here in about ten minutes. What's it all about?'

Linus smiled sweetly. 'I'd rather not have to go through it all twice,' he said. 'If you don't mind, we'll wait till he gets here.'

'Please yourself.' She opened the tin and held it out to him. 'Have a digestive,' she said. 'Most men like them.'

Linus resented being lumped with the vast – and, he suspected, inferior – majority of his sex and he was on the verge of taking a custard cream instead, but the fact remained that he preferred digestives, especially when they were chocolate ones, and there was such a thing as cutting off your nose to spite your face. He took a digestive.

James Erbistock's ten minutes turned out to be only five.

Whatever Mrs Jones-Drybeck had told him, he must have come at once. If Linus didn't look like a vet, then neither did James Erbistock. If that young man looked like anything, it was a harassed schoolmaster. He was tall and thin, a direct contrast to his employer, but he didn't look as if he had the strength that most vets in general practice are likely to need, especially if that practice extends to cattle and horses, as was probable in any rural area. He was about thirty but would probably, Linus thought, look exactly the same when he was fifty. If there was a great deal of resolution about Mrs Jones-Drybeck's mouth, there was none at all in the face of her supervising vet. His qualifications were excellent, so he must have stuck at his studies. Nevertheless, he had the face of a weak man.

'This is a bit unexpected, isn't it?' he said. 'I didn't think we were due for an inspection yet. Still, if that's what the Ministry wants . . . ' His voice trailed off.

'It's a bit more serious than that, I'm afraid,' Linus told him. 'You've a kennelmaid called Gail Thatcham, I believe?'

'Yes, we have.' It was Mrs Jones-Drybeck who answered and she seemed surprised that the visit should be connected with the girl. 'You won't be able to see her, though. She's off sick at the moment. Her boyfriend rang in and said it was 'flu. She's a good girl. Very conscientious. One of the best I've had, as a matter of fact. I hope she's not in any trouble.'

'She certainly won't be coming back, I'm afraid. She's in the Churchill. She's got rabies.'

'Oh my God!' Mrs Jones-Drybeck went pale and sank back on to her stool.

'Are you sure?' Erbistock asked.

'They're as sure as they can be this side of a post-mortem,' Linus told him. 'And they don't think it will be long before they can do one.'

'Obviously you think she got it here.' Mrs Jones-Drybeck was not one to shy away from unpleasant facts.

'It is – naturally – our first assumption. Did you know she hadn't been vaccinated?'

'No. Of course I urge the girls to have it done but I can't force them to. I seem to remember her saying something about its being a minimal risk and I told her not to be such a fool. Obviously she didn't listen.'

'You've seen no sign of anything in any of your dogs?'

Mrs Jones-Drybeck and her vet exchanged glances and there was a noticeable pause before she answered. It might have been due to the need to review in her mind the inmates of the kennels. 'No, Mr Rintoul. None.'

'What about the epileptic retriever, Lucky?' Linus wondered if a certain wariness in Mrs Jones-Drybeck's eyes followed the question but dismissed it as imagination.

'What about him?'

'Gail says he had a fit Friday week ago and accidentally bit her.'

'She said nothing about it at the time.'

'That's right. She says she thought nothing about it – it was just one of those things. I gather if it hadn't been in a fit, she might have thought more of it. As it was, she bathed it in disinfectant and put a plaster on it.'

Mrs Jones-Drybeck gave an exasperated sigh. 'What fools these girls can be! I'd have thought Gail would have had more sense, too! You think she caught it from Lucky?'

'Do you blame us?' Linus turned to the vet. 'Mr Erbistock, she told me the dog was vomiting on Friday. She said she left a note about it. She assumed the dog had a digestive upset. Presumably you looked at it?'

'Of course I did. It wasn't anything serious. I gave it some antibiotics to be on the safe side but there was no recurrence. It's all in the records.'

'I'm sure it is but you'll appreciate I have to check. I'd like to see the dog, if you don't mind.'

Mrs Jones-Drybeck stood up. 'Of course not. What a fortunate chance you came at lunch-time. At least we don't have to scare the girls just yet.'

She took a bunch of keys from a hook by the door and

led the way across the main gates of the quarantine complex, waiting briefly while Linus collected his protective gear from the car. 'My, you do take this seriously,' she commented, the faintest hint of a sneer in her voice.

'Unlike your kennelmaid, I have an aversion to risk,' he told her. 'Especially when there is one.'

Linus dipped his booted feet into the bowl of disinfectant outside the gate and stepped through, noting with approval that Mrs Jones-Drybeck and her vet did the same. The gates were locked again behind them and she led the way to the kennel block where Lucky was being quarantined.

The kennels were of the design most usual where large numbers of dogs had to be housed. Each block consisted of a long shed with a central door leading to a central corridor running the full length of the building. The kennels went off from either side and each kennel consisted of three sections.

First, there was the indoor section with one door on to the corridor and another to the outside run. Dogs were shut into here at night and provision was made for infra-red heating in the event of really severe weather. The walls were covered in ceramic tiles so that they were easily cleaned, the floor was concrete and each dog had a bed, the nature of which depended on the size of the occupant. The bedding used for most dogs was shredded paper although a few had blankets. Some of the pet dogs also had their favourite toys.

Immediately outside this section was a covered outdoor run. This was the same width as the kennel and about the same length, and it led directly into the uncovered outside run. Both of these had slightly sloping concrete floors which were easily hosed down and the gate between the two sections was more often open than not: only in very high storms was a dog likely to be restricted to the covered run. The walls of each run were constructed of concrete blocks to about waist height and these were surmounted by stout angle-iron and wire mesh and roofed over with chain link. There were no gates in the runs and contact between one dog and the dogs on either side was prevented by the fact that, whereas in a boarding kennel one stretch of mesh between each run would have been perfectly satisfactory, in a quarantine kennel there were two with a gap of several inches between them.

Each block of kennels and runs was enclosed in its own security fence, the gate of which was locked behind everyone who went in, no matter how brief their stay was likely to be. In the same way, the door into the kennel building was also locked. Dogs are adept at slipping past a kennel-maid when their kennel is opened but if that were to happen here, the dog would only be able to run up and down the central corridor. If, by some careless mischance, the door to the building was unlocked and someone came in, allowing the dog to slip out, it would still be contained within the perimeter fence of that block and in the even more unlikely event of its getting through that, too, it would be contained behind the perimeter fence that encircled the whole complex. It would require a human error of some magnitude or an act of sabotage to enable a dog to escape into the world at large.

At the end of each block furthest from the door was the kennel kitchen for that block. The dogs' meals were prepared here, their dishes washed up and, at this establishment, sterilized. Outside the whole complex was a cold-store and a building where dry foods and tins were kept. Rigid co-operation with the public health department of the local council kept the place free of rats and an incinerator of specified design dealt with rubbish. The type of incinerator was specified by the Ministry because, if a dog died in quarantine, the head would be sent to the Rabies Section in Surrey but the rest of the carcase, after a normal post-mortem, would be incinerated. Since some dogs are very large indeed – almost human-sized, in some breeds – this item had to be able to cope with them.

Linus looked briefly at the label on the door of Lucky's kennel. It was correctly filled in. He had known it would be. He looked through the bars of the door. The dog had been out in his run but as soon as he saw he had visitors, he came running up, his golden feathered tail waving happily. He looked entirely normal. Linus had never seen a dog in the final stages of rabies – the condition this one was supposed to be in – but he had seen film of it and there appeared to be nothing whatever wrong with Lucky.

He turned to Mrs Jones-Drybeck. 'This *is* Lucky?' he asked. 'The kennelmaid hasn't moved him and forgotten to change the label?'

She shook her head. 'There's only one other Golden Retriever on this block and that's a bitch. This is Lucky.'

'I suppose I'd better go in.' Linus slipped the door catch free of its connection. Like kennel doors everywhere, it opened inwards so that the occupant could not burst it wide open and escape. He had no problem easing himself in while Lucky waited behind the door. Mrs Jones-Drybeck fastened it firmly behind him.

It is not easy in heavy gauntlets to examine a dog thoroughly and several times Linus came close to discarding them. Common sense prevailed and he persevered. He had seldom seen a more healthy-looking dog. Even its temperature at 101 – Linus had no time for Celsius figures – was about as normal as one could find. He would have sworn there was nothing wrong with it. There was only one thing about the dog that struck him as strange and that was its teeth. It was true Lucky was only three years old but he was a pet dog and it was unusual to find a pet dog of that age without a hint of tartar. Had he been only two, Linus would not have been surprised. It indicated that Mr and Mrs Milton paid far more attention to such details than most pet owners. This, in turn, suggested that they would have been unlikely to overlook the dog's rabies jabs when they were in Germany which, coupled with the course of injections that was compulsory for every dog on arrival in quarantine, made it all the more unlikely that Lucky was rabid.

He indicated to the two observers that he was ready to come out and as he gratefully removed his protective clothing, he said, 'How many dogs did Gail have responsibility for?'

'All the dogs on this side of the block,' Mrs Jones-Drybeck told him. 'Twenty when we're full up.'

'What happens when it's her day off? Or when it's someone else's day off? Who does them then?'

'I've got one girl who only does relief work. We have a problem at the moment because she's doing Gail's dogs and I'm having to cover the other girls' free time, but we're coping.'

'I'm sure you are.' Linus couldn't quite imagine Mrs Jones-Drybeck in a situation with which she couldn't cope. 'I don't think you'll be jumping the gun if you advertise for a replacement. There doesn't seem to be much chance of her recovering.' He looked around him. 'I've seldom seen a healthier-looking dog than Lucky. We know he bit Gail — in one of his fits, she said — but it's beginning to look to me as if it must be one of the other dogs. Have any of them been under the weather lately?'

Erbistock shook his head. 'Nothing that isn't easily accounted for. Very occasionally we get a bit of enteritis but nothing that doesn't respond to treatment. You'd better examine the books. They'll bear out what I say.'

'I'll do that — and not because I doubt your word. First, though, I'll have to examine every dog in this block fairly thoroughly. Then I'd like to have a quick look at the others, especially any Gail has had to look after recently.' It occurred to him that, if the bite from Lucky wasn't the source of Gail's infection, and with an incubation period that could range from ten days to two years, he would be very lucky indeed if, in the end, he didn't have to do a full clinical examination of every dog in the place and then face the further possibility that he might have to try and follow-up every dog that had been through this kennel since Gail first started there, which Sean had told him was eighteen months ago. 'I see you've one empty kennel down at the end on this side?'

'That's right. A Boxer that went home three or four days

ago. It's reserved for a couple of mongrel pets coming in next Tuesday.'

'Could you put them in another block?'

Mrs Jones-Drybeck considered. 'I could, I suppose. Why?'

'Two reasons. At the moment we would be wise to consider that quarantine may have to be extended for a further six months for all the dogs on this side. No need to warn their owners yet: we may be able to limit it to the dogs on either side of the affected one. What I'd like you to do is to leave Lucky and the dogs on either side where they are. One of them's in an end kennel anyway, so he's got nothing on his other side. Move the dog that's next door but one to Lucky into that empty kennel. That way we have an infection-proof space between these three and everything else.'

'We'll do it now, before the girls come back from lunch,' she said decisively. She unhooked the lead that hung outside the dog's kennel and without preamble went straight in and brought out the dog, which might have been an Airedale and again might not. It trotted happily beside her down to the empty kennel. Mrs Jones-Drybeck returned for its bed, its water bowl and a rubber deck-quoit. Once those had been put in the new kennel she removed the label and Linus peered over her shoulder. The dog rejoiced in the somewhat improbable name of Savonarola.

'Good God!' he exclaimed. 'Savonarola! What on earth does the owner actually call him?'

'Savonarola,' Mrs Jones-Drybeck replied. 'The man's barmy, of course. One of these academics with more brains than common sense. We call it Bill.'

Linus spent the rest of the afternoon thoroughly examining the rest of the dogs in that particular block. Most welcomed the extra attention. Some did not. None exhibited any symptoms worthy of alarm.

'I'll be back tomorrow to check on Lucky again and to look at the other dogs. It won't have to be quite so thorough, thank goodness, but I'd be grateful if you'd check on whether Gail had anything to do with any of them. Until Lucky shows some symptoms, there's still a question-mark over whether he's the one.'

Linus got back to the office in time to make a full report to Trevarrick. He learnt that Gail was worse and the hospital was in even less doubt about her complaint than they had been before.

'I don't understand it,' Linus said. 'I've gone over all the dogs she looks after and there's nothing wrong with any of them. As for this Lucky, he's positively bursting with good health – yet, according to the book, he shouldn't even be alive.'

'What was Jones-Drybeck's reaction?'

'She was undoubtedly shaken to learn that the girl had rabies but she pulled herself together very quickly. I'm quite sure it had never crossed her mind that that might be why she was off. Which in turn suggests she had no reason for thinking any of the dogs was ill.' He paused and frowned. 'Even when she knew, it didn't seem to bother her. She made it perfectly clear what she thought of me for bothering with protective clothing and when it came to moving Savonarola – '

'Who?' Trevarrick interrupted.

'Savonarola. The kennels calls him Bill.'

'I'm not surprised. Go on.'

'When I asked her to move him she didn't even bother to put on any gloves. Just handled him as she would any other dog.'

'He's not the one who's supposed to have bitten Gail,' Trevarrick pointed out.

'But the one we know *has* bitten her shows no signs of rabies, which suggests there's a strong possibility it's one of the others. I wouldn't have handled it in my bare hands.'

'What are you implying?'

'I don't know. Nothing, I suppose. She was probably just demonstrating her superiority over mere mortals like me.'

'What's your assessment of the situation? Will you need

any help tomorrow? Or would you like someone else to take it over?'

'No, I'd like to carry on. I've an uncomfortable feeling that there's something here that's just eluding me. As for a situation – well, quite honestly, we haven't got one. Certainly not one that calls for us to alert any other departments. I suppose Gail hadn't been abroad lately – feeding stray cats in the Colosseum?' he added hopefully.

'I'm afraid not. The hospital has already looked into that. Seems the last holiday she took away from home was two weeks in Weston-super-Mare with her sister. Hardly a high-risk area.'

'Pity. If only she'd been hiking in Nepal or riding a bike round India, I'd be inclined to let Highnoon off the hook, despite Lucky's bite. I'll go straight out there in the morning, if that's all right with you.'

'Fine. I suggest you do your report tonight, though, while it's fresh in your mind.'

'I'm going to. I'll drop it in when I've finished tomorrow.'

Linus's first act when he got home was normally to put the kettle on. Today he poured himself a large whisky and sank into an armchair, suddenly exhausted. He sipped his drink and leant back, his eyes closed and his mind restfully blank. Gradually, as the alcohol seeped through his system, he felt himself relax and then his brain began to function again. Weston-super-Mare. If they'd been to Cowes, he'd have been prepared to consider whether Gail had come into contact with something on a visiting yacht, but not at Weston-super-Mare.

It had to be the kennels. It had to be Lucky. Gail herself had said if it hadn't happened in one of his fits, she'd have reported it. It was only the fit that had induced her to disregard it. What if it hadn't been an epileptic fit but a rabid convulsion? He doubted very much whether a kennelmaid would know the difference – or most vets, if it came to that. But if Lucky had been having convulsions . . . How long ago, now? Twelve days? . . . If he was having convulsions nearly a fortnight ago, how come he was still alive – and not only alive, but bouncingly healthy? It didn't add up. Nothing did. The sooner he put the day's events on paper, the more likely he was to spot some inconsistency, some little point he had previously overlooked. He looked at his watch and sighed. Should he do it now and eat later or should he get a meal inside him first?

He sat up straight, his eyes suddenly wide open. A meal. Clarissa. He was taking her out to dinner. Blast! No sooner had his recognition of the inconvenience of his date struck him, than he reprimanded himself. No man in his right senses – and most assuredly not a man of forty-eight tending to *embonpoint* and with no great track record at meeting even moderately attractive women – would risk standing up for a second time one of the Clarissa Pensilvas of this world. Missing their lunch date had not inconvenienced her – or, if it had, she had disguised that fact most tactfully. No woman would stand being put off twice in a row. Even a wife, who wouldn't have much choice about it, could cut up rather nasty, as he knew all too well.

He picked up the phone and booked a table at the Windmill. Then he sat down and, with his usual punctiliousness, recorded the day's events.

It was well past seven o'clock before he had finished and he knew he could not fail to be late for his meeting with Clarissa. His instinct was to rush upstairs, get ready as quickly as possible and hope he didn't keep her waiting too long. No, he thought. Better to let her know. He rang the Randolph and left a message putting the time back half an hour. This way, she would have time to get over any annoyance and, with any luck, he might even be a little early.

He made it and, because all the parking spaces were occupied by the evening's theatre-goers, he risked the double yellow lines. Clarissa was not, as he half-expected, waiting for him in the lounge but a call to her room brought her down with no more delay than was to be expected from any female.

'I've booked a table at the Windmill,' he told her. 'I hope you like it. I thought it might make a change for you to get away from the city.'

'Let me guess,' she said. 'It's either an olde worlde pub that does delicious meals or it's a converted windmill.'

'Neither. It's a converted barn with straw-fired central heating.'

'You're joking.'

'Not at all. The food's good, too. Not haute cuisine, but very good.'

'Then why the name?'

'There's a windmill outside it. Not one of those romantic historical monuments with stately sails. Just an ordinary one like a pylon with a wheel at the top. It's a pity it'll be dark. You'll just have to take my word for the spectacular views. I'm sorry I had to cancel lunch,' he went on. 'Sorry I was late this evening, too. I'm afraid neither could be helped.'

'At least you let me know. There's nothing worse than a man who keeps you hanging around wondering if he's coming or not.'

Linus silently congratulated himself on his forethought. Perhaps, at last, he was learning. 'It was the least I could do,' he said modestly.

They were shown to a quiet corner table which suited Linus admirably. 'I can recommend the devilled whitebait,' he said.

She screwed up her nose and shook her head. 'No, thank you. I don't like all those little faces looking up at me.'

Linus, who was rather partial to whitebait, had never thought of them like that. It was really rather off-putting when one did and he was not at all sorry that so beautiful a woman should be so squeamish. It fitted his fundamentally romantic view of women, a view all too often proved false. Perhaps he'd better have something else.

They both opted for the duck and conversation was general until well into the main course, when she asked him without preamble whether his practice was a large one.

'I don't have a practice,' he told her. 'I did have once, many years ago, but my wife didn't like the hours, the constant interruptions to what she called our "private life", so I sold it.'

'Your wife?' It was a perfectly natural question.

'We're divorced. It's been some years now.'

'So now you're involved in research, I take it. The University and all that.'

He laughed. 'There's no veterinary school in Oxford. It's at Cambridge. No, I'm a civil servant now.'

'You mean you've given it up altogether? I thought you said . . . ?' Her voice tailed off as if she were unwilling to accuse him of equivocation.

'I'm still a vet. For the Ministry of Agriculture, Fisheries and Food, if you want the full details. I'm what's called a Veterinary Officer.'

'Which means you do what?'

Linus wondered whether she really had no idea or whether the question was an excuse to get him talking about himself. He also thought she sounded a little guarded. She was probably calculating that a civil servant wouldn't make as much money as a GP vet. Well, that was true enough and there was nothing he could do about it. If it mattered to her, this could be a very short acquaintance. 'I inspect cattle markets and slaughterhouses,' he said. 'Quarantine kennels, too. Then there's all the TB testing of cattle. TB and Brucellosis. We ensure the conditions under which animals are exported are humane and we deal with notifiable diseases like foot-and-mouth.'

'So what cropped up today?' she asked. 'Foot-and-mouth?'

'No. We haven't had any of that for a long time, thank goodness.' He decided it was time to turn the questioning round. No city girl was going to panic at the thought of a foot-and-mouth epidemic. Rabies was another matter altogether. He would have quite liked to be able to discuss it with someone not involved. A fresh mind might be able to hit on the one point which he had missed and which might explain everything. But he couldn't. If the infected animal was proved to be Lucky, there would be no need for news of the incident to get any further than the files of the departments involved – unless Gail's parents decided to talk to the Press, of course. That might come yet. No, better to turn the conversation and find out a bit more about Clarissa. He knew precious little about her at the moment.

'You know something about me,' he began. 'What about you?'

'Like you, I divorced some years ago. He was an American so it was probably just as well there were no children.'

'Would you have liked children?'

'It's not a thing I feel passionately about. Besides, there's plenty of time yet. One day, perhaps.'

'When you find the right man?'

She laughed. 'Something like that. Tell me, do you spend a lot of time in art galleries and museums?'

'I like paintings. If you absorb the qualities of the very best, you develop an eye for what's good, even if you've never seen anything like it before.'

'What use do you put this eye to when you've developed it?'

'I buy a few pictures from time to time.'

She opened her eyes wide, obviously surprised. 'Really? I know it sounds rude to say so but I shouldn't have thought a vet on a civil servant's pay could afford to collect.'

'You'd be surprised what you can afford when you've only yourself to support. I don't buy Old Masters, naturally, but sometimes I come across something nice by a lesser artist and there's always the chance to buy something good by a living painter.'

'And is that your only vice?' Her tone was light and it was the sort of question people put in this sort of situation, yet Linus had a feeling she was perfectly serious.

He thought about it. 'Do you know, I really think it may

be? I don't smoke. I rarely drink. Don't gamble. Don't drive particularly fast. Rather a negative list when you think about it.'

'Women?'

He smiled. 'One or two. I like their company. I wouldn't regard that as vice, would you?'

'Not the way you put it. You sound as if you lead a life of unadulterated rectitude.'

Put like that, it sounded tedious and uninteresting, yet Linus didn't see his life like that at all. Neither did he see himself like that. It was a depressing thought that others might do so. 'By some people's standards, I suppose I do,' he replied defensively. It occurred to him that he was really no nearer learning very much more about his companion. Clarissa had succeeded in turning the conversation once more away from her. It was very flattering that she was interested enough to ask, but he had the odd sensation it wasn't entirely a personal interest, which was ridiculous.

'What about you?' he said. 'What are your vices?'

'Clothes,' she said instantly. 'I spend a lot on clothes. And success. I very much enjoy making a success of my business. I've always been ambitious.'

'And your spare time? Your hobbies? What do you do when you're not being successful or buying clothes?'

She became vague. 'Not very much. I travel quite a bit – I enjoy going abroad. I suppose I go to the theatre quite often. It depends what everybody recommends. If enough people say something's worth seeing, I usually go.'

'What sort of places do you pick when you go abroad?'

'I go for sun, sea and sand, mostly. Except in winter, when it's skiing, of course. In the spring I like to take a break in a city – Paris, Rome, Venice, San Francisco. Anywhere where the shopping's good.'

'You were saying you'd been in art galleries all over the place.'

'Oh, I have. You can't go to Paris and not visit the Louvre, can you? I mean, one doesn't.'

Linus was conscious of a pronounced sense of disappointment. Clarissa was undoubtedly beautiful but it seemed she was shallow. She thought he was the strange one. Perhaps he was: there were plenty like her, after all. He wondered if a deeper, less superficial acquaintance with her would reveal more intellectual depth. She could be so used to meeting people with nothing to offer beyond the immediately satisfying moment, the currently fashionable 'thing', that she was unaware there might be more.

'How long will you be in Oxford?' he said.

'I had expected to be able to go back to London tomorrow,' she told him. 'Now something's come up and it seems unlikely. I'm going to have to stay a few days more.'

'Good,' Linus said and meant it, despite his disappointment. 'Does that mean we'll be able to meet again?'

'Oh, I'm banking on it,' Clarissa replied.

Linus had had an ulterior motive in taking her to the Windmill. It meant that when he drove her back to Oxford, he could very easily take the road that led past Osney Island and what would be more natural than that he should ask her in for coffee? It was a gambit that had been known to produce results on more than one occasion and it didn't sound as if she intended to drop him. If her beauty had rather overawed him when they first met, her brain – or the use to which she put it – certainly didn't and he felt more confident, less afraid of a rebuff.

He broached the subject after they crossed the toll-bridge and were heading into the city.

'By the way,' he said casually, as if it had only just occurred to him, 'I live not far from here. Just off this road, as a matter of fact. I don't suppose you'd like another coffee? Or another brandy, for that matter?'

She made a point of looking at the clock on the dashboard, tracing its hands with a beautifully manicured finger. 'I'd love to,' she said, 'but not tonight, I'm afraid. I'm going to have to make an early start tomorrow. Do you mind terribly?'

Linus wondered what would happen if he said, 'Yes'.

Mutual embarrassment, he supposed. 'Not at all,' he told her. 'Perhaps another time.'

'Another time would be lovely. When you know how you're situated, maybe you could give me a ring and we can fix a date?'

'I'll do that.' He kept his voice normal so that his disappointment didn't show. It sounded suspiciously like the big brush-off. He'd heard it before in one guise or another. It never failed to hurt.

He passed the road that would have led to coffee, a night-cap and maybe more, drove under the railway and swung left, past Worcester College and into Beaumont Street. He pulled up opposite the Randolph and leant over to open the passenger door. She put a hand on his arm.

'I meant it,' she said. 'Do call me. I'll be expecting it.'

Linus drove home in a more optimistic frame of mind.

Chapter Four

When he reached the kennels next morning, it was apparent that something had been said about Lucky. Sharon, who was looking after Gail's dogs for the time being, was wearing gloves and a balaclava. Linus himself made do with the gauntlets and the helmet. He studied the dog through the bars first and could detect no change from the previous day.

'How's his appetite?' he asked.

'Fine.'

'Is he drinking? What was his reaction when you hosed down the run?'

'He's drinking normally but we shut them into the inside kennel when we're hosing down and don't let them out again till most of it's dried off, so he wasn't in contact with that.'

It was a sensible practice, Linus knew, but a pity in a

case like this where the dog's reaction to water was crucial. 'What about his epilepsy? Has he had a fit since you took over?'

'No. Not a hint. In fact, I've been quite agreeably surprised. Gail was quite fond of him – I think she felt sorry for him – but she always said he was a funny cuss. A bit wary of being friendly, if you know what I mean. I've not found him like that at all. Quite the reverse. Look at the way he greeted you – like a long-lost friend. That's not the way Gail used to describe him.'

'You've looked after him before, though, haven't you? When Gail's had her days off? What was he like then?'

Sharon shrugged. 'To be honest, you don't take much notice of them, not as individuals, when you've only got them for a couple of days. It's different when they're part of your daily life.'

Linus was thoughtful when he came out of Lucky's kennel. There was still no sign of ill-health but what Sharon said had a certain significance. The popular picture of the rabid dog wasn't always correct. Most people visualized such an animal as running berserk, frothing at the mouth and biting anyone who came within range. More often the telling early symptom was simply a change of personality. The ebullient dog might become shy, what the Germans called an *Angstbeisser*, a word for which there was no entirely satisfactory translation. On the other hand, the shy, retiring dog could become more adventurous, more willing to approach strangers. Was that what was happening here? It couldn't be discounted. The thing that still didn't fit was the time factor. If Lucky had been rabid when he bit Gail, why had no other symptoms shown until now? It didn't make sense.

He examined Lucky's immediate neighbours thoroughly and then did a quick examination of the others in the block. They all appeared entirely normal. When he had finished he paused outside Lucky's kennel again, studying the dog within.

'It doesn't seem possible, does it?' Sharon said.

'Be careful all the same,' he told her. 'If there's been a change in his character it would be unwise to take risks. Ask Mrs Jones-Drybeck for some heavy gauntlets and some facial protection that can't be punctured by teeth.'

'She thinks it's all a to-do about nothing,' Sharon said.

'Does she, now? I don't think Gail would agree with her, do you?'

Mrs Jones-Drybeck was waiting for him when he had finished and he could see James Erbistock hovering behind her, uncertain whether he should be offering to help or not. He looked quite anxious, which was more than could be said for his employer.

'Well?' It was the tone she might have used to a disobedient child from whom she expected an apology.

'Sharon tells me Lucky's character is not as Gail described him. He's become more friendly. Couple that with the vomiting and we may at last have some significant symptoms. He needs to be handled with great care. All the others seem to be all right. There are no outward signs yet, anyway. Let's hope there won't be. I'd better look at all the other dogs.'

'All of them? It will take you all day! Apart from that, it's completely unnecessary. There's been no contact between any of the blocks.'

'I'm sure there hasn't but I'd be failing in my duty if I didn't and you know it. I told you yesterday I'd be doing so.'

'That was when you'd decided Lucky wasn't showing any symptoms. Now you think he is, what's the point in looking at the others?'

Linus didn't like Mrs Jones-Drybeck. He didn't like being treated like a fool and he had a civil servant's dislike of being told how to do his job. Hiding his feelings did not come easily. 'Come, come, Mrs Jones-Drybeck. You know better than that. I know how carefully this place is run. In terms of cleanliness and efficiency, it's one of the best but even you must admit there's always the possibility that something – a rat, for instance – might be the vector between one block and another.'

'So you intend to go over every dog on the place with a fine-tooth comb?'

'I intend to examine every dog to establish its general state of health, yes.'

'Making a record of it, I suppose?'

Linus nodded. 'Naturally.'

'If you reckon on five minutes per dog, have you the slightest idea how long it's going to take you?'

'I've already worked that out. When I need reinforcements, I'll send for them. In the meantime, I'll waste no more time chatting. Do you wish to come round with me?'

There was a fleeting exchange of glances with her own vet before she said, 'No, I do not! I've plenty to get on with without playing nanny to you. I presume you can manage on your own?'

'All I need is the kennelmaid for each set of dogs. Apart from that, just let me get on with it. I'll let you know soon enough if there's anything wrong.'

'There won't be.' It was a dogmatic statement of fact. 'You'd better get started. If you've got time to have any lunch, there's quite a good pub down the road. Most of the girls go there.'

So much for hospitality, he thought wryly and began a long and inconclusive day's work.

He made his way down the list, observing each dog first, checking the details on each label, recording temperatures, peering into mouths, examining eyes and finding only healthy dogs. The Pit Bulls were an ugly lot. They reminded Linus of paintings of the old-fashioned Bulldog. They had solid, straight legs, broad fronts, strong bodies with well-developed musculature, though those due to leave in the next month or so had become flabby through the enforced idleness of quarantine life. Their heads had something of the pushed-back nose of the bulldog but without the exaggeration. He supposed they were pretty close to the Staffordshire in general type, but bigger and he didn't much like them. He supposed this must be due to the knowledge of what they were used for in the States and the strong presumption that at least some of them were destined for the same illegal end over here. His jaw tightened. He loathed the thought of animals being abused. These were, without exception, perfectly friendly and gave him no grounds on which to base his dislike which should, he knew, be directed at the people, not their victims.

When he left one of the Pit Bulls, the dog was so anxious not to lose his company that he jumped against the door, leaping high enough to enable him to see through the grille at the top.

'It's a good job the runs are covered, if that's how they can jump,' he commented.

'I read a book about them,' the kennelmaid told him. 'They train them to leap up and down by hanging their meat well above their heads. They say it strengthens their leg muscles.'

Linus shuddered at the implications. 'It would,' he said, continuing to peer at the excited dog. With his eyes still on the dog, he drew the girl closer to the kennel. 'What's that?' he asked.

She peered through. 'What are you looking at? I can't see anything odd.'

'It looks like a scar.'

She lost interest. 'Lots of them have scars. They've been used for fighting, I suppose, so they would have, wouldn't they?'

'This isn't a fighting scar. Open up again. I want a closer look.'

The girl did as she was bid and the dog, delighted to have his visitor back, demonstrated his pleasure with tongue and tail, making it quite difficult for Linus to get a close look at his underside. He finally succeeded and what he saw confirmed what he thought he had glimpsed. Alongside the dog's penis and running parallel to it was a perfectly straight scar about two inches long. It had been stitched and had healed perfectly.

'What's this?' he asked the girl.

'That? I don't know for sure. They've all got them. The dogs, at any rate. I did ask Mr Erbistock and he said he didn't know, either. He thought it was probably some trick of the dog-fighting fraternity. He said he supposed it was either some sort of implanted steroid that worked slowly and saved having to dose the dog, or perhaps something to make it aggressive.'

Linus had no idea how feasible the theory was but the scar was certainly manmade and looked relatively recent: he could still see quite clearly the marks where the stitches had been. 'How fresh are these scars when they come in?' he asked.

'I couldn't say. Mrs Jones-Drybeck looks after them for the first week or so. She says there's some funny customers among them and she likes to settle them in herself. Then we share the chores for a few days so that the dogs get used to me and then I take over.'

Linus looked around him. 'There seem to be a lot of them,' he said. 'I've never seen so many at other kennels.'

'Some won't take them. It's a bit of a speciality here. Some specialize in show dogs or whelping bitches. Mrs Jones-Drybeck does Pit Bulls. You'd have to ask her why.'

Curiosity did not seem to be the girl's besetting sin, Linus thought, and she wasn't too bright, either. Still, she seemed efficient enough and there was certainly nothing wrong with the dogs in her care.

By the time he had finished, the girls had gone home and he was working by artificial light with an impatient Mrs Jones-Drybeck and a still-hovering James Erbistock to let him into kennels and out of gates. Long before he got to that stage, he was wishing he had asked Trevarrick for another pair of hands. He heaved a sigh of relief when at last the gates of the main perimeter fence closed behind him. 'Thank goodness that job's done,' he said. He turned to Erbistock. 'How do you manage to look those over every day and still have a private practice?'

'It isn't easy,' the younger man admitted. 'Of course, it

isn't a very big private practice. Just the villages in the immediate area.'

'What's the verdict?' Mrs Jones-Drybeck cut in. She had a tendency to eliminate anyone else from a conversation, Linus noticed. It was as if only her contribution could be of any interest.

'They all appear to be perfectly healthy,' he told her. 'It's Lucky we need to watch – and the ones on either side of him.'

'Will you extend their quarantine?'

'Almost certainly, but we needn't let that be known just yet. Are the owners likely to visit in the next few days?'

'None of them has made arrangements to. If they do, I'll say there's a bit of a tummy bug going round and we'd rather they didn't come for a day or two.'

'Won't that worry them? I'd have thought it would make them more anxious to see their dogs.'

'It takes some owners like that. Not these. They don't visit all that often.'

'I thought Lucky's owners were devoted?'

'They are, but they said something about being away on holiday. Look in the book. You'll see they haven't visited recently.'

Linus sighed. 'I suppose that's the next chore to do: check all the visitors to that block. There's always the chance someone wiggled a finger through the grille.'

'There most certainly is not!' Mrs Jones-Drybeck exclaimed. 'My girls are under very strict instructions that there is to be no contact with any dog except the visitor's own.'

'Good. I'll need the names and addresses, all the same. Tell me one thing, Mrs Jones-Drybeck. Why do you have all those Pit Bulls? Your kennelmaid says you've made them your speciality but I can't for the life of me see why.'

'Can't you? It's perfectly straightforward. Most kennels won't touch them. That means there's a premium to be had by taking them. They're a profitable line. Very profit-able. As you undoubtedly noticed, they're not at all aggressive with people so they're not really the problem other people think they are. Still, that's their loss and my gain.'

'Doesn't it bother you to think that they're going to be used for dog-fighting?'

'I'd not have taken you for someone who reads the gutter press,' she said scornfully. 'Who's going to spend a small fortune bringing a dog over only to have it torn to bits? No one, that's who. I don't believe all these alarmist stories. I suppose there may be a lunatic fringe involved and maybe one or two offspring of these might get into their hands, but that's all. They make very nice pets, you know, and there's quite a demand.'

'Expensive pets,' Linus commented laconically. 'Do you think they've been used for fighting before they come over here?'

'Sure of it. You must have noticed the battle scars. All the more reason why they should have a nice retirement as somebody's pet, don't you think?'

She made it sound as if she were running a charity, Linus thought. 'What about the other scars?' he said.

'The other scars?'

'In the posterior ventral abdominal wall. Manmade incision about two inches long.'

'Oh, those. We think they must have been the site of some sort of implant. Steroids, perhaps. Whatever it is, it's always been removed shortly before they come over. The stitching is quite fresh when they arrive. It always worries me in case infection sets in. I don't like losing a dog. I always look after them myself to start with. My eye is keener than their girl's.'

Linus didn't doubt it. 'She said it was because you said they were funny customers and needed careful settling in,' he said.

'Cross-questioning the staff, are we?' she remarked without animosity. 'That's what I told her. She's not one of my better girls – not really all that bright – and like a lot of her kind, she'd be deeply offended if she thought I was implying she wasn't observant enough. But she's not.'

Since this opinion tallied with the one he'd already formed, he had no quarrel with Mrs Jones-Drybeck's policy even though it struck him as uncharacteristically tactful. As for her reasons for taking Pit Bulls – well, he couldn't admire them but they made economic sense. He wondered just how much more it cost to quarantine one of them than, say, a Savonarola, but he didn't fancy asking Mrs Jones-Drybeck. It was none of his business and she was more than capable of telling him so, loudly and in public.

When he had left home that morning, he had had some idea of phoning Clarissa to see if she would be free that evening. He thought about it now and abandoned the idea. Even if she were free, he was – what was the expression one of the girls in the office used? Knackered. Yes, that described it pretty well. He stopped at a Little Chef on the way home and felt a lot better afterwards. It gave him the strength to tackle the paperwork. He told himself it was stupid to go on covering this case single-handed. Quite apart from anything else, other Veterinary Officers needed the experience. Let's face it, it wasn't available often. He still hadn't visited the halal place.

When he got home, he hesitated briefly before picking up the phone. He knew Gail hadn't died yet: that was something he would be among the first to know. He had been so busy that he had given scarcely a passing thought all day to Sean. There was little he could say to comfort the boy and nothing he could do to remove his distress, but Sean had turned to him – and not entirely, Linus hoped, because of his professional expertise. He was not about to let that frail bond snap for no better reason than pressure of work. The friend with whom Sean shared rooms was guarded. Sean wasn't there and hadn't been for a day or two but there was nothing for Mr Rintoul to worry about. Obviously the boy knew the situation that existed between father and son. Possibly he was unaware that there had been a slight improvement.

'Is he still at the Churchill with Gail?' Linus asked.

Sean's room-mate sounded relieved. An honest boy who

doesn't like having to hedge, Linus thought. 'Yes, he is. I don't know when he's likely to be back. I gather it's quite serious and her parents are there, too. I don't suppose he'll be back until she turns the corner.'

Or dies, Linus thought. Aloud, he said, 'Thank you. I'm sure you're right. I won't bother them at the hospital. If you see him, would you let him know I called? Tell him I'll be in touch.'

He put the phone down and debated once more whether to ring Clarissa. He could ask her what sort of a day she'd had. He thought better of it. An accidental meeting and one dinner did not give him the right to make that sort of inquiry. Far better to get on with his paperwork.

He called in at the office to leave his reports and discuss the situation with Trevarrick.

'We're going to have to extend the quarantine on those other two,' Linus told him. 'I think we're going to have to put Lucky down but I'd like to hold off on that for the time being. We do have some symptoms – of a sort – now but I'm curious. None of it seems quite right, somehow. I'd like to remain responsible for inspecting the dogs in that block, especially Lucky and the ones on either side, but if you think it's necessary to continue examination of the others by us in addition to the supervising vet's daily inspection, I'll need another pair of hands or two.'

Trevarrick pursed his lips. 'I don't understand this time factor, either, though I'm not at all clear how delaying destruction is going to get us any further. Still, you're the vet on the ground. We can certainly leave it at least until the girl dies. I suppose we'd better keep an eye on everything else for the time being. I'd like to go out there myself but I don't dare leave here right now. I'll send out there the first two Veterinary Officers to arrive in the morning.'

'I'm not sure whether that's a punishment for punctuality or a reward,' Linus commented. 'It's a tedious chore, I'll tell you that. I'll be back here by lunch-time. If they want me to fill them in, they can speak to me at the kennels but it's routine, really. Every dog on the place appears perfectly normal. They'll notice soon enough if one looks wrong.'

The inspection was without incident. Sharon greeted Linus as an old acquaintance and Lucky clearly regarded him as an old friend. There was still no obvious sign the dog was ill. Even Mrs Jones-Drybeck was little in evidence. She expressed irritation at pettifogging bureaucrats who held up her girls' work and it wouldn't have surprised Linus if she had told him to put the dog down so that they could get on with their routine in peace. It would have been in character. Instead, she left him to get on with the job and only when he said he was going did she make any further comment.

'I looked at that Retriever before you came,' she said. 'If you ask me, there's nothing wrong with him.'

'He certainly looks normal enough,' Linus agreed cautiously.

'It's my opinion she's been bitten on holiday. I don't suppose you've thought of that, have you?'

'We're well ahead of you, there.' It gave him some satisfaction to tell her that. 'The only holiday she's had was at Weston-super-Mare. Not what you might call a hotbed of rabies.'

'What about those day-trips to Boulogne? Couldn't she have contracted it on one of those?'

Linus stared at her. 'Is that where she used to go?'

'Sometimes. Always just before Christmas, I believe, but two or three times a year in all. So she always said, anyway.'

Linus's drive back to Government Buildings was executed automatically. His mind was fully occupied with Mrs Jones-Drybeck's information. Why hadn't they thought of that? Yet it had never occurred to any of them. All the same, he had a strong suspicion that the knowledge got them very little further. Those day trips were carried out on a huge scale. Did the ferries keep passenger lists? The police could deal with that, of course, but how far forward would it get them? There was a chance she had gone with a friend and if so, that friend just might remember whether or not Gail had had any physical contact with a dog or cat. More likely there'd be no recollection at all.

He told Trevarrick what he had learned but his boss shook his head. 'We'll get the police to look into it but I don't think it will make much difference in the end. Not to Lucky, at any rate. Sooner or later he's going to have to be destroyed because we *must* know whether he's rabid. If he's not, I suppose it lets all the others – and the kennels – off the hook and we shall have to assume something happened on one of those trips.'

The phone rang. Trevarrick said, 'Excuse me,' and picked it up. When he put it down, his face was thoughtful.

'Gail's dead,' he said.

Chapter Five

'Inevitable,' Linus said. 'Even so, at the back of my mind I was still half-hoping it wouldn't happen.'

'We all were,' Trevarrick replied. 'It's human nature to go on hoping against reason, I suppose. Now there's no question: we put that dog down. Do you want to go out and do it or shall I ask one of the others?'

'I'll do it,' Linus said, 'but I'd like to leave it at least until tomorrow. Can we do that? There's something about this case which still bothers me. I don't know what it is and I can't pin it down but I *know* something's not right. It just feels wrong, somehow.'

'I can't keep a possibly rabid dog alive indefinitely just because you have some sort of hunch. Tolworth are going to want that dog's head – and soon.'

Linus nodded. The Ministry's rabies department was located at Tolworth. It was where all information on imported animals was collated and it was to Tolworth that the heads of all animals that died in quarantine were sent in order that microscopic examination to determine whether or not the dog had rabies could be carried out. 'Can you give me another twenty-four hours to worry at it?' he asked.

Trevarrick hesitated. The answer should be 'no' but it was perfectly true that there were a number of features to this case that didn't add up. 'All right,' he said at last. 'Twenty-four hours – but no more.' He looked at his watch. 'I'll get the letter written to the owners of the two dogs that are going to have to stay here for another six months and I suppose there's no point in delaying a letter to the Miltons letting them know that Lucky is going to have to be destroyed. I'm afraid it means we're likely to have them on our backs once they get it, but that can't be helped. Better if they don't meet you, since you're the one who will be doing it.'

His secretary had been getting the files out as he spoke. 'But the Miltons live in Abingdon,' she exclaimed. 'Just round the corner from me. Why don't I drop the letter in on my way home? I know it's not usual but this isn't a usual situation, is it?'

Trevarrick shook his head. 'I don't think that's a good idea at all. If they see you deliver it and recognize you, you could have them pestering you about it at home and that's really not on.'

'By all accounts, they're very fond of Lucky,' she insisted. 'If I were in that position, I'd want to know as soon as possible. In any case, perhaps they'd like to see him again before it has to be done.'

Trevarrick shuddered. 'A sentimental, tear-strewn parting is something any vet can do without,' he said.

'In most cases I'd agree with you,' Linus commented. 'This is a bit different. That dog has always been a liability to them yet they've demonstrated their affection for him in no uncertain terms and we're not even sure the dog is rabid. If that's what they want, I'm perfectly prepared to put up with a bit of honest grief.'

'In that case, OK, you can do it, Lisa. I just hope it doesn't rebound on you this evening.'

'Remember, we don't even know if they'll be there,' Linus reminded him. 'Mrs Jones-Drybeck said they were on holiday and hadn't been able to visit. If they're still away, they've got a miserable homecoming in front of them but we can't do anything about that. If we follow Lisa's plan, at least we'll have shown willing.'

It had been Linus's intention to arrange another date with Clarissa but Gail's death changed that: Sean had been upset at her illness and its implications; he must be shattered by her death even though it was expected and Linus's place was with his son – if Sean wanted it that way. Linus was optimistic that he would. The very fact that Sean had sought him out was an indication that he wouldn't reject an overture of comfort from his father now. He telephoned Balliol but Sean wasn't there and no one seemed to know where he might be. This was worrying but there was nothing Linus could do about it for the time being except go home and try again later.

It was all very well to tell himself there was no point in worrying about something over which he had no control but that didn't stop him doing so all the way home. Students were strange animals, up in the clouds one day and suicidally melancholic the next and there was no denying that Oxford offered the choice of two rivers, a canal and a railway line as well as more sophisticated means of topping oneself, such as a drug overdose.

When he opened his front door and was greeted by the smell of freshly made coffee, he heaved a sigh of relief. Only Sean and his cleaning woman had spare keys – and she only made the instant sort.

The boy was sitting on the sofa, a mug in his hands, his elbows on his knees, staring unseeingly at some spot straight in front of him. He looked up just after Linus came into the room, as if there were a delay-switch on his reflexes. His face as he looked up at his father bore the blank expression of one looking at a perfect stranger in whom one had no interest whatever.

'Gail's dead,' he said flatly.

'I know. I heard. Is there more coffee in the pot?' The question required no answer and Linus was on his way through to the kitchen to find out for himself before one could have been given.

He came back into the sitting-room with his mug and hesitated. He wanted to sit beside his son, to be close enough to offer real comfort if it were asked for, but it didn't seem right, somehow. Not yet. There had been too much antagonism between them over the years to permit that sort of intimacy. He sat in an armchair opposite and at a slight angle to Sean and sipped his coffee.

'Were you able to be with her at the end?' he asked eventually.

Sean nodded. 'Mr and Mrs Thatcham let me come in. They didn't have to but they did. It was nice of them. They're good people.'

'They sound it. I expect they were glad to know there was someone else who cared as much about their daughter as they did.'

'Some parents wouldn't have wanted to share those last moments,' Sean said.

'I don't know that I would have,' Linus admitted.

For the first time there was an expression in Sean's eyes. It was surprise. 'Why should it bother you?' he asked.

'Maybe past circumstances make a difference,' Linus said, trying to put his feelings into words. 'Maybe if we'd been closer before something like this happened, I'd be willing to share, too. As it is, I'd want every moment for myself. It's selfish but it's how I'd feel.'

'But you let us go!'

'You think I had much choice? Which do you think was best for you – a messy custody hearing with all the inevitable recriminations or an out-of-court agreement?'

Sean looked abashed. 'I thought you didn't care,' he said.

'You were wrong. I cared.'

Sean was silent for a long time, staring down into his mug of cold coffee. His face had reverted to its former blankness and Linus had no idea what he was thinking about. When his son spoke again, it was clear his thoughts had returned to the more immediate situation.

'Why did Gail have to die?' he asked.

Linus hesitated before answering. 'Do you want the truth? Even if it's unpalatable?'

'Of course I want the truth – especially if you know it.'

'I know it all right, and it's prosaic enough, so if that question was in anticipation of a metaphysical, Meaning-of-Life answer, you'll be disappointed. Gail died because she was careless.'

He saw his son bristle with anger at this blunt criticism of the girl he had loved and wished he could give him some all-embracing answer relating Gail's death to a wider cosmic purpose.

'Gail had two chances of not dying,' Linus went on relentlessly. 'If she had been vaccinated from the day she started at that kennels and kept her boosters up to date, she wouldn't have contracted the disease. That was her first chance. If, having been bitten, she had reported it and had had the vaccination immediately, it is almost certain the disease wouldn't have developed. By the time she knew something was wrong, even if she had known what it was, it was too late. That was her second.'

'But she thought the risk was statistically minimal!' Sean protested.

'If it were that minimal, there'd be no quarantine,' his father said bluntly.

Sean stared down at his mug again, unable to look his father in the eye. 'I suppose there wouldn't,' he agreed in a forlorn whisper. He got to his feet and took his mug out to the kitchen.

Linus could hear him washing it up under the tap and resisted the impulse to go out and commiserate with him. At a time when most people offer sentimental platitudes, Sean was having to face up to the unpleasant fact that free will enables us to make choices which are not only disastrous but occasionally fatal. It wasn't an easy lesson but it was one which needed to be learnt.

It took Sean a long time to wash up his mug and put it away and when he still didn't return to the sitting-room, Linus took his own mug into the kitchen. He tried to exhibit the nonchalance of someone who has no purpose other than the apparent one, desperately anxious that Sean shouldn't think he was prying. As he came through the door, he saw Sean, whose back was to him, hurriedly wipe his eye with his sleeve. Good, Linus thought. That's the best thing he could do. He put the mug down on the worktop and glanced at his son.

'Forget the stiff upper lip,' he said. 'That never did any good.' He put a tentative arm on his son's shoulder, half afraid that, after so long an estrangement, any physical contact might be resented, and was almost overwhelmed by relief when, instead of brushing him aside, Sean turned to him like a child and buried his head against his father's shoulder.

The outward manifestation of Sean's grief was not short-lived and Linus knew that the ensuing days would see renewed bouts of undisguised mourning. He knew, too, that Gail's death would not have been entirely without purpose, for a bond had been forged between him and his son which could never now be totally severed.

When Linus reached his office next morning, he smiled perfunctorily at the elderly man who was pacing the corridor outside and gave no thought to the matter of who he might be or what he might want. He had barely had time to take his coat off when Lisa, notepad in hand like a dutiful secretary, slipped in, carefully closing the door behind her.

'Mr Milton's outside,' she told him.

The name didn't immediately register. 'Milton?' Linus queried.

'Lucky's owner – remember?'

'Oh my God! The last thing I expected was to find him on the doorstep first thing. Still, I suppose I'd better see him and make it seem as if I don't mind. He must be back from his holiday. What a homecoming!'

'You haven't heard the half of it,' Lisa said. 'He claims Lucky's been dead for a week.'

Linus stared at her. '*What* did you say?'

She repeated it. 'He's got a letter saying so. I've seen it. He wants to know why we've upset his wife again by sending another one telling them he wasn't dead after all but will be soon. By the way, they haven't been on holiday.'

Linus sat down heavily, totally unable to grasp the implications of what he was hearing. 'You'd better send him in – and don't forget the coffee. Trevarrick's got some whisky in his filing cabinet. Third drawer down. Lace mine with it.'

Mr Milton was both angry and upset and when Linus had read the two letters he was waving in his hand, he didn't blame him. One of them was the letter Lisa had delivered by hand the previous evening. The other was from Mrs Jones-Drybeck and was dated the previous Sunday, the day Gail had first stayed away from work and, he calculated rapidly, nine days since she had been bitten. It said, quite simply, that Lucky had died of an epileptic fit the previous day, that the body had been disposed of in accordance with Ministry of Agriculture, Fisheries and Food regulations, and that Mrs Jones-Drybeck sent her sympathies to Mr and Mrs Milton in their loss. It was a perfectly straightforward letter which left no room for misunderstanding. Linus found it incomprehensible.

'Excuse me,' he said and hurried to Lisa's room. 'Double check the files,' he told her. 'Then get on to Tolworth and find out whether by some cock-up they've been notified and we haven't.'

'I've done that. Nothing on our files and no cock-up,' she said.

'Then what the hell's going on?' The question was purely rhetorical and he returned to his office without waiting for the disclaimer such questions usually elicit.

Facing Mr Milton once more, Linus made a quick appraisal of the man and the situation. His visitor was justifiably upset but he wasn't stupid. There was a limit to how much any member of the public needed to be told about the incidence of rabies in quarantine kennels, but Linus rather thought a frank statement of the position now might prevent Mr Milton's feeling thwarted and going to the Press. It began to look as if there were elements to this story that were better kept under wraps.

Linus resumed his seat. 'I'm going to need your co-operation,' he began, hoping that his explanation would finally eliminate the suspicion on the older man's face. 'The facts are these. The Friday before Mrs Jones-Drybeck says Lucky died, he bit his kennelmaid in what she took to be an epileptic fit. It may have been just that or it may have been a rabid convulsion. I say that because she became ill and died yesterday – of rabies. She had been very foolish in not having been vaccinated and she compounded that folly by not telling anyone about the bite – which, of course, she took to be an inadvertent one by a dog who had no control over his reflexes. She developed symptoms far sooner after the bite than is usual but, even so, we would have expected the dog to have died by now. What has been puzzling us is that there is a Golden Retriever in those kennels, in the kennel allocated to Lucky and bearing his label, which appears to be perfectly healthy. That is the dog we have to destroy.'

It was hardly surprising that Mr Milton looked confused. 'I don't understand,' he protested.

'Neither do I,' Linus told him. 'The first thing we have to establish is whether the dog is Lucky or not. If it is, we have to find out why you were sent that letter. If it isn't, we have to find out what happened to the real Lucky. The obvious explanation is that perhaps your dog escaped and Mrs Jones-Drybeck, afraid of losing her licence, substituted another to keep the Ministry happy but told you Lucky had died, knowing that, if she didn't, you would realize the dog was a different one.'

'That would mean that a rabid dog is roaming the countryside,' Mr Milton pointed out.

'Precisely. One of our problems is that we have to prevent a general panic. Obviously something will have to be said but it needs to be very carefully worded and first of all, we must make sure whether or not the dog in Highnoon Kennels is Lucky.'

The old man nodded. 'You can rely on my discretion,' he said. 'If it's all the same to you, I'd rather not bring my wife into this. She's upset enough. Will my identification be sufficient?'

'Certainly – for identification of the actual animal. We have a second string, of course. Lucky is – or was – epileptic. An ECG will soon show whether the dog in his kennel suffers from that condition.' Linus hesitated. 'I don't suppose you have any veterinary evidence that Lucky was epileptic?'

Mr Milton felt in his inside pocket. 'I most certainly have,' he said. 'Will a letter from our vet in Germany do? I'm afraid it's in German but I'm sure you can get it translated.' He produced a folded piece of paper and handed it to Linus.

'*Fallsucht*,' Linus read aloud. 'I'm no German scholar but there's not much doubt about that. All the same, I'd like to get a proper translation of the whole thing if you don't mind my hanging on to it for a day or two. What I'm going to have to do now, Mr Milton, is to tell my boss of this latest development. I'd hazard a guess this isn't a situation the Department's ever had to face before. We shall certainly want you to identify the dog but it's not going to be as straightforward as it might seem. Do you mind waiting a bit longer? Lisa is already getting you some coffee.'

Mr Milton expressed his willingness to put himself at the department's disposal if it would help to clear up the confusion surrounding his dog and Linus made his way to Trevarrick's office. He passed Lisa with a mug of coffee.

'I've told him,' she said, nodding her head in the direction of the Regional Veterinary Officer's door.

'What the hell's going on?' were Trevarrick's opening words as Linus entered.

'I wish I knew. At best, Lucky was rabid and died and they've substituted something else. At worst he escaped and they've substituted something else.'

'Isn't there a third choice? What if Lucky died of nothing particularly sinister and the dog they've substituted is rabid?'

Linus considered it briefly and shook his head. 'No. The dog that bit Gail was rabid. He had to be. She knew the dog well. She saw him every day. She'd have noticed a substitute.'

'One Golden Retriever looks much like another.'

'Maybe, but no two dogs behave exactly the same. It might fool Sharon who only saw Lucky occasionally. It would never fool Gail – and even Sharon has commented that he doesn't behave as Gail said Lucky did.'

'If we have definite evidence Lucky was epileptic – I mean veterinary evidence, not his owner's say-so – an ECG will soon prove whether the dog there now is the same one. Then we'll have to put it down and find out whether it's rabid.'

'It's my guess it almost certainly won't be,' Linus told him. He put the German vet's letter on the desk. 'There's our evidence about the dog's epilepsy. I suggest we get it properly translated. Milton's willing to help by identifying the dog but he doesn't want his wife upset any more.'

'Fair enough.' Trevarrick walked over to the window and looked out. 'But why a substitution at all? It's no reflection on the kennel if an inmate develops rabies.'

'It is if it escapes,' Linus pointed out.

'Surely they'd realize that the risk to public health out-weighed the possible damage to their reputation?'

'That might be so if they had reason to believe the dog was rabid. I don't think they did. I'll swear Mrs Jones-Drybeck was genuinely shocked to learn what was wrong with Gail.'

'You realize what this means, don't you? We've got to alert the police and the Local Authority. If that dog escaped, it's been on the loose for a week. It could be anywhere! God knows how big an infected area we're going to have to declare!'

'There is a more optimistic scenario,' Linus suggested. 'Let's say Lucky just died and they didn't suspect rabies. They knew the Miltons would notice a ringer so they told them the truth but they didn't want us nosing around so they put in a substitute. When the time came for Lucky's release, the new dog would simply come out and go to a pet home somewhere.'

'The only nosing around we'd do is to send an Animal Health Officer to remove the head and take it to British Rail for despatch to Tolworth. It's standard procedure. Why should that worry them?'

'I don't know,' Linus admitted. 'Look up their files. They've not been going more than about four years. See how many other fatalities they've had. Maybe not enough to realize just how routine it is.'

Trevarrick frowned. 'On the other hand, it could suggest they've something to hide.'

'It could, couldn't it? It would also suggest the carcase was incinerated. I imagine the forensic chaps can identify bone ash, don't you?'

'Bound to.' Trevarrick reached for the telephone. 'Might not be able to distinguish canine bone ash from human, though. Still, that's not the problem. I'd better call the police.'

'Not yet,' Linus said. 'Give me time to go over there and get that dog. I'd hate anything to happen to him before I do: once he's dead, we've no way of finding out whether he's epileptic. Find me a crate and a licensed carrier and I'll get that dog to the Veterinary College at Potters Bar. Warn them we're coming. When the College has done the ECG, they can euthanase him and the head can go off in the normal way. Jones-Drybeck must be expecting us to authorize his destruction and if she's not faced this situation too often, she won't realize we don't usually take the whole dog. Nor does she realize we suspect it's not Lucky. Let the police turn up after I've got him safely crated.'

'What about Mr Milton? Do you expect him to drive all the way over to Potters Bar?'

Linus hesitated. 'I know it's not usual but then, nothing about this case is. Why can't you take him to Police HQ at Kidlington? He can see the dog in its crate there. You, and half a dozen policemen should be adequate witnesses to the identification, don't you think?'

Mrs Jones-Drybeck was not surprised to see Linus but she was instantly suspicious of the carrier he had brought with him.

'What's this?' she said. 'We have our own carrier's licence. Why bring in someone else?'

'Red tape,' Linus said vaguely. 'Ministry instructions. You must realize the dog has got to be examined.'

'Nonsense! Do you fondly imagine I haven't read the procedures? All you have to do is put the dog down and send the head off to Tolworth.'

'In the normal course of events, that's so,' Linus said cautiously. 'This case is rather puzzling. The dog has no symptoms so it's all going to be looked into a lot more thoroughly. There's always the possibility it's a more virulent strain,' he improvised cheerfully. 'That would account for Gail's showing symptoms so soon.'

'But not for Lucky appearing to be so healthy,' Mrs Jones-Drybeck commented acidly.

'That's right. As I said, it's all very puzzling. Now perhaps you'd open the gates so that we can get the vehicle as close as possible to load the dog. We wouldn't want to take unnecessary risks, would we?'

Mrs Jones-Drybeck had no choice but to obey the man from the Ministry but she did so in a way which left Linus in very little doubt that she would have preferred to send him and his carrier packing. He was very tempted to ask her why the Miltons had been told their dog was dead but he knew the police were on their way with that precise question and forewarning this overbearing female that MAFF was aware of irregularities was no way of establishing the truth. Far better to let her think, at least for the present, that bureaucracy had gone mad. James Erbistock was there, hovering in the background as usual, long and thin and looking worried. If Linus's suspicions were right, he had every cause to look worried but it had to be admitted that at no time had Linus ever seen him exude confidence.

Once the dog was crated and the crate sealed and loaded, Linus led the way off the premises, pulling over in a lay-by to have a final word with the carrier. There was no point in Linus's accompanying the dog to Potters Bar: as soon as the Veterinary College had the ECG results, they would telephone Trevarrick. Linus had every intention of following the police into the kennels. He would almost certainly be exceeding his brief by doing so and might even have no right whatever to be present, but he wanted to watch Mrs Jones-Drybeck's reaction and – possibly more revealingly – James Erbistock's as well.

Quite apart from any professional interest, he had considerable natural curiosity to hear her explanation for the letter reporting Lucky's death to his owners and a more clinical curiosity to see how long it took her to come up with it. If the police insisted on excluding him, so be it, but since they would be needing to cooperate with MAFF in the long-term investigation of this business, he rather thought there was a good chance they'd turn a blind eye to his presence. He pulled out of the lay-by and swung round in the road. He drove the short distance to the kennels and backed into a convenient field entrance. He could watch comings and goings from here without himself attracting attention.

When two police cars swung into the private access road, he turned in after them, his identification ready to show the constable who was at his side before he'd had time to put the hand-brake on.

'I'm afraid the kennels is temporarily closed, sir. Perhaps you'd like to come back another day,' the young man said before noticing the proffered card. 'Oh, I see, sir. My apologies. You're the vet dealing with this, are you?'

'That's right, Constable. I've just supervised the removal of the dog in question.'

Linus got out of his car and approached the most senior policeman present. 'Linus Rintoul. MAFF,' he said. 'The dog's safely on its way. I'd like to hear their excuses.'

'Inspector Lacock. I imagine we're likely to be working together for a while. Just leave the questioning to us. OK?'

'Wouldn't dream of interfering, Inspector.'

Mrs Jones-Drybeck was surprised to see the police. James Erbistock was quite clearly appalled. Inspector Lacock appeared to notice neither reaction.

'Mrs Jones-Drybeck?' he asked. She nodded. 'A routine visit, Mrs Jones-Drybeck. I'd like to inspect your quarantine records.'

Mrs Jones-Drybeck threw a quick glance at the far from routine policemen now standing by every security gate and nodded. 'In the office. This way,' she said, leading them across to the neatly painted building.

'You have an Order from Ministry of Agriculture, Fisheries and Food ordering the removal of a Golden Retriever called Lucky, I believe,' the Inspector went on.

Mrs Jones-Drybeck shot Linus a glance. 'As Mr Rintoul can confirm,' she said, extracting the relevant file and withdrawing the paper referred to.

Inspector Lacock scrutinized it. 'And the dog that has been removed is the Golden Retriever, Lucky, belonging to Mr and Mrs Milton?'

Mrs Jones-Drybeck smiled. Quite suddenly Linus knew that, while she might have been worried before, she was much less so now. Almost relieved, in fact. 'That's right,' she said. 'As you must know, there's a suspicion our former kennelmaid caught rabies when he bit her. Personally – as I have already told Mr Rintoul – I think she must have been bitten on one of her trips to France but I appreciate that MAFF has to make sure.'

'Yet you wrote to the Miltons telling them their dog was dead?'

There was no mistaking the fact that Mrs Jones-Drybeck was momentarily taken aback. She made a very rapid recovery.

'Oh no! Don't tell me that letter went off! Of all the stupid . . . ! Perhaps I'd better explain.'

'Perhaps you had,' the Inspector agreed.

'The dog was very ill, you see. Very ill indeed. Nothing to do with its epilepsy. A very severe attack of enteritis. James here treated him – he'll confirm what I say. I really didn't think the dog would live and since I was going to be short-handed the next day, I wrote the letter to save the bother of trying to fit it in when the dog died. You appreciate that I expected to find it dead when I came in next morning. Well, Lucky finally responded to the antibiotics and I should have destroyed the letter. How it ever came to go out, I can't imagine. Poor Mr and Mrs Milton! How upset they must have been! Lucky means so much to them, too.'

Inspector Lacock looked across at the vet whose anxiety did not appear to have diminished. 'Do you confirm this, Mr Erbistock?'

'That the dog had been ill, you mean? Oh yes. Yes, of course. I didn't know about the letter,' he added hastily.

The phone rang. Inspector Lacock's hand reached it before Mrs Jones-Drybeck's.

'Speaking. Yes. Thank you.' He put the phone down. 'How very interesting,' he said blandly. 'Mr Milton has just been shown the dog that Mr Rintoul removed from here a short while ago. He says it is definitely not Lucky. I'm afraid I shall have to ask you and Mr Erbistock to accompany me for further questioning. I must caution you . . .'

'Don't bother with all that,' she snapped. 'I'm not stupid enough to say anything at all until I've seen my solicitor – and neither is James.'

As they were led out of the office, Linus picked up the phone.

Inspector Lacock frowned. 'We'll be going over this place with a fine-tooth comb. We don't want the phone tied up. Will you be long?'

'Only as long as it takes to ring the deputy supervising vet, David Thelwall,' Linus told him. 'There's a lot of dogs here to be inspected each day, you know. And don't forget the incinerator,' he called after the disappearing uniform.

Gail's death, Sean's distress and the strange circumstances surrounding Lucky had almost driven Clarissa from Linus's thoughts. Almost, but not quite, and when he did think of her as he drove back to Oxford, it was to tell himself that she must have left the city by now. Hadn't he been going to ring her? He had good enough reasons for having forgotten to, but try explaining that to a woman. Perhaps he'd ring the Randolph when he got home, just on the off-chance, even though he knew it would be no good. If she was still there, she'd be out of all patience with him. By the time he turned off the Headington roundabout, he'd decided to forget all about her despite the little voice that told him to ring the Randolph, anyway. He concentrated on the traffic until he reached Marston Road and parked in front of the unsightly buildings whose only saving grace was that they were alleged to be temporary.

He put his head round Trevarrick's door and gave him a brief résumé of the day's events. He looked at his watch. 'I don't suppose that poor dog will get there till tea-time,' he commented. 'It'll be tomorrow before we know any-thing. Pity. Still, it gives me time to get the paperwork done.'

'We'll know before that,' Trevarrick told him. 'They've given him a police escort to Potters Bar, so he'll not be held up in the traffic. They're going to do the ECG tonight and the police are going to take the head straight down to Tolworth. Staff are staying there to do the fluorescent antibody tests straight away. By the time we get here tomorrow we should have a ninety-nine per cent probability rating on whether or not this particular Lucky has rabies. We'll have to wait longer for the back-up tests but at least we'll be almost certain.'

Linus whistled. 'My, we are pulling out the stops.'

'What do you expect? It's a bit different from the usual death-in-quarantine case, don't you think?'

Trevarrick sounded testy, Linus thought with satisfaction and wondered if anyone would write 'cracks under stress' on his boss's annual report. Then he chided himself for being unfair. It was all very well for Linus to find the whole thing exhilarating – he was at least able to get out and do something about it. Trevarrick was paying the penalty of rank: he was obliged to stay on the end of a phone and organize. If Linus was condemned to that, no doubt he'd be tetchy, too. He withdrew his head and made his way up the sloping corridor to his own office and immersed himself in the tedium of the necessary paperwork.

It was nearly five o'clock when the phone rang. So unexpected was Clarissa's voice that he failed to recognize it at first.

'Very flattering, I must say,' she commented when he had asked her to repeat her name. 'If it weren't for the fact that I quite enjoy your company, I'd take deep offence and ring off.'

'Don't do that,' Linus said hastily. 'It's just that I didn't know you were still in Oxford. I've had so much work on that I've not had time to call you and I suppose I wasn't expecting you to call me here. It doesn't mean I'm not pleased to hear you.'

'Good. Then why don't you take me out to dinner tonight?'

Linus was a bit taken aback at the suggestion. He was perfectly willing to take her out to dinner. Delighted, in fact. It was just that he had a deep-seated feeling the suggestion should have come from him. He wasn't used to women who initiated the advance and now that he was experiencing it, he wasn't sure he liked it. On the other hand, he enjoyed her company, so why not?

'I can't think of one good reason why not,' he said. 'Half past seven?'

He hesitated briefly before booking a table at the Bay Tree. It was further than the Windmill but less gin-and-Jag and the return journey offered the same advantage – if Clarissa concurred. He packed the remaining paperwork in his briefcase. He had time to work on it at home before he went out. He must make sure it was up to date. Once they knew the verdict on poor old Lucky, he would have work to do whichever way the tests went. If Mrs Jones-Drybeck and young Erbistock were detained for very long, there was a whole quarantine kennel to sort out. The chances of dispersing two hundred dogs to other kennels were remote. Life would be a lot easier if the police found some simple explanation for what had been going on but, even in his most optimistic mood, Linus couldn't imagine what that simple explanation could possibly be.

As he left the office, it occurred to him that it was odd Clarissa had telephoned here. It would have been much easier to find his home number: there was only one other Rintoul in the book. MAFF, on the other hand, wasn't listed under 'M' for Ministry but under 'A' for Agriculture and then the entry gave the numbers of several departments.

The Bay Tree proved a great success and it seemed to Linus that Clarissa's friendliness had acquired a warmth that hadn't been there before. Perhaps not ringing her had been a good move, even if it had been inadvertent. The prognosis looked decidedly more hopeful than it had done the last time he took her out. It was over coffee that he remembered the phone call.

'What made you ring me at the office?' he asked quite suddenly.

'Are you not allowed to receive calls?' she asked. She sounded guarded but that was probably because the question had been so unexpected.

'No, nothing like that. It's just that I should have thought it was easier to find my home number and leave a message on the answering machine.'

'If I'd known you had one, maybe I would have done. As it was, all I had to find was the Ministry's number. Much easier than ploughing through a list of names, especially when I wasn't sure of the address.'

Linus let the subject drop. He was the only one of the two Rintouls listed who lived in Oxford. She couldn't possibly have looked him up at all. Maybe she had just assumed there would be several. He found himself wondering, quite illogically, where she had rung from. He told himself it didn't matter. It was none of his business, anyway, and even if he knew, what would it signify? He allowed the conversation to revert to uncontentious matters.

When he suggested a nightcap this time, Clarissa was happy – quite flatteringly eager, in fact – to agree and Linus turned off the road and over the little bridge on to Osney Island with a lighter spirit than he had known for several days.

He saw her look with some diffidence at the plain front of the little terraced cottage and suspected that there was an element of relief in her 'Oh, what a charming room!' when he ushered her into the sitting-room. He guessed that anyone who went to the Louvre because it was the thing to do might well look slightly askance at an artisan's cottage. She had probably expected mock-Georgian.

On his way through to the kitchen, Linus switched on his answering machine. There wasn't much on it. Sean had rung to say he was all right and his father wasn't to worry about him. The woman who cleaned for him once a week said her Fred's back was playing him up something rotten and would Mr Rintoul mind if she came the day after tomorrow instead of tomorrow. The only other call was from David Thelwall, the vet who was Erbistock's deputy and upon whose shoulders fell the responsibility of supervising the health of the animals at the Highnoon in Erbistock's absence. He clearly took his duties seriously. He had examined every dog on the place and they were all fine. There was just one feature which puzzled him and on which perhaps Mr Rintoul could throw some light. There was a block of some breed listed as Pit Bulls which, he added, he couldn't find in any book, and all the males had a healed incision in the posterior ventral abdominal wall to one side of the penis. So far as he could tell from the scar tissue, the incisions had been made at roughly the same time as the dogs came into quarantine. Could Mr Rintoul throw any light on this?

'Can you?' Clarissa asked as he switched the machine off. 'I'm sorry. It's none of my business, I know, but I could hardly help overhearing.'

Linus shrugged. 'It doesn't matter,' he said. 'It's outside my field, anyway. These dogs have been used for fighting before they came in. Some of them will be used for it again. I'd noticed the scars myself. The most likely explanation is that they've contained some implant to make them fight or to put on weight. Something like that. Whatever it is, it's not there now so it's nothing to do with me. My responsibility is purely and simply to ensure that no rabies enters the animal life of this country through the quarantine kennels in this area. What happened to the dogs before they came here and what happens when they leave is, happily, none of my business.'

'Not even if it's illegal?'

'Let's put it this way: if I saw one man murdering another, I'd tell the police but I don't consider I have any sort of duty to go round the country looking for people committing murder.'

'So you won't be going over there to look at these scars?'

'I don't need to. I've already seen them. I'll tell Thelwall what I think and I imagine he'll find his time so taken up with the statutory daily examination that he'll soon have too much on his plate to spend much time thinking about them himself.'

She sank back more comfortably into the sofa and sipped

her coffee. 'That sounds eminently sensible,' she said. 'Come and sit down beside me.'

Distinctly encouraged, Linus did as he was bid. He did have the fleeting impression that in some way which he couldn't quite make out, he was being used but he pushed the thought away. Why not? he told himself. After all, wasn't that precisely what he was doing? He certainly wasn't pursuing the acquaintance because he was hellbent on marrying her. Perhaps this was just another manifestation of the modern, liberated woman. He didn't altogether approve but that didn't mean he was going to reject the opportunity.

An hour or so later, it became clear that there was a limit to Clarissa's liberation. She announced her intention of returning to the Randolph.

Linus made no attempt to hide his disappointment. 'You don't have to. There's no reason why you can't stay here.'

'What will they think at the Randolph if I turn up around breakfast in the dress I went out in for dinner?'

'It won't be the first time a guest has done it and the chances are someone quite different will be on duty anyway. Do you really care what a receptionist thinks?'

'Yes, I do. I may want to stay there again.'

'There are other hotels in Oxford,' Linus pointed out reasonably.

'Not like the Randolph. Now, are you going to run me back or do I call a taxi?'

Linus put his jacket back on. 'Of course I'll run you back – if you're quite sure that's what you want.'

She stood up and kissed him on the cheek. Once again he had the uncomfortable feeling he was being used. 'It's very difficult for business women on their own, you know,' she said. 'Thank you for not being nasty about it. So many are.'

Linus didn't think he liked the inference that he was one of many but he let it pass and escorted her out to his car. The very faint hope that she might invite him in when they reached her hotel died with her very final good-night kiss. Clarissa was no believer in lingering farewells. Linus watched her cross the road briskly and disappear into the hotel before driving home once more, his sexual ego firmly placed back in its normal position around his boots.

Chapter Six

When Linus woke up next morning he felt depressed. He was uncertain to what extent this was due to what he regarded as his failure to persuade Clarissa to spend the night with him or whether the probable degeneration of the Lucky case into a routine exercise was to blame. If it was discovered that the real Lucky had escaped, then there would be nothing routine about the next few days but Linus rather thought it unlikely. He knew this judgement was based on a pure hunch and therefore unreliable. Nevertheless, that was how he assessed it.

He switched on the radio, as much for the weather forecast and the company as for anything else and paid only superficial attention to the news, none of which related to Oxfordshire and all of which was depressing. An airliner had crashed into the Atlantic but no group had claimed responsibility. The Prime Minister had made a speech deploring the naivety of those who believed the Soviet Union's protestations of a desire for peace. The President of the United States did not have cancer and a cabinet minister denied sleeping with a Page Three girl, claiming he only met her to discuss helping her to get into films. The Home Office had rejected claims that Frank Teramo, the alleged Mafia godfather, should be banned from Britain. A certain Lord Sangobeg had said there was no evidence to support the allegations. The name conveyed nothing to Linus. He supposed the President was relieved and wondered when it would dawn on that gentleman that this was at least the fifth occasion on which he was said not to have cancer of one sort or another, which almost certainly meant that he did have but they were keeping him going anyway. As for the cabinet minister – well, if he thought anyone believed that yarn, he deserved all he got.

By the next bulletin, the plane was identified as American and the cause of the crash was not known, a fact which didn't stop 'experts' speculating on which terrorist group was responsible for it. Libya had specifically denied responsibility. Linus wondered how long it would be before the Americans took that as an admission of guilt. He switched off. There was unlikely to be anything new. He contemplated the impact on the nation if the PM announced that the Russians were our wonderful natural allies or the cabinet minister said yes, he did sleep with her and it had all been worth the ensuing scandal.

Punctual, efficient Lisa was, as always, in the office before the rest of them. She looked up as Linus passed her door.

'The College rang, Mr Rintoul,' she called out.

He back-stepped and put his head round the door. 'And?' he said.

'No epilepsy.'

'So that confirms it. Good. I take it there's a report in the post?'

'They're sending it by messenger. They didn't want to risk its being mislaid. It should be here by lunch-time.'

'You'd better get on to Inspector Lacock. At least we now know that the dog which is supposed to be Lucky and reports of whose death seemed to have been greatly exaggerated, isn't. Jones-Drybeck and Erbistock are going to have to talk their way out of that one and it won't be easy. I'd like to be a fly on the wall when they try to explain what happened to the real Lucky.'

'Are they both necessarily involved?' Lisa looked doubtful. 'I mean, couldn't it just be Mrs Jones-Drybeck working on her own initiative?'

'It could, but it isn't. I'm sure she's the organizing genius behind whatever's been done but I'm certain he's in collusion with her. If ever I saw a worried man, it's James Erbistock. He's got the sort of face every poker player dreams of playing against. No, he's involved, all right. I'm off to Banbury. Tell Trevarrick when he gets in. I'll go on to the Highnoon from there. I don't know if I'll make it back here today.'

Once he was past the ring-road, Linus encountered remarkably little traffic and turned his car radio on. Now it appeared that the airliner had lost altitude at a significant rate. Flames had appeared when it was a few feet above the sea and seconds later the plane had exploded. The crew of an aircraft carrier had seen it. Terrorist attack was still the favoured theory but it no longer seemed feasible to assume there had necessarily been a bomb on board. There were strong adherents to the possibility of metal fatigue and at least one expert was claiming always to have had doubts about the basic design of that particular aircraft. The Prime Minister's views on the Soviet Union had ceased to be newsworthy and the President had dropped to one sentence but the cabinet minister still rated three. His explanation had been dropped.

When Linus reached the stockyard, he felt restless. He exchanged a word here and there, kept an eye on the loading and unloading and found nothing amiss. He was quite unable to account for the way he felt. It was that strange, empty restlessness that occurs when one should be doing something but can't remember what it is. Or something left undone that matters. Linus chased the elusive something round in his mind and failed to pin it down. He thought it might have something to do with Lucky but he couldn't even be sure of that.

'Had a heavy night of it, have we?' said a voice behind him and he turned to see the friendly grin of Fred Grinton, the RSPCA inspector who made the stockyards one of his regular beats.

'No such luck,' Linus told him. 'Maybe that's the problem.'

'Fancy a ploughman's?'

'Why not? It's the only lunch I'm likely to get.'

The two men made their way to a pub that served a noted ploughman's lunch which was such good value that it was even worth suffering the television in the bar. Linus took his plate and his pint to a table in the corner, suddenly aware of just how hungry he was. The piece of French stick was warm and crusty, the wedge of Cheddar had been cut from a farmhouse cheese, not some pre-packed plastic slab, and the garnish was a side-salad in itself. He attacked it with gusto while above the bar some female attacked the hand that was feeding her by expressing her disgust of what had been on the telly the night before. She almost made Linus wish he had seen the programme that had so offended her except that he had a strong suspicion that the copulation of the Lesser Spotted Nittlethwit was probably a lot less exciting than she made it sound.

'Hear you've been having a spot of bother,' Fred said when the first pangs of hunger had been assuaged.

'Have I?' Linus answered.

'Not you personally. The Department. Spot of bother over Enstone way.'

'You should know better than to listen to rumour.'

'I don't. Well, I do: it's part and parcel of the job, but not in this case. I've got a boozing pal in the cop shop.'

'Born liars, the police,' Linus said without acrimony. 'Thought everyone knew that.'

'So you wouldn't be interested to learn of a stray Golden Retriever round Enstone way?'

'Why? Is there one?'

'Not that I've heard of,' Fred admitted. 'Thing is, I'll hear before you do. If there's a stray dog making a nuisance of itself, they'll phone me before they go to the police – and it wouldn't occur to them to ring the Ministry at all. You might like to bear that in mind.'

'I will. Keep your ears open, will you?'

'How likely is it?'

'Not very. That's pure guesswork on my part. I think it's

84

already dead. Proving it is another matter. You could try telling your boozing chum to keep his mouth shut.'

'Don't worry about him. He was just giving me the nod. I'd not call him a blabber.'

Disgusted of Tunbridge Wells had made way for the news headlines and both men automatically stopped talking to watch.

The air crash was still the leading item and mystery still surrounded its cause but the aircraft carrier, HMS *Invincible*, had already reached the scene and by some miracle had picked up a survivor. A Bulldog in a not-quite-submerged crate had been fished out of the ocean but was not expected to live.

'If it does, they'll make it the ship's mascot,' Fred said.

'More likely the owner will turn it into a celebrity,' Linus amended.

'Depends whether the owner was on board, too.'

One of the auctioneers joined them and the conversation became rural and a great deal more general until Linus, looking at his watch, realized he should be on his way to see Thelwall and have another look at the two dogs who had been kennelled on either side of Lucky. He stood up as the one o'clock radio news was announced. It was automatic to stay for the headlines. The dog – which was now a Bull Terrier – had been christened Sailor by an imaginative crew and was now on its way back to Culdrose in a Sea King helicopter, together with several of the larger pieces of debris.

Fred Grinton snorted. 'In one hour that poor dog's grown a nose. What's the betting that by the time they land it'll be called a St Bernard?'

'Not a St Bernard,' Linus told him. 'An Alsatian. That's the only breed the newspapers can identify. Alsatians and Dobermans. If it doesn't quite fit either of those – like a Pekinese, for instance – it becomes a cross-bred Alsatian. Tell them it's a German Shepherd and you've thrown them completely. I'll bet you a fiver they call it an Alsatian once it lands.'

'You're on,' Fred agreed. 'Want a side bet as to what it really is?'

Linus considered. 'It seems to have stayed afloat against the odds,' he said at last. 'Something must have buoyed it up. I'll go for a Poodle. The pockets of air in its coat kept it afloat.'

The laughter of the other two followed him out of the pub while the sense of camaraderie stayed with him during the drive to Enstone, though it somehow didn't quite succeed in quieting his feeling of restlessness.

The police were still in evidence though their activities were limited to the office and the incinerator.

'Have they found anything?' Linus asked Thelwall as they walked to Lucky's kennel block.

'I don't know what they're looking for in the office,' the other man admitted. 'I'm not at all sure they do, either. I've tried to point out that they can't just walk off with the visitors' book. How else are we supposed to keep a record of people who may need to be tracked down? They don't seem to realize that we're not keeping records for the fun of it, or even for their convenience, but because we're obliged to and writing things on scraps of paper until they let us have them back just won't do. So far as the incinerator is concerned, they've taken away every last particle that was inside it. Fortunately the council dustcart only comes up this access road once a fortnight, so the dustbins had two weeks' rubbish in them – and it included plenty of ash. How much of it was from the house fire and how much from the incinerator, I've no idea. Still, that's their job. They've no doubt at all they'll be able to identify bone ash and they reckon they'll be able to tell whether it's from a dog or not.'

'I suppose no other dog's supposed to have died in the last couple of weeks?' Linus asked.

'They've been remarkably fortunate,' Thelwall told him. 'As far as I can make out, no dog that's been through this kennels has ever died. How's that for a record?'

'Unbelievable,' Linus said shortly.

There was nothing wrong with Lucky's neighbours but Linus decided they'd have to do extended quarantine. 'It's hard on their owners,' he said, 'but I can't see we've any choice. Even if the Lucky we took away yesterday is clear – as he almost certainly will be – the other one equally certainly wasn't.'

'Come and look at these Pit Bulls,' Thelwall told him. 'I'd like your opinion.'

'I've seen them – and I'm no wiser than you are. Their kennelmaid says she was told the scars were something to do with fighting and it's quite likely. It's not an area I know anything about. Do you?'

Thelwall shook his head. 'Only what I read in the papers and that isn't much. There seems to be a feeling there's big money involved, which may explain why so few convictions seem to be obtained.'

'I've heard that, too. Can't see it, myself. Not really big money. That would suggest a really well set up organiz-ation. I'd have thought it was little local enclaves of fanciers, wouldn't you?'

Thelwall looked doubtful. 'There's an awful lot of them coming through this kennel for a little local enclave,' he said. 'Did you know we had another due in today?'

'I must have seen the licence,' Linus replied, 'but I can't say it registered. Dog or bitch?'

'A dog. From New York. I'd like to look at him but he was on that plane that went down. Pity.'

Linus was silent for a moment, looking at him. 'You know, of course, that a dog was rescued from the crash?' he remarked.

'I heard the midday news. A Bulldog, I gather.'

'An hour later it had become a Bull Terrier. What's more, they've called it Sailor, so it's a reasonable bet it's male. I wouldn't place too much certainty on the accuracy of the breed description but I think we can assume an aircraft carrier full of sailors knows male from female. I'd say there's a good chance this dog is the one due here today and if it's really a Pit Bull – and you couldn't blame anyone for not identifying that breed – it will be interesting to see if it, too, has an incision and whether that incision is as fresh as we think it might be.'

Thelwall looked at him. 'Are you thinking what I'm thinking?'

'I expect so but I'd rather find out for myself, wouldn't you? If we're right, this could be the tip of a rather nasty iceberg. In the circumstances, I can't recommend a police vet should handle one of these beasts – they're a far cry from his usual patients.'

The young vet grinned. 'I like it,' he said. 'Is it possible?'

'Of course it's possible. I'm the man from the Ministry, remember?'

Linus phoned Trevarrick and told him the dog being flown in on the Sea King was almost certainly booked into the Highnoon. Even if there had been more than one dog on that plane, there was a place at this kennels for it, a fact which would save Tolworth a lot of running around. He proposed going down to Culdrose with Thelwall straight away, using the Highnoon carrying vehicle. He knew that neither he nor Thelwall was, in fact, a licensed carrier but this was an exceptional situation, so why not?

Trevarrick hesitated. He liked to do things by the book but there was no denying it would be easier all round this way. Rintoul was a cautious man, not given to irresponsibility and he, Trevarrick, could certainly clear it with Customs and with Tolworth for this one occasion.

'OK,' he said eventually. 'You get on down there while I sort out the red tape this end. And Rintoul – '

'What?'

'Don't do anything like let the dog out for a run, will you?'

Linus controlled his irritation with an effort. 'Is it likely?' he asked, deliberately keeping his tone mild.

'No, I suppose not. Sorry. This Jones-Drybeck business has got on my nerves.'

And it's beginning to show, Linus thought as he put the phone down. He turned to Thelwall. 'Come on,' he said.

'We need a Pit Bull sized crate. There must be one around and I shouldn't think the one he was picked up in is in a fit condition to be used. It wouldn't surprise me if they've got him on the chopper with just a collar and lead.'

'What do we do if we get there and find he's been landed and whisked off somewhere else?' Thelwall asked.

'Not very likely. It depends how far out in the Atlantic the *Invincible* was. Do you know the range of a Sea King?'

Thelwall shook his head. 'No idea, but it's going to take us at least four hours to get down to Culdrose.'

'I think those big ones have quite a range – and they're not supersonic, you know. Anyway, if the dog has been collected, we just go along and collect it back. We've got the import licence, after all.'

When they finally reached the Royal Navy's helicopter base in Cornwall, they found they were expected and Linus's MAFF identity card was enough to get them through the gates, although the sentry refused to allow Thelwall through until he had made a phone call confirming that it was all right to do so. A military jeep led them to a place where various interested parties were assembled. It was dark now but the night was clear and they were told there was no reason to doubt that the Sea King would get there. He was already within radio contact of the base.

Linus introduced himself to the two Customs officers. 'Do you expect there to be anything here for you?' he asked.

'Only the dog, unless they've picked up dutiable odds and ends, which isn't very likely,' one of them replied. 'At least with you here we'll be able to send the dog on his way and get back home. I had visions of having to sit up all night with the damned thing until the powers that be had decided what to do with him. I bet he's not crated.'

'That's what we thought likely,' Linus agreed. 'If we're right, I take it you'd prefer us to go on board and crate him there?'

The Customs officer nodded. 'That's right. Let's do it by

the book. We don't want him setting foot on English soil and spreading rabies, do we?'

'No, we'll let him bite the hand that pushes him into his crate instead,' Linus said, and they both laughed.

The landing area was swamped with powerful lights that illuminated it as clearly as if it had been day. Linus and Thelwall stood on the periphery of this area among groups of people, each of whom was there because of his own particular field of expertise. Everything outside the wide circle of light seemed tar-black by contrast and Linus noticed that people seemed unwilling to venture back into the dark that surrounded them, much as prehistoric man must have been reluctant to leave the circle of light cast by his fire.

A young naval officer moved up beside him. 'Are you the quarantine chaps?' he asked.

It wasn't quite how Linus would have described himself but it was accurate enough. 'That's right. Is there a problem?'

'Pity you've got the name of the place splashed all over that Transit van. Couldn't you find a plain one?'

'I'm not sure I follow you,' Linus said.

'Didn't you see the Press at the gate? It's the dog they want to see. Barring a few dead bodies – which so far we haven't got – that dog's tomorrow's front page. They're going to want photos of him. Until you turned up they didn't know where he'd be going. If they don't get their pictures tonight, they'll be swarming all over the place tomorrow.'

Linus groaned. The prospect of intrepid journalists scaling security fencing to get into a kennel where, unbeknown to them, a dog had just died of rabies was not one to be viewed with equanimity.

'I suppose you're right,' he said. 'I'd better get in touch with the police at my end. The last thing we want is over-eager news-hounds inside the perimeter. Unlike you, we don't run to armed guards.'

It didn't take long to leave a message for Lacock and

when Linus returned to Thelwall's side, he could just make out the distant sound that soon proved itself to be the Sea King's rotors.

Linus had known the Sea King was a big machine but he had never seen one except on television and was quite unprepared for the size of the helicopter that descended from the night sky. He and Thelwall stayed where they were while the ground-crew rushed forward, each man knowing his specific role.

'We'll get the dog off first,' an authoritative voice called out. 'Bring your vehicle alongside.'

Thelwall drove the Transit up to the Sea King while Linus and the Customs officer followed on foot. They peered in. Sure enough, Sailor was secured to the side of the helicopter by a makeshift collar and a length of rope that would have held a Limousin bull in check. Of two things there was no doubt: Sailor was a Pit Bull and he was a very sick dog. Linus took the import licence from his inside pocket and handed it to the Customs officer. Meanwhile Thelwall and a rating were manhandling the crate into the Sea King.

'Close the doors,' Linus ordered. 'I'm untying this rope and we don't want to risk him suddenly taking fright.'

It was a necessary precaution though it didn't look as if there was much danger of Sailor even being able to stand up. The Customs officer backed away as Linus guided the sick animal towards the crate and pushed him in.

'What's wrong with him?' he said. 'Why is he like that? Is it rabies?'

'Hardly,' Linus said pityingly. Didn't the man have the first idea of the symptoms? 'Most of his trouble is exhaustion and exposure. It's quite likely he was sedated before he left and that would make him woozy. It's probably a combination. Are you going to seal this crate?'

This the Customs Officer did and when the helicopter door was opened, several men in fatigue overalls came forward to lift the crate back into the Transit. One of the pilots came forward.

'Take care of him,' he said. 'We all got very fond of the poor tyke while we had him on board.'

'We'll do what we can,' Linus told him. 'Don't be too optimistic, though: he doesn't look good.'

He climbed in beside Thelwall and they bumped across the turf to the road that led off the base. As they approached the gates, Linus was aware of the cameramen standing there. They must have been there when they had arrived but their presence hadn't registered. The seamen at the gate pushed the onlookers back as they opened the gates to let the Transit through.

'Can we see Sailor?' someone called out. Another man, closer to the window, said, 'Is he really a British Bulldog?'

'No,' Linus called out as they drove past. 'Alsatian.'

Thelwall flashed him a startled look. 'What did you say that for?'

Linus chuckled. 'Private joke. They won't know the difference.'

They had driven several miles before Thelwall spoke again. He had been looking in his mirror rather more often than might have been judged necessary. 'I think we're being followed,' he said.

'The Press, I expect. Now you know what it feels like to be a celebrity.'

'Shall I lose them?' Thelwall asked doubtfully.

'Whatever for? They know where we're going and I've no desire to prolong the trip. You've been watching too much TV.'

There were reporters waiting at Enstone, too, but fortunately the police had them well under control. A middle-aged sergeant, a classic example of the almost extinct village bobby, followed them in.

'We'll keep up a patrol for a few nights,' he told the two vets. 'Inspector Lacock suggests that the best thing to do is to have a photocall in the morning. Let them take all the photos they want of the dog and they'll go away happy. He says it'll help if he's got a pretty kennelmaid to hold him.'

'It makes sense,' Linus agreed. 'Trouble is, the dog may not make it.'

'Don't tell them that, for God's sake!' the policeman exclaimed. 'They'll vie with each other to bring down world experts on this and that if they think he won't live. They'll hang around inventing bulletins and climb over fences trying to get "exclusives". Just tell them the dog's being sedated for tonight after his hectic day and there will be a photocall in the morning. Tell them to go and find a nice comfortable hotel and be back about ten. So it's stretching it a bit. If it gets them off your back, who cares?'

'You'd better do the talking, then,' Linus told him. 'You've a nice, reliable manner about you. They'll believe you more easily than me.'

'Especially when they realize he's no Alsatian,' Thelwall murmured.

Between the three of them, they carried the crate through the security gates and into the little surgery that was, happily, hidden from anyone outside by the bulk of one of the food stores.

'Thank you, Sergeant,' Linus said. 'Perhaps you'd be kind enough to do what you can to get rid of the spectators?'

'It'll be a pleasure, Mr Rintoul.' He stared into the crate. 'Poor bugger,' he went on. 'I think you may well have a grieving nation on your hands tomorrow. Good night, sir. Good night, Mr Thelwall.'

Linus broke the seals and opened up the crate. 'I'm very much afraid he may be right. Help me get him on the table. Easy, now. We don't want to make him any worse.'

As gently as they could, for the dog was very heavy, Linus and Thelwall lifted him out of his crate and on to the examination table. His body was limp because he was almost too weak to move but the dark brown eyes watched the two men trustingly. They laid him on his side and Linus gently lifted one hind leg.

'He's got the incision, all right, and it looks fresh,' he said. Carefully, anxious not to cause the dog any pain, Linus palpated the area around the cut. He had been surprised to see it still had stitches which must mean it was less than a week old. He stood back. 'What do you make of it?' he asked Thelwall.

The younger man palpated with equal care. 'There's certainly something there,' he said at last. 'What's more, it's not part of his anatomy.'

'Let's go in there and find out what it is,' Linus suggested.

Thelwall hesitated. 'Will he survive a general anaesthetic? He's in a pretty bad way.'

Linus shook his head. 'The post-operative shock would kill him even if the anaesthetic didn't. No, we'll give him a local. He still won't feel anything and he's too weak to struggle. Tell you what, though. Before we start, rig up an infra-red heater in his kennel and make sure the bedding's thick. He's going to need all the warmth we can give him.'

While Thelwall took care of this, Linus stayed with the dog, stroking its head gently and playing with the uppermost ear. He talked to it, too, and was disproportionately flattered to find an unhealthily pale tongue licking his hand.

'Sailor,' he said scornfully. 'What sort of name is that? Let's see what your owner calls you.' He reached into his pocket for the rest of the dog's documentation and for the first time took note of details other than the dog's breed. The owner was one Henry Lewdown and the dog's name was given as Ripper. Linus groaned. That was almost as bad.

When Thelwall came back he held the dog while Linus surrounded the incision with small injections of anaesthetic and then, while they waited for them to take full effect, the two vets took it in turns to scrub up. Their task was neither onerous nor lengthy. The stitches were easily removed and very little healing had taken place between the tissues they joined.

'I'm no pathologist,' Linus commented, 'but I doubt if those stitches have been in for longer than twenty-four hours. Aha! What have we here?' He slipped his gloved fingers into the small cavity that he had just opened up and withdrew a small, flat, plastic-wrapped package, now slippery with blood. He laid it on the table, to one side of the dog's head. 'I don't know about you, Thelwall, but I'm not altogether surprised at that.'

David Thelwall grinned. 'I don't think I am, either. What do you think it is – precisely, I mean?'

'No idea, but I'm reasonably sure it won't turn out to be self-raising flour. Come on. Let's get this poor dog sewn up again. The foreign body can wait.'

Linus sewed the dog up swiftly and efficiently. It was a long time since he had had to do anything like this and he was quietly proud that his old skills had not deserted him. He even found himself wondering whether it was too late to set himself up in private practice again but he knew he had become accustomed to undisturbed nights and a largely nine to five routine for too long to break the mould now. When he had finished, he stripped off the surgical gloves and stood looking down at the dog for a few minutes. 'Poor sod,' he said. 'I hope you make it, chummy. You deserve to.' He turned to Thelwall. 'I'll bring the dog. You lead the way.'

Thelwall opened the door for him and stood aside as Linus carried the heavy brindle body through. Then he slipped past him so that he was in front of him at the next entrance. The door from the kennel to the run was firmly closed and a fair heat now permeated the tiled sleeping-quarters. A rectangular wooden dog-bed, its edges metal-covered against chewers, was filled with a deep layer of shredded absorbent paper. The infra-red lamp hung on its chain immediately overhead, its more usual function to give added warmth during the winter months to the smaller breeds. Thelwall opened the door and Linus went through with the dog which he laid carefully down beside the heat-source. He looked around.

'Get him some water, Thelwall. The chances are he'll not be up to helping himself to it, but it needs to be there, in case. If he makes it through the night, the kennelmaid can try him with a little warmed milk in the morning. There's not much more we can do now.'

'I thought I'd check on him on and off through the night,' Thelwall said.

'Could you? That would be nice, though I doubt if it's going to make much difference.'

'I don't suppose it is, but I'd like to all the same. I feel involved with this one, somehow.'

They made their way back to the little surgery and Linus picked up the packet and balanced it in his hand. 'Where's the scales?' he said. 'I wonder what this weighs? A couple of ounces, at a guess.'

He rinsed the blood off the packet while Thelwall found the little medicine scales in a cupboard. Together they watched the needle.

'Not a bad guess,' the younger man said. 'Seventy-five grammes. What do you think it's worth?'

'I haven't a clue. Depends what it is, I suppose. We'd better take it back to the office and ring the police.'

'On television they put a finger in it and lick it and then they know what it is,' Thelwall said helpfully.

'Do they now? Well, if you want to dip your finger in something that's just come out of a dog's inside and then lick it, that's fine by me. I take it you're familiar with the different tastes of all the possible drugs?'

Rather shamefacedly, Thelwall admitted that he had no idea and that, put like that, he didn't much fancy it, either. Instead, they carried the little packet to the office and Thelwall put it in the somewhat inadequate safe while Linus telephoned the police.

He more than half expected that one of the police cars patrolling the kennels would be detailed to come in and collect the little parcel and take a quick statement. He was therefore none too pleased to have to wait for another car to come out from Oxford.

Detective-Sergeant Denbigh was brusque and suspicious. He made no attempt, Linus noticed, to taste the white powder in the packet they handed him.

'Inside a dog, you say? Bit far-fetched, isn't it?'

'Not really. Not once the idea's occurred to you. It pre-supposes a crooked kennel-owner, of course – and a crooked vet. Not an easy combination to find but once you've found them, anything's possible.'

'What made you open the dog up?'

'Several of them have these incisions. I'd wondered why. The chance to get one straight off the plane wasn't one to be missed. If whatever had been implanted was connected with the fighting, it would have been removed before the dog came in. There would have been a week-old incision but no stitches.'

'If it's what we suspect it is, why wouldn't sniffer dogs at the airport find the drugs?' the policeman demanded.

'You're the expert,' Linus said. 'You work it out. My guess is they keep sniffer dogs well away from contact with animals that may be rabid. This is a scheme with a lot of possibilities, you know. False bottoms to the crates, for a start. You could put drugs or explosives in there, not to mention less sinister contraband.'

'Then why the hell hasn't MAFF devised a more secure system?' Denbigh demanded.

'MAFF's brief is to prevent the import and spread of rabies,' Linus pointed out. 'We do that pretty well, con-sidering. I shouldn't think it's ever occurred to anyone that a crooked set-up could be used like this. What's that stuff worth? Multiply it by all the male Pit Bulls that have gone through this kennels since it opened and my guess is they've more than repaid the cost of importing them, so that anything they're sold for in the dog-pits is pure profit.'

Detective-Sergeant Denbigh snorted. 'Peanuts com-pared with the drug value,' he said. 'It must have cost them a bomb to set up this little lot to start with.'

'I think you'll find the kennels makes a tidy profit on its own account,' Linus said, 'and I think if you ask around, you'll find the dog-fighting game produces a healthy crop of peanuts. Say a dog costs £500 to buy in the States and about £400 to ship over. Quarantine at cost – say another

£500. The dog, whether as a fighter or a stud dog, is going to fetch something like £1500 if he's sold. If he's not, he'll make £300 a time at stud, and goodness knows what in bets if he's used in the ring. This packet of drugs oils the wheels – it increases the profits but it isn't huge in itself, I dare say. You'd be a better judge of that than me. All the same, you're left with a nice little number: a profitable, crooked set-up that has the capability of being adaptable to other purposes.'

'You know a lot about these things,' Denbigh said suspiciously.

'I don't, as a matter of fact, but I do know the sort of prices we're talking about in the other section of the dog fancy – the legitimate part – and believe me, I've underestimated, if anything.'

'So you reckon this Erbistock must be bent. D'you reckon there are many bent vets?'

'Rather fewer than there are bent coppers, I'd say,' Linus told him and found great satisfaction in the look of annoyance on the man's face.

David Thelwall felt it was time to intervene. 'Are you going to tell the Press about this?' he asked.

'Why?' Denbigh snapped.

'Because if the dog lives through the night, we were planning a photocall to get them off our backs once and for all. There's no need to say anything about it but if they've seen you arrive . . .'

Denbigh nodded. 'True enough. No, we'll say nothing. If you're asked, I'm here in connection with – let's see – the discovery that a dog has been destroyed in contravention of the rules. Or hadn't you heard?'

'Heard what?'

'I spoke to Lacock before I came out. It seems a dog *was* incinerated so we're assuming we don't have a rabid monster roaming Oxfordshire.'

Chapter Seven

Linus drove home with more care than he customarily used. He was tired and he knew it. He opened the driver's window to get a supply of cold air round his head and he made himself concentrate. He found that no amount of cold air and will-power was enough to keep his mind exclusively on the road ahead. Part of it kept wandering off to think about Ripper. Ugh, what a name!

He would make a point of seeing this Mr Henry Lewdown. He wanted to know what sort of a person went in for dog-fighting — and what sort of a person allowed his dog to be so abused as to risk its life carrying such a foul cargo as drugs. Linus supposed it was possible that Lewdown knew nothing of that side of it. It would be perfectly easy for the exporters to make the implant and, since no one was allowed to visit their dog for two weeks after its arrival, the stitches would be out and the wound largely healed by the time the owner first saw the dog. Furthermore, the wound was not in a place which caught the eye, so they might not notice the scar until the dog was home. By that time it would be so well healed that most owners, if they noticed it at all, would assume it had been caused by some injury inflicted before they bought the dog. He was prepared — just — to give Lewdown the benefit of the doubt so far as the drugs were concerned. The fighting was something else.

Linus's professional experience told him that dogs which seized any opportunity for a scrap seemed thoroughly to enjoy the fight and no amount of torn skin and subsequent stitching stopped them diving right in the next time they had a chance. He remembered with a respect bordering on affection a little mongrel terrier he must have stitched up half a dozen times because its greatest delight was in challenging something larger and heavier than itself and never running away when its challenge was accepted. The difference was that Bob's owners had done nothing to encourage him. On the contrary. They sank wire into the ground under their fences and put barricades along the top, but still Bob managed to get out and their distress when they brought him to Linus's surgery to be stitched up was acute.

No, the fact that the dogs might well enjoy the fight was irrelevant. It was the depravity of the owners who set up the fights that Linus found incomprehensible. How could sentient human beings find either pleasure or vicarious excitement in seeing animals torn apart? The ancient Romans had sunk to such levels – and worse – but we flattered ourselves we had progressed since then. Not all of us, it seemed. Centuries of moral education leading gradually to what should be a humane society must still have had no effect on a minority. Such people presumably walked around the streets looking just like anyone else yet inside their heads was a deformed mind that gained pleasure, not just from watching two dogs tear each other apart, but from putting them through a regimen of exercise and training designed to toughen them up and heighten their natural aggression in order to make the ensuing fights as savage and brutal as possible. The very thought of such people, such activities, produced in Linus a sickening, angry revulsion. Yes, he would be very interested to meet Mr Lewdown.

It was three o'clock in the morning when he finally got home. He very nearly went straight to bed but then he decided his mind was churning over at a speed that would preclude sleep so he went into the kitchen and made himself a mug of cocoa. While the milk boiled, he switched on his answering machine. There was a call from a relieved Trevarrick giving him the news which Denbigh had already passed on, one from a local gallery to say they had a little watercolour he might like to see, a wrong number – and a call from Clarissa to say that tomorrow (which Linus reminded himself was now today) was likely to be her last day in Oxford and could they meet? Perhaps he'd give her a ring at the Randolph around breakfast-time. Linus looked at his watch and groaned. He had intended not to set the alarm but to get up when he woke up. That was unlikely to be 'around breakfast-time'. He didn't have to contact Clarissa, of course, but he couldn't deny that he wanted to. Deep down, he found it really quite amazing that she wanted to go on seeing him. He rinsed out his mug methodically and stood it upside down to drain before going upstairs. He set the alarm for half past eight.

The effort of getting up so early after the lengthy exertions of the day before was entirely worthwhile when Clarissa sounded genuinely pleased to hear him. They arranged to have dinner again and Clarissa intimated that she had particularly liked the Windmill.

'It seems a long time since I've seen you,' Linus told her. 'The trouble is, I really have been extraordinarily busy but, with any luck, that phase is over for the time being.'

'Good,' she said. 'I wouldn't like anything to crop up to stop tonight's date. How can you be sure it won't?'

'Virtually certain,' he told her. 'By the way, do you recall the message on my answering machine the other day?'

'What message was that?' She sounded cautious. Linus thought she had probably forgotten all about it but was unwilling to let him know she was so totally uninterested in something that obviously interested him.

'The one about some dogs with signs of an incision.'

There was a silence as if she were trying to remember the incident. 'Oh, that. Yes, I remember something about it. Why?'

'Another one came in today and we found that tucked up behind the wound someone had inserted a packet of drugs.'

'Good heavens! What did you do?'

'There was only one thing we could do – tell the police. They're dealing with it now.'

'Yes, I suppose so. How exciting! I'll see you tonight. About a quarter to eight?'

Linus felt a slight sense of disappointment that, despite her words, she had sounded not at all excited — scarcely even intrigued. Was she really as incurious as she sounded? Or did she not really believe him? It was a bizarre enough story by any standards but surely not one that anybody would invent.

Linus debated whether to go back to bed but he didn't seem that tired now that he was awake so he had a leisurely breakfast and went in late to the office. Lisa greeted him with an air of resignation.

'The police are going through the files,' she said, 'and the preliminary news from Tolworth is that the head we sent them is clear. Of course, they've the biological test to do yet and a histology, but it seems pretty certain.'

'I thought that would be the result,' Linus commented. 'A bit hard on the poor dog. No need for him to have died at all, really. I suppose we had no choice but I don't like unnecessary destruction. Never have. Any news from Thelwall?'

'Not yet. Shall I get him for you?'

Linus didn't really expect Thelwall to be at the kennels yet — after all, he had had just as tiring a day as Linus and probably hadn't had the incentive of a Clarissa to get him out of bed, but he soon realized he had underestimated the stamina of youth.

'Sailor's doing fine,' were the young man's first words and Linus felt guilty that he had forgotten Thelwall's intention of sitting up with the dog. 'He's very weak but he's drunk some milk. Keep your fingers crossed and I think he'll make it. Are you coming over for his encounter with the Press? They're already gathering. TV, as well, by the look of it.'

'No, thanks. I'll leave that delight to you. Don't say anything about the rabies: by some miracle we've managed to keep it out of the papers and now the scare's over, we don't want them to get hold of it. I seem to remember the police don't want the drugs mentioned either.'

'That's right. They're crawling all over the place.'

'How do they propose explaining their continued presence to the media?' Linus asked, intrigued. 'Is it still the illegal destruction?'

'They've improved on it. I gather the story now is that they want to ensure no pressman puts himself – and society – in danger by penetrating the quarantine area in a fit of professional zeal. Our sergeant of last night tells me they've already started asking villagers how they feel about having a place like this on their doorstep.'

'Does that mean we can expect a close-it-down campaign?'

'I don't think so. People round here are pretty level-headed. I gather one journalist was told that at least the dogs stayed on the right side of the fence which was more than the speaker could say for some and he had a shotgun for unwelcome visitors, whether they had four legs and rabies or two and a notebook. I'm going to take police advice and get one of the girls to pose with the dog. His weakness is easily explained by the aircrash. I'm not sure what to tell them he is, though. They're not going to believe "Alsatian", you know. He looks even less like one standing on all fours.'

'Nevertheless, I'd be inclined to avoid the truth. Say he's a Bull Terrier. If someone suggests he looks more like a Staffordshire, that's all right. Tell him you wouldn't be surprised if there was a bit of that in him, too.'

'I've already been told not to identify the owner: the police want to get hold of him first. I thought I'd say we weren't giving his name until we'd been able to tell him and at the moment he's away on holiday. That ought to hold them off for a while.'

Inspector Lacock came in while Linus was enjoying his first cup of coffee and Linus looked at him in some surprise. 'I thought your job was finished once we'd cleared up the rabies business,' he said. 'What brings you here?'

'We're underplaying the drugs side of it, for the time being. We're still looking for the evidence with which to nail Jones-Drybeck and Erbistock over the rabies business. Of course, there's no doubt they're up to their necks in this, too, and it's our guess the reason for the secrecy over Lucky's death was to avoid the risk of the police poking their noses in, for reasons now understandable. They've got a tricky lawyer, too, and it's my belief she's as bent as they are. The longer they think we know nothing about the drugs, the better.'

'Will you have enough to hold them?'

'We already have. They've been charged with contravening the Rabies (Importation of Dogs, Cats and Other Mammals) Order of 1974 (as amended). That can net them an unlimited fine and up to one year in jail. Trouble is, it's not the kind of thing that gets them remanded in custody and the last thing we want right now is them on the loose.'

'With that hanging over them, MAFF won't want them back on the premises at all,' Linus told him.

'Don't worry. We've managed to stall. Further charges expected, etc. They're out of your hair for a few more days yet but that solicitor of theirs is cutting up rough.'

'What have you found out about the Pit Bulls?'

'Not much that you couldn't have found out for yourself if you hadn't been otherwise occupied,' Lacock told him. 'It's quite clever. They belong to various people – there's no case of one or two importers bringing in a whole lot of them. Just individual owners in different parts of the country bringing in the odd two or three over a period of time. It gets more interesting when one compares the licences with the visiting books: hardly any of them visit their dogs.'

'That's odd,' Linus remarked. 'Most owners go regularly – once a month at least, and quite a lot go every other week. Every week if they're local.'

'That's right. That's why the different pattern of Pit Bull visiting is so interesting. There's another thing, too. Something you wouldn't have been able to spot. A lot of the addresses are phoney. Not all of them, but some. Any Pit

Bull that gets visited has a genuine address but none of the phoney addresses visit and, to be fair, not all of the genuine ones, either. Yet they're all collected when their quarantine is over.'

'Who by?'

'That's the irony of it. Once they've finished their six months, MAFF rules about signing the book don't apply – the dog is no longer a danger.'

'So anybody could collect the dog?'

'That's right. In the case of a legitimate operation, if anyone except the owner came to fetch the animal on its release, the kennel operator wouldn't let it go: they know the owners quite well after six months of visiting. But in this sort of set-up those principles don't apply. We'll be talking to the kennelmaids, of course, but it's my guess that either Jones-Drybeck handed them over or there will have been so many of them that the girl won't remember any faces.'

'I'd bet on it,' Linus said thoughtfully. 'She struck me as one of the least curious females I'd ever met.'

'Which brings me to Mr Henry Lewdown,' Inspector Lacock went on. 'Do you know the name?'

Linus shook his head. 'Should I?'

'It's possible. He's a second-hand car dealer. At least, that's his official business and he runs it absolutely clean. We've never found so much as an illegal tyre there – and, believe me, we've looked. We know he sails close to the wind in a number of areas but we've never been able to pin anything on him. He's brought in quite a lot of Pit Bulls over the last four or five years: half a dozen, in fact. Ripper – or Sailor – is one of two in at present. The other's a bitch. Which brings me to why I'm here – it wasn't to fill you in out of the kindness of my heart.'

'I thought you were being remarkably frank,' Linus told him. 'What's the catch?'

'Lewdown's Pit Bulls. By all accounts they're nasty brutes, but Thelwall seems to think you've got a way with them. Our dog-handlers have no experience of that sort of animal. Obviously we've got to pick up Lewdown and examine the rest of his dogs. We'll take a couple of police handlers along, of course, but I'd be grateful if you'd come too.'

Linus was about to point out that it was only with other dogs that the Pit Bulls could be expected to be aggressive and that they certainly didn't need him, when he recalled that he would not be averse to meeting Lewdown and he was unlikely to get another opportunity. 'All right,' he said. 'When do we go?'

'Now.'

Henry Lewdown lived in an ostentatious house of obtrusive red brick to the north of the city. It was the sort of house that had been built in the 'thirties before planning laws imposed some measure of reserve on architectural design. It stood boldly out in its manicured lawn, very square and red with white window-frames in the pseudo-Georgian style, a Queen Anne mansard roof and – the ultimate anachronism – very new sliding patio doors leading on to an equally new and very stark patio. An attempt had been made to lessen the impact of the concrete slabs by placing tubs of plants at intervals along it but, since the tubs were of exceedingly white plastic, the resulting effect was hardly sympathetic. Nor was it the sort of house where one expected to see any kind of dog other than a manicured poodle. As they went up the asphalted drive, Linus looked about him for any indication of Pit Bulls. There were none. There was a raw, new, timber-built stable block but no kennels. There was a small paddock with a collection of brightly painted new jumps, but nothing that could possibly be a dog-compound. If it hadn't been for the name on the import licences, Linus would have discounted any possibility of finding Pit Bulls here.

A Spanish maid who understood English better than she spoke it opened the door and visibly blanched at the uniforms.

'A work permit I have,' she said. 'You want I get it?'

'Not at this stage,' Inspector Lacock said, not unkindly.

'Later, perhaps. We've come to see Mr Lewdown. Would you tell him we're here?'

Her face cleared. 'Mr Lewdown is out,' she said. 'Mrs Lewdown is upstairs. You want I get her?'

There was no need for an answer to this because at that precise moment they were joined by someone who was very clearly the lady of the house. Mrs Lewdown was built on what used to be called Junoesque lines. She was closer to forty than thirty and her blonde hair had been coming out of a bottle for so long that it looked as if it could no longer breathe on its own. Every inch of her that they could see (and, Linus suspected, every inch they couldn't) had been tanned in the Bahamian sun. Quite literally tanned for, like so many women no longer in the first flush of nubile youth, the combination of sun, salt water, gin and tobacco had given her skin the colour and texture of a mature saddle. She wore a lot of gold and a dress in a shiny jersey fabric that didn't exactly cling but nevertheless left little to the imagination. Her opulent vulgarity matched the house perfectly.

'And which policeman are you?' she asked. The accent, Linus decided, would have fitted a barmaid in an up-market pub, which in all probability was where Lewdown had met her.

Inspector Lacock introduced himself and asked if they could speak to Mr Lewdown. Mrs Lewdown ignored the question and stared at Linus.

'Who's this?' she asked.

'Mr Rintoul from the Ministry of Agriculture, Fisheries and Food,' Lacock told her.

'You what?' Her astonishment was unfeigned. 'The Inland Revenue I could understand, but the Ministry of Agriculture? We're not farmers!'

'Mr Rintoul is one of the Ministry's vets.'

'I don't care if he's the Ministry's pet monkey,' she snapped. 'He's no cause to be here. There's only the children's ponies and we've a perfectly good vet of our own.'

107

'Who might that be?' Linus asked. It was none of his business but the chances were she didn't know that.

'Someone my husband knows. Sold him a car once, or something. Erbistock. Yes, that's the name. I don't like him much but he seems competent enough.' She looked Linus up and down. 'You don't look like any vet I've ever seen,' she remarked. 'Too well-dressed by half. Are you sure you're a vet?'

'I don't actually have my qualifications with me,' Linus said apologetically, 'but I assure you Inspector Lacock has checked me out. Tell me, does Mr Erbistock look after your dogs, too?'

'Dogs? What dogs? We don't have any dogs. Nasty, messy things, all muddy paws and moulting hairs.'

'Oh, come, Mrs Lewdown,' the Inspector broke in. 'Your husband has imported several dogs over the last few years. Pit Bull Terriers.'

Mrs Lewdown looked bewildered and Linus could have sworn her bewilderment was genuine. 'Pit *whats*?' she asked.

'American Pit Bulls,' he told her on the unlikely off-chance she might only know the other name for the breed.

'Never heard of them,' she said positively. 'And we've certainly never had any, that's for sure.'

'Yet import licences for them have been issued in your husband's name,' Lacock pointed out.

'Then either someone is giving a false name or he's keeping them somewhere else because they're certainly not here. In fact,' she went on magnanimously, 'you can search the place if you like and I shan't insist on a warrant.'

'That won't be necessary,' Inspector Lacock told her, as sure as Linus that she was telling the truth. 'All we need is to have a few words with your husband and that will clear the matter up.'

She smiled smugly. 'There, I'm afraid, you're going to be disappointed, Inspector. As I think I heard Maria telling you, he's not here. Gone away on business for a few days.'

'Perhaps you'd be kind enough to let me have an address

or a phone number where I can contact him,' the Inspector persisted civilly.

The smile grew broader. 'I'm sorry, Inspector. I'm no wiser than you. He left very hurriedly this morning with absolutely no advance warning. Something had come up, he said. That sort of thing happens in business, you know.'

'So I believe. I take it it would be a waste of time asking you when you expect him back?'

'Completely,' she agreed. 'I'd love to tell you, of course, but I quite simply don't know myself.'

Both men considered there was a very good chance this was true but, either way, it was no help to them.

'Perhaps I could ask you to let us know when he comes back or when he gets in touch with you,' the Inspector suggested.

'Why bother? You're going to leave someone to watch the house and I don't doubt you'll tap the phone,' she said acidly. 'You'll know his whereabouts before I do, I dare say. But I don't mind telling him to ring you when he gets back.'

Inspector Lacock thanked her and asked if she minded their looking over the grounds just to make his report neat and tidy. She was not the least disconcerted by the request and both men knew before they set out that they would find no evidence of dogs at all, let alone Pit Bulls.

'What do you make of that?' Linus said as they left the premises.

'Whatever her husband's up to where the dogs are concerned, I'm sure she knows nothing about it,' the Inspector replied. 'We'll watch the place all the same, and, since there are drugs involved, I dare say we'll have no difficulty getting permission to tap the phone. Neither he nor she will get in touch with us voluntarily. Unless they're burgled, of course, and then they'll come running.'

Linus was so tired that the rest of the day was like living in a slow-motion film. Everthing he did seemed to take three times as long as it normally did and even his brain was functioning in bottom gear. Even frequent lubrication with coffee did little to ease the process. The prospect of bed became infinitely seductive and it was a prospect which did not include Clarissa, a sure sign, he suspected, of the advance of age. He even considered cancelling his date and more than once his hand hovered indecisively over the telephone. He withdrew it every time. If Clarissa was leaving Oxford, another opportunity of seeing her was unlikely to present itself. He enjoyed her company. More accurately, perhaps, he enjoyed being seen in her company. Middle-aged men, especially wealthy ones, were not infrequently seen with beautiful, if vacuous, dolly-birds and more frequently with their expensively befurred middle-aged wives. Very rarely did a man like Linus, who might be middle-aged but certainly wasn't wealthy, come by the company of one of the Clarissas of this world and this Clarissa was a real humdinger. He knew himself to be neat, tidy, presentable – he might almost venture to call himself well-dressed – and at least he didn't eat his peas off his knife, but he had to admit to himself that he had no very clear idea what Clarissa saw in him or why she was so keen to maintain the acquaintance. Clarissa came into the category of gift-horses into whose mouths it was better not to look, and he would be foolish not to enjoy her company while he could.

He had decided to follow her hint and go back to the Windmill and, since it was to be a last assignation, he asked for a secluded table, knowing that this would mean one of the little booths tucked under the stairs and well screened from the vulgar gaze.

Clarissa always dressed well but on this occasion, Linus had the feeling she had made a particular effort. She wore a simple shirtwaisted dress of softly pleated black crêpe de chine that buttoned down the front and bloused over the belt. Her ballerina's chignon was studded with pearls – he supposed they were sewn or stuck on to a fine net. She looked extremely elegant and very beautiful and he almost regretted having asked for a secluded table. For some reason, her resemblance to the young lady in the Leonardo was even more marked.

She seemed in some indefinable way to be in what Linus could only call a 'softer' mood than usual. She looked at him more often and when she did so there was a softness in her eyes that had not been there before and when, between courses, her hand lay on the cloth, it seemed entirely natural to cover it with his own. She smiled when he did so and his apprehensions melted away.

'I *am* glad I met you,' she said. 'It was sheer chance that took me into the Ashmolean that day.'

'So am I. Perhaps we should drink to your American friends.'

She looked at him blankly. 'My who?'

'The American friends who wanted you to look at Powhatan's mantle.'

Her face cleared. 'Oh, them. Do you know, I'd almost forgotten all about them. Yes, we should. I wonder what made me pick that particular day?'

'I suppose that's something we shall never know.' Linus hesitated. 'I've enjoyed our assignations,' he went on, uncertain whether he might say too much or too little.

She smiled – a shade indulgently, Linus thought. 'How delightfully old-fashioned,' she said. '"Assignations": a lovely word.'

'I'm sorry if I strike you as old-fashioned,' Linus said rather stiffly. 'I'm not very fond of the word "date".'

'I didn't mean to imply that you were old-fashioned,' she said hastily. 'Only the choice of word. Though you do have what one might call an old-fashioned charm. It's what I like about you.'

Linus supposed this was meant as a compliment and decided to accept it as such. 'Then in that case, I'll consider myself flattered.'

'Can I be absolutely honest with you?' Clarissa asked.

Privately reflecting that absolute honesty was a non-existent commodity, Linus assured her that she could.

'There have been times when I wished you were a little less old-worldly,' she told him.

'In what way?'

'Well . . . you don't have to be *quite* such a gentleman, you know. I mean, if you really want something badly enough, you don't have to give up at the first "no".'

Linus was considerably taken aback though he tried not to show it and hoped that the dim lights made that possible. Then he decided he was glad she had said it. It considerably enhanced his expectations of the evening. 'I see,' he said. 'I'll try and bear that in mind.'

They rounded off the meal with Irish coffee and when they rose from the table, Linus put Clarissa's coat round her shoulders and guided her to the door, oblivious of their fellow-diners. Even had he noticed the man in the quiet suit at the bar, it is unlikely Linus would have recognized him: one seldom does recognize a person seen out of context. Inspector Lacock recognized Linus, though, and whistled softly through his teeth but he made no attempt to draw the vet's attention. That could wait.

'I take it you'd be happy to come in for brandy – or another coffee,' Linus said as they drove back towards Oxford.

'I was half afraid you wouldn't ask,' Clarissa said and they both laughed.

She opted for brandy and Linus joined her, delighted that the exhaustion of the day seemed to have evaporated. He felt tired, to be sure, but it was a warm, pleasant glow of tiredness induced by good food, good company and a little alcohol. When he took her in his arms, he was not expecting to meet reluctance but neither was he anticipating quite such a full-bloodedly sensual enjoyment as Clarissa demonstrated.

He no longer felt middle-aged and wished only that they could have reached this degree of intimacy earlier in their acquaintance and before she was about to be snatched from him by the demands of her business. The brandies remained unfinished by the sofa and Clarissa preceded him up the stairs, leaving her dress in a little heap on the sitting-room floor.

Consummation came quickly and Linus knew her satisfaction had not been feigned. He made to withdraw but she held him close.

'No,' she whispered. 'Not yet. You'll come again and I want to feel it happen.'

'I'm heavy,' he protested.

'Not that heavy.'

Her slender fingers caressed his body as he kissed her lips, her neck, her breasts and, as she stirred beneath his touch, he felt his vitality return and he plunged still deeper inside her, delighting in her groans of pure ecstasy.

They rested then for a long time, talking little but touching often, with fingers and lips exploring the quiet, sensuous corners of their bodies until the need was upon them again, but this time, when the tide ebbed, they slept.

Linus woke first and wondered how long it had been since he woke with a woman in his arms. Unwilling to disturb her, he began to calculate it but the answer looked like being a depressingly long time. Instead, he eased his arm out from under her and slid as unobtrusively as he could from the bed. He picked up his robe and went downstairs.

When he returned with a tray of tea, Clarissa was stirring and he kissed her gently as he put the tray down on the table beside the bed.

'How awake are you?' he said. 'I thought you might like some tea.'

She sat up then and he was quietly pleased that she felt no need to cover her breasts. She smiled at him. 'Better than room service,' she said. 'Your wife trained you well.'

He frowned. That last comment struck a discordant note. He didn't make early morning tea automatically, like a dog trained to bring in the paper. It had been . . . an offering, a small gesture of appreciation and that aspect had quite escaped her. He smiled but said nothing and slipped back in beside her.

113

Sensing his sudden slight reserve, Clarissa leant across and kissed him. 'I wish I didn't have to go today,' she said.

'So do I,' he replied, and meant it.

'What will you do today?'

'Oh, I don't know. Take it fairly easy, I suppose. Monday was pretty fraught: I didn't get back till the early hours and yesterday's early night didn't materialize.'

She chuckled. 'Are you sorry?'

'Not in the least, but it means I shan't feel up to much today. Maybe I'll go out and see that dog.'

'That dog? Oh, you mean the drug-smuggling one. What's happened about that?'

'Nothing much. The owner's gone away on business. I suppose they'll have to wait for him to come back. It's not my pigeon, thank goodness. It was odd, though: his wife knew nothing about the dogs at all. A whole section of his life of which she was totally ignorant.'

'I dare say she has secrets of her own.'

Linus grimaced. 'Quite likely. I don't think I'd be very happy in a relationship that incorporated large-scale concealment.'

She kissed him again. 'You're just old-fashioned,' she said. 'It's your greatest charm but it's not very realistic.'

Her almost patronizing cynicism struck another false chord in Linus's mind but this was not a morning when he wanted false chords so he changed the subject. 'Are you sure you have to leave today?' he asked.

'Virtually certain. I shan't know for sure until I get back and make a few phone calls. You could ring the Randolph later and check, if you like.'

'There's nothing to stop you making the calls from here,' Linus pointed out.

She shook her head. 'You're very kind, but I never mix business and pleasure.'

'I just thought it would enable you to let me know straight away if there was any chance of your staying on.'

'You're really very sweet.' She got out of bed. 'No, I'll have a shower and get back to my hotel. Will you ring?'

'Of course. If you do have to go, you'll leave a number where I can contact you?'

'Don't worry: I've every intention of seeing you again. Will you book a taxi for me for, say, half an hour's time?'

'Aren't you staying for breakfast? I can drop you off on my way in.' Linus was startled at this abrupt end to the interlude.

She looked as if she was thinking about it. 'No,' she said at last. 'I'd rather get on, if you don't mind. Besides, I never eat breakfast.'

'Not even at the Randolph?' Linus asked, remembering that there had been occasions when she most certainly had.

'The Randolph doesn't count. If you're paying for bed and breakfast, you may as well eat the breakfast, don't you think? I won't be long.'

When she had gone, Linus was conscious of a faint feeling of disappointment. It certainly didn't relate to the night's activities. Far from it. In fact, Linus had risen, so to speak, to heights of which he hadn't known he was capable. Perhaps a sense of anti-climax was inevitable, yet he knew it wasn't quite that, either.

He was late in again and he could tell from his manner that Trevarrick was less than delighted although no comment was made and, when Thelwall rang to suggest he ought to go in and see Sailor, Linus was happy to have an excuse to go out.

'That dog must have the constitution of an ox,' Thelwall told him. 'You won't believe the recovery he's made in so short a time.'

Sailor was on his feet and looked perfectly well. He was a little thinner than he should be and probably, Linus thought, than he had been when he was shipped out, but his thin, whip-like tail lashed from side to side when he saw his visitors, its tip touching its ribs every time it swung to the full extent of its range. Linus opened the kennel door and went in. Now the whole of the dog's rear end joined in the delight at seeing him.

Thelwall laughed. 'You'd think he knew you were the one who removed his cargo,' he said.

'He was conscious at the time. Remember? Though all he'd recall was that I'm the one who opened him up and stitched him together again. You're the one who's been nursing him. I hope he's equally grateful to you.'

'Nothing like that,' Thelwall told him. 'I'm quite put out.'

Linus enjoyed the dog's company. There was something comfortingly genuine about the dog's pleasure in seeing him. He fondled the dog's ears and slapped its sides in that hollow-palmed slap that dogs love.

'Let's hope for his sake they find Lewdown,' Thelwall commented.

'Why? I can't say I'm at all keen on anything as nice as this going to the fighting fancy.'

'If Lewdown doesn't turn up, the dog will have to be put down. Someone's got to pay his quarantine.'

Linus looked up. 'Surely the kennel can carry one passenger?'

'Tell that to your people. MAFF is running the place until the Jones-Drybeck-Erbistock business is sorted out. My instructions are that the accounting has to be spot on.'

'I didn't realize you were taking it over.'

'Someone's got to run it and I don't mind having a go, though it's none too easy to keep a private practice going as well. No wonder Erbistock didn't have much of a practice. When I've found out all the wrinkles, I might even make them an offer for the place. What do you think?'

'If you can raise the capital, you could do worse. There's a good living to be made from a well-run quarantine kennel but it's a twenty-four-hour-a-day job.'

'So's a veterinary practice.'

When they returned to the office, they found Inspector Lacock there. 'Good morning, gentlemen,' he said. 'I hope you found everything routine, unexciting and entirely unexceptional today.'

'So far it has been,' Thelwall replied. 'I've a feeling your arrival here is going to throw a spanner in the works, though.'

'I heard Mr Rintoul was out here, that's all. Have a nice evening, Mr Rintoul?'

'Very pleasant, thank you, Inspector. Did you come all this way to ask me that?'

'No. I came out here to tell you we've found Mr Lewdown.'

Linus's heart sank. He realized there was nothing he wanted to be told less. The dog belonged to Lewdown and there was no way by which he could stop the man using him for anything he liked. 'I can't say I'm delighted,' he said. 'That dog deserves a good home and he won't get one there. What does Lewdown say about the drugs? It came as a complete surprise, I suppose?'

'Mr Lewdown had nothing whatever to say about drugs. Or anything else, for that matter. He was fished out of the Camber last night.'

The two vets exchanged glances. 'What's the Camber?' Thelwall asked.

'You're obviously land-lubbers like me. Good. Now I can make you feel as small as the Portsmouth police made me. Apparently it's a small commercial dock in what's called Old Portsmouth. They get the odd fishing-smack there, the occasional schooner, that sort of thing. Not a place for pleasure-craft, I gather. There are some warehouses and a fish-packing place. They think Lewdown slipped on ice from there and fell in. It must have been after working hours or someone would have seen him, but once they've all gone home, it's pretty deserted.'

'So who found him?' Linus asked.

'Chap walking his dog. Said if it hadn't been a clear night and a full moon he wouldn't have noticed a thing.'

'And they're sure it's Lewdown?'

'We are now. His wife identified him this morning. We'd warned all ports, naturally. Mind you, we were thinking more of ferries to the continent, but the Portsmouth police reckon he might have been trying to cadge a quiet lift on

117

something going out from the Camber. It's mostly only locals who would think of going out from there: most people would make for the regular ferries and hope not to be noticed in the crowds.'

'Are they sure it was an accident?' Thelwall asked. 'I'd have thought with drugs involved it might well not have been.'

'That has occurred to us, Mr Thelwall,' Inspector Lacock said drily. 'I assure you it is being thoroughly looked into. The fact that he had no identification does tend to raise one's suspicions. At least they have a starting-point: he had booked into the Dolphin earlier that day – under another name, of course – so he wasn't necessarily expecting to leave straight away.'

'All of which means,' Linus said thoughtfully, 'that this poor dog belongs to Mrs Lewdown.'

'Who isn't going to want it.' Lacock concluded Linus's thoughts for him. 'On the other hand, she may be very interested in the news value of being the owner of a dog with such a tragic recent history. It survives a mid-air explosion, two operations to enable it to transport cocaine and then, just as it's getting better, its owner floats upside down in a bit of dirty sea-water. The Press will have a field day. You've met her, Rintoul. Can't you just see her wallowing in it? Yellow curls all over the front page?'

Linus could. It was not an appealing picture. Furthermore, when all the publicity was over, she'd ditch the dog without a second thought. 'Hang on!' he said suddenly. 'She doesn't know about the dog. If no one tells her, she won't claim it.'

'Of course she knows about it,' Lacock retorted. 'We told her when we were there.'

'No, we didn't. Cast your mind back. We told her he'd imported several over the years. She denied it. We made no mention of this particular one.'

'It doesn't alter the fact that it's her dog and although we intend to go on keeping it quiet for the time being – we don't want the people behind this drug-smuggling to know how much we know – sooner or later she'll have to be told.'

'Anyone who can use a dog to smuggle in drugs should be barred from keeping dogs,' Linus said.

'I think we could probably arrange something along those lines,' Lacock agreed. 'Will that suit you?'

'For the time being,' Linus conceded.

They walked out of the office and back to their respective cars together. 'You're something of a dark horse, Rintoul, aren't you?' the Inspector said.

'Am I?' Linus was surprised. 'In what way?'

'I was at the Windmill last night. I don't think you recognized me in civvies. Interesting companion you had. Very interesting. Known her long?'

'Not terribly,' Linus said cautiously. 'She's quite a stunner, isn't she? Not sure why you should describe her as "interesting", though. Not that she isn't, but it's a funny word to use.'

'Perhaps the reason I used it was because it was seeing her in your company I found interesting,' Lacock said.

'I have my moments,' Linus said modestly. 'But that's not what you meant, is it?'

'Didn't you know that Mary Calshot is the solicitor acting for Jones-Drybeck and Erbistock?'

'She didn't mention it,' Linus said cautiously. 'Are you sure?'

'Quite sure. There's no room for mistaken identity with a woman who looks like that.'

Chapter Eight

By the time Linus had fastened his seat-belt, Lacock's words were gnawing away inside him, corrosive and destructive. He could not delude himself that Lacock had mistaken Clarissa for anyone else. As the Inspector himself had said, it simply wasn't possible to mistake a woman as stunning as Clarissa. Or Mary. If she was a solicitor, then Mary Calshot must be her real name: there would be a register of solicitors just as there were registers of vets, doctors and clergymen, and presumably the police would have checked the credentials of any solicitor representing those against whom charges were being preferred.

He had begun this day feeling six feet tall and with more spring in his step than he could remember for a long time. Clarissa had made him feel like that. Now it began to look as if she had taken him for the middle-aged, besotted fool he had proved to be and that was not a comforting thought. He took a bend too fast and his heart skipped several beats as it lurched about in the region of his stomach. Slow down, he told himself. That was too close. He eased his accelerator foot and concentrated on the road until a lay-by came up. He pulled in. He needed to think.

He went back to the beginning. Had Clarissa been sent for because the kennels knew they had a rabid dog? Probably. The original Lucky might well have died by then and, given the illegal nature of one side of the kennels' business dealings, it was perfectly understandable that Jones-Drybeck should seek advice from her masters before deciding whether to let MAFF know. He wondered whether their first meeting had been entirely fortuitous. It was chastening to have to consider that he was being used even then but it was a possibility he had to face. Reflection reassured him on that point. She could not possibly have known he was going to the Ashmolean. No one could. He had gone there on the spur of the moment. He supposed she could have been following him in anticipation of his future usefulness but he was inclined to dismiss the idea: it didn't make sense to select one particular Ministry vet before anyone but the kennels knew about the rabies. If another vet had been detailed to deal with it – and the kennels at that time had no reason to believe MAFF knew anything about it because they didn't know what was wrong with Gail – an acquaintance with Linus would have been virtually useless.

Linus remembered that he hadn't even mentioned the rabies to her. They had been so anxious to keep the scare out of the Press that he had said nothing. He now guessed that rabies was the least of her concerns. He had told her about the incisions and later about the discovery of the drugs. These were things the police were keeping entirely to themselves so that the villains concerned wouldn't know how the case against them was developing. Linus had handed them that information on a platter. He reddened with mortification as he thought of it. His comments to Clarissa had been the sort of innocent remark one makes to a wife or a very close friend. He had told her of the discovery of the drugs almost as soon as he had told the police – and Lewdown had promptly vanished. At break-fast-time he had told her the police were going to have to wait for Lewdown's return. It wasn't a crucial piece of information. Indeed, common sense would have told anyone that if they couldn't track him down, they would have no option. All the same, it meant that, thanks to Linus Rintoul, the villains were aware of police progress at every stage. He supposed her willingness to spend the night with him had been in order to encourage him to make more inadvertent revelations. He was obliged to concede that the old saying about there being no fool like an old fool was pretty accurate.

He did toy briefly with the idea – and it was an appealing one – that Clarissa was innocently involved in all this; that she was a perfectly legitimate solicitor who just happened to have been implicated by some very nasty people. It was a theory he couldn't sustain. No solicitor acting innocently gives a false name and Clarissa had not only given Linus her alias, but she was also booked into the Randolph under that pseudonym. No, Clarissa Pensilva – or Mary Calshot – was fully implicated and Linus Rintoul was a fool.

He turned on the ignition and put the car angrily into gear. He had no more liking for being used than the next man and it didn't make it any more bearable that the user had been a beautiful woman. It might have been some satisfaction if he could have kidded himself that at least he had seduced her but he knew that all the serious advances had been made by her. He had been too 'old-fashioned' to push his luck.

There was another thing to bear in mind, too. The whole drugs scene was one about which he knew nothing but, if the newspapers were to be believed, it was a very nasty one indeed. That meant that Clarissa – or perhaps, he thought hopefully, it was just Clarissa's connections – were very dangerous people. He felt that slight frisson of fear that comes from knowing one is swimming out of one's depth, but it was quickly overtaken by anger that what had, he was convinced, started out as an innocent and casual acquaintance, had been corrupted and used. A woman of integrity would have dropped the association when she realized there was a conflict. A woman of integrity, he reminded himself, wouldn't have been involved with drug-running in the first place. He felt an urge to get his own back. He regarded such an urge as childish but that didn't lessen its strength. The trouble was, where did he begin? Getting his own back – revenge was a stronger word for it – was not something he habitually did.

He headed out into the Oxford-bound traffic but then, on an impulse, crossed the road and pulled into a filling-station. He drew up away from the pumps and sought out the telephone. Three minutes later he was in his car and driving back the way he had come.

Fred Grinton was waiting for him in a small country pub which mercifully did not provide its customers with non-stop television. Linus bought the RSPCA inspector another half and one for himself and sat down opposite him.

'What's all this, then?' Fred said. 'Mysterious phone calls, sudden haste and goodness knows what else? You are lucky to catch me in – and I haven't got time to sit around here till they close, either.'

'Dog-fighting,' Linus said briefly. 'I want to know everything you know about it, however unimportant it may seem.'

'That won't take long, then. I don't suppose I can add much to what you've probably already picked up one way or another. Tell me what you know and I'll fill in any gaps I can.'

'I've no details at all,' Linus confessed. 'It's illegal but on the increase. There seems to be a general idea there's big money involved – mostly in the form of betting, I suppose. The breed most often used is American Pit Bull Terriers but they use Staffordshires if they can get them and maybe Bull Terriers as well. That's about it.'

Fred nodded. 'Accurate enough. It's said it's not only big money but also big names and that's why the police are reluctant to be too energetic. It's very well organized and there's more of it in the North and Midlands than in the South. As far as I can make out, there are little unconnected outfits but most of it is fairly carefully co-ordinated. I did hear that there's organized crime behind it, too, but that may just be melodramatic exaggeration.'

Linus thought of the drugs and the whole crooked set-up at Mrs Jones-Drybeck's, but said nothing.

'In the early days, when Pit Bulls were more scarce, there were a lot of cases of Staffordshires and Bull Terriers – but particularly Staffordshires – being stolen. Registrations rose dramatically as a sort of sub-culture bred both breeds for the ring and serious breeders were very worried. The stealing seems to have eased off a bit. Quite a few of the game little terrier breeds began to disappear, too. No good for fighting themselves but just the thing for throwing into a training pit to let the dog get the hang of the game. There was a move to ban the import of Pit Bulls – you probably heard about that – but it failed.'

'That's right,' Linus agreed. 'There were two arguments, I seem to remember. One was based on the fact that anyone is entitled to import their pet dog of any breed and that if you ban the breed, they'll just apply for licences as something else. The other was that Customs men can't be expected to tell the difference between one breed and another especially when they're similar, and Pit Bulls are very like Staffordshires to the non-expert. Besides, if the owner swears it's one thing, how can you disprove it? There's been a case in another area of a quarantine kennel taking in a little white dog described as an American Eskimo and then a few weeks later taking in another Eskimo Dog which turned out to be four times the size and a proper husky. Both owners claim to be right and it's none of MAFF's business that the dogs are so different. What's more, it doesn't matter: both came in legitimately.'

'There've been several books published, too,' Fred Grinton went on. 'If you want to find out more, you could dip into them. You won't find them in any library, though, and I've heard the firms that supply books to the dog fancier won't touch them. They purport to be written as a disinterested exercise in widening the knowledge of all aspects of the dog-game but they can be used as training manuals. Very nasty.'

'So how does someone get hold of a Pit Bull?' Linus asked.

Fred looked at him with curiosity mingled with distaste. 'With great difficulty, I should imagine. Why the interest? It doesn't sound like you at all – and I hope it isn't.'

'That Jones-Drybeck woman has a lot of them in her kennels. Said she specialized in them because other kennels wouldn't touch them. They seem to be a profitable breed but I've never seen them advertised.'

'Depends where you've looked. They won't be in *Country Life* or *The Field* or even the local papers. At one time the canine press accepted adverts but the outcry was so great they stopped. *Exchange and Mart* is where you'll see them.' He drained his glass and stood up. 'I don't know what use you intend to put this information to, Linus, but I'd advise you to be very careful indeed. If you're not, MAFF will have a vacancy to fill.'

Linus laughed. 'Come on, Fred. You've been watching too much television.'

'I wish I got the chance,' Fred said bitterly. 'Make a fool of yourself, if you must, Linus, and a dead fool if you really can't help it, but do make sure it's all going to be worthwhile before you start meddling, won't you?'

He was perfectly serious and Linus was conscious again of that little prickle of fear.

When he got back to Oxford, Trevarrick had heard the news of the discovery of Lewdown's body on the radio and had already taken steps of his own in relation to the two Pit Bulls being quarantined in the car dealer's name. He called Linus into his office.

'It's a tricky situation,' he said. 'I've spoken to Mrs Lewdown. Naturally, she's upset at the death of her husband but she's quite adamant that she knows nothing about these animals, has no interest in them and absolutely no intention of paying for their quarantine. She's sending me a letter authorizing their destruction, so that's two less to bother about.'

'I don't think the police will want that done,' Linus told him. 'Certainly not to the dog. He's evidence.'

'Then the police can pay his bills,' Trevarrick said. 'The sooner we can empty that kennel, the better. We don't have the manpower to run it ourselves any longer than we have to.'

'Right now young Thelwall's running it – and doing a good job. He's even thinking he might take it over if he can raise the capital. Now that the rabies scare is over, I'm the only one who's been going over there.'

'Right, and you should be doing other things. But that bitch can be put down as soon as we get the letter even if the dog has to be kept.'

'I don't like putting down perfectly healthy animals. It's not what I trained for,' Linus protested, 'particularly not that dog. We've worked hard to save him and he's making a good recovery. If Mrs Lewdown doesn't want him, I'll take him – and pay for his quarantine.'

'What in heaven's name do you want with a dog like

that? Or any dog, for that matter. It's not quite your style, is it?'

'Maybe I'm changing my style. Any other objections?'

'No, none,' Trevarrick said doubtfully as if he felt he should be able to find one.

'Then get back to Mrs Lewdown and get her to change her mind. If she says the dog has to be destroyed then, sooner or later, that's what we'll have to do. I know we can't find it a home contrary to the owner's specific instructions. We probably can't do anything about the bitch without bringing in the media to work up a sob story and I don't think the police want any more media attention than we've got. Just don't expect me to put either of them down, because I won't.'

Trevarrick reached for the phone and dialled.

'Mrs Lewdown? Trevarrick here. Ministry of Agriculture.'

Linus couldn't distinguish the words at the other end but he had no difficulty recognizing exasperation when he heard it.

'Yes, I know, Mrs Lewdown,' Trevarrick went on. 'I'm sorry to be bothering you again, especially in the circumstances, but I think I may be able to save you some bother. One of my Veterinary Officers would be happy to give a home to one of your husband's dogs.' There was a pause. 'Yes, Mrs Lewdown, he'd pay the quarantine charges. He seems to think we may be able to find someone to take the other one. If you're prepared to make them over to the Ministry, we won't have to bother you again – and, of course, there won't be the risk of the newspapers getting hold of the story.' There was another pause, longer this time. 'Of course, we wouldn't say anything, but things do have a habit of getting out, as I'm sure you know, and there's no denying that "grieving widow puts down husband's pets" doesn't look good at all.' During the next pause, Trevarrick was obliged to hold the handset well away from his ear. 'How very sensible, Mrs Lewdown. Yes, just a letter handing ownership over to the Ministry – that's all we need and I can't see any reason for you to hear from us again, can you?'

He put the phone down. 'Satisfied?' he asked.

Linus grinned. 'I had no idea you could be such a devious bastard,' he said.

'Your problem is that you're not,' his boss told him. 'That's why it's me who's Regional Veterinary Officer and not you.'

'You're welcome to it. I prefer to get out a bit more.' He started to leave the room and hesitated at the door, then turned back. 'I've some leave owing to me,' he said. 'Mind if I take it? A week should be enough.'

Trevarrick tried to hide his irritation. He didn't like people who took their leave at short notice. It mucked up the schedules. 'Starting when?' he asked.

'Tomorrow.'

'Tomorrow! Cutting it a bit fine, aren't you?'

'Sorry about that. Thing is, this business has been getting to me more than I expected. First there was Sean's distress to deal with, then all the brouhaha about a rabies scare and now this drugs business. To be perfectly honest, I've just about reached the end of my tether. I could use a few days.'

Trevarrick couldn't argue with that. Rintoul had borne most of the burden of the rabies business himself. Not the office work, perhaps: the preliminary liaison with the local council, the health authority and the police – but certainly the sheer physical slog of examining all those dogs, not to mention the psychological stress of knowing that one of them had the power to kill him if he took the smallest hint of a risk. 'I suppose we can manage,' he said at last. 'I'll expect you back on Thursday.'

Linus drove home with no very clear idea why he had asked for some leave or what he was going to do with it. He'd go and see the dog, he decided, and he'd better see how Sean was coping. Apart from that, about the only thing he wanted to do was sleep. If he slept for long enough, the police would sort the whole thing out. They'd find

Lewdown's killer or discover that it really had been an accident; they'd track down the people behind the drug-smuggling and, with a little bit of luck, they'd clean up the dog-fighting, or at least one corner of it, all before he, Linus, got back to work. He supposed he'd had some idea that morning of doing something about the fighting himself but Fred's warning had been sincere enough and, when he analysed it, what hard facts did he have? None. The only positive contact with the 'game' he had was Lewdown, and a fat lot of use he was now.

As for some half-baked idea of getting his own back on Clarissa, well, it seemed less important now. In any case, her involvement was more likely to be connected with the drugs than the fighting and the police were the people to deal with that.

When he got indoors, the first thing he saw was the tray of early-morning tea which he had uncharacteristically not washed up before leaving the house. It brought memories flooding back, some of them pleasant enough but superimposed on those were others. No one likes to be made a fool of and no one likes to be reminded of it. It made him feel very slightly sick to recall how thoroughly he had been duped. One way to overcome the feeling was to get rid of the evidence. He washed up.

The fact that there was nothing he had to do, nothing tomorrow for which he had to prepare, left Linus feeling restless and his thoughts wandered more and more to Clarissa. Had she left the city? Or was that just her excuse for not having to see him again? She hadn't said she was definitely going, he recollected. There had been some doubt. This would enable her to have an alibi if they happened to bump into each other. Hadn't she said she intended to see him again? It hadn't seemed an odd thing to say this morning, not after last night, but he had no idea whether it meant anything or was just something else she said to keep him happy. He even wondered if it had more sinister implications. He rang the Randolph.

The receptionist was polite and apologetic. She was

afraid Miss Pensilva had booked out. No, first thing in the morning – well, after breakfast. No, Miss Pensilva had left no forwarding address and no telephone number. She regretted that it was not hotel policy to divulge the address under which people had booked in. She really was most awfully sorry, but there was no message for a Mr Rintoul or, indeed, for anyone else.

Linus put the phone down. It struck him that Clarissa's resemblance to Leonardo's Lady with an Ermine was not a purely physical one, though that was what he had taken it to be. There was a sharpness in both faces that had more to do with character than with physiognomy. It was a sharpness that was almost a slyness. He could see that now. He had always appreciated the beauty of the Leonardo without actually liking the sitter. He had allowed himself to be seduced by Clarissa's beauty without reflecting on the character behind it. Where that was concerned, he had got no further than deciding she was rather shallow. He took more care analysing the character of people in paintings than he had done for a living being. In short, he had been a fool and as a consequence had been treated like one. The only redeeming feature of that unpalatable truth was that at least he was the only one who knew it. Clarissa did, of course, but she was gone and with her, the urge for some small revenge.

He slept well that night and awoke more refreshed than he had expected to be. He had no doubt at all about his first activity on this first day of his leave. He would go out and see 'his' dog. Thelwall was pleased to see him and the dog was delighted.

'I'm glad,' Thelwall told him. 'I think you'll find him a handful but you'll cope and at least we both know he won't end up in the fighting-pits.'

'He needs a new name,' Linus said. 'I'm damned if I'll own a dog called Sailor and I'm none too keen on Ripper, either.'

'I don't suppose you fancy Rover much, either, even if it is appropriate.'

'You don't suppose correctly,' Linus said shortly. 'Nor am I much enamoured of Fido, Prince or Rex.'

'Prince and Rex are only for Alsatians,' Thelwall commented. 'I take it you've decided against Savonarola, too.'

'You've met him, have you?'

'More to the point, I've met his owner and, believe me, I don't envy the dog.'

Linus laughed and pulled the dog's ears, to that animal's ecstatic pleasure. 'I'll call him Ishmael,' he said. 'Tell the kennelmaid to get him used to it. I'm taking a few days' leave. Look after him. I'll pop in when I get back.'

'Lucky you. Are you going anywhere interesting?'

Linus shrugged. 'Haven't given it much thought, to be honest. I suppose what I need is a change of scene and a complete rest, though I've an idea that might bore me to tears. I'll probably just play the whole thing by ear.'

He drove home in an uncertain frame of mind and put a frozen lasagne in the oven. He needed this leave even if he hadn't any very clear idea what to do with it. He pottered about the house, wasting the rest of the morning and the first part of the afternoon and despising himself for doing so. A week's leave wasn't very much. It ought to be used, not frittered away.

When the idea came to him, it came suddenly. He ran upstairs and packed an overnight bag with his customary punctiliousness. He threw the bag on to the back seat of his car and headed away from Osney Island towards the bypass and then south down the A34.

It was a bright and sunny afternoon and his spirits lifted as he put his foot down on a good road. Whether his improved spirits were due to the weather, to the fine bursts of downland scenery or simply to the fact that he was actually doing something, he neither knew nor cared. All that mattered was that he felt better.

South of Winchester, he turned off the dual carriageway and headed south-east through strings of villages whose core might be old but which had been swamped by a sea of post-war neo-Georgian red-brick gentility. Eventually these largely dormitory villages serving the two great ports of Southampton and Portsmouth were left behind and he shifted to a lower gear to climb the three-hundred-foot high outcrop of chalk, the last and westernmost trace of the South Downs, that stood sentinel over the island below.

Linus had chosen his route from a roadmap and this road, cutting diagonally across country from the A34, had looked more direct than heading to Southampton and then east along a featureless motorway. There had been nothing to tell him there would be this spectacular view and, since he was on leave, there was no reason why he shouldn't stop and enjoy it.

It must have been raining here because the light had that clarity which in England always follows rain. The tide was in, making the pencil-line of water that divided the city from the mainland clearly visible. To his right and facing the great naval port of Portsmouth he could make out a castle keep within a fortified wall and Linus wished he had thought to bring binoculars and an Ordnance Survey map so that he could identify what he saw. Due south, across another stretch of sea, lay the crouching bulk of the Isle of Wight and off the eastern marshes of Portsea Island itself bobbed the ubiquitous flotilla of small pleasure boats.

Linus drove carefully through the confusing streets of the unfamiliar city, grateful that someone had had the forethought to signpost 'Old Portsmouth' and even, later, 'Camber'. There was nothing edifying in the architecture he passed and he concluded that any opportunities wartime destruction had given the city fathers had been largely wasted. Old Portsmouth looked more promising, though to one accustomed to the untouched and often medieval splendour of Oxford, he suspected that this place might prove to be an acquired taste.

He found the Dolphin without difficulty and was reassured to find the deep carpets and dark panelling of a quiet, traditional hotel. As the receptionist turned the book round to face him, he was pleased to see his name was to be at the bottom of the double page. He took his time over signing it so that his eye could wander over the page. This was a slack time of year and the two pages covered nearly a week of visitors. No one had signed their name as 'Lewdown' but that was hardly surprising: a person trying to evade the police would be extremely foolish to use his own name. Linus wondered why he himself had bothered to come here. What did he fondly imagine he could find out about Lewdown that the police didn't already know? Then, as he was about to hand the pen back to the receptionist, his eye caught another signature. C. Pensilva. It was followed by a London address.

'Good gracious,' he exclaimed. 'What a coincidence!' He pointed to the name. 'I don't suppose that is a *Miss* Pensilva? A Miss Clarissa Pensilva, to be exact?'

The receptionist was cautious. 'It was a lady, yes. I'm afraid I didn't ask her first name.'

'If it's who I think it is,' Linus went on, 'it's a former friend of my wife's. Obviously she's moved – it must be at least ten years. A tall woman, very beautiful, extremely elegant. Used to make my wife hopping mad, as a matter of fact. Clarissa could pop into Marks and Spencer and come out with something quite ordinary, looking a million dollars, whereas my wife could spend hundreds and look very nice but still quite ordinary, if you know what I mean.'

The receptionist unbent. 'It sounds as if it's the same woman, Mr Rintoul – and I know *exactly* how your wife felt. I'm afraid Miss Pensilva is no longer with us. In fact, as it turned out, she needn't have booked in at all: she had a phone call at about six o'clock the same day and had to leave in a hurry. The porter brought her car round, I remember. It was just what I'd have expected her to drive – a black BMW. Very elegant. I dare say she'd be interested in renewing her acquaintance with your wife.'

'Oh, I shan't contact her,' Linus said, having memorized the address. 'It's rarely advisable to try to renew old acquaintance, don't you think? Besides, it was my wife she was friendly with and I'm afraid Susan died some years ago.'

The receptionist was immediately embarrassed, as Linus had known she would be. 'I'm so sorry, Mr Rintoul. I had no idea. Do forgive me.'

He smiled and patted her hand in a fatherly manner. 'No need to apologize,' he said. 'As I said, it was a long time ago and there was no way you were to know, now was there?' He took his key and picked up his bag, then hesitated as if he had just recalled something. 'Didn't I read something about one of your guests in the paper this morning? Or was it yesterday? Recently, anyway. Had an unfortunate accident?'

The girl was delighted to be able to make amends for her gaffe with some harmless information. 'You mean Mr Denham,' she said. 'Tragic, that was. He fell into the Camber and was drowned, or so they say. Funnily enough, he knew Miss Pensilva, too. Well, I don't know that they knew each other exactly, but they struck up an acquaintance in the short time she was here. They shared a table at lunch-time. I wouldn't have thought he was her type, though – a bit flash, if you know what I mean.'

'When you're on your own in a strange hotel, I don't think it much matters,' Linus commented. 'You're just pleased to have someone similarly placed to chat to.'

She nodded. 'That's very true. I've often noticed that. I hope you enjoy your stay, Mr Rintoul.'

Linus assured her he would do his best and made his way to his room where he unpacked his bag and laid his clothes neatly in the chest of drawers. Then he went out for a walk.

He was really quite pleased with the results of his chat with the receptionist. He had found out Lewdown's alias, something the police must certainly know and something the use of which was not immediately apparent but which it was gratifying to have discovered. He had also discovered that Clarissa had been here and that was something which the police almost certainly did not know. They knew her

133

as Mary Calshot and Linus was sure, casting his mind back over his conversation with Lacock, that the Inspector had no suspicion she might be using another name, nor had he, Linus, told the policeman she was. He had also found out that Clarissa's visit to Portsmouth fitted neatly in between his telling her the police were looking for Lewdown and meeting him for dinner. He had no idea where the phone call she had received fitted in unless it was some prearranged means of giving her the excuse not to be around when Lewdown's body was found and he wondered whether, if it had not come, she would have stood him up. Almost certainly, he decided. At all events, her presence in Portsmouth must implicate her thoroughly in Lewdown's death.

He strolled down the High Street to the Sally Port and stood on the little fishing jetty, looking out on a sea that was fast becoming grey and cold. He glanced up. The sky had clouded over and the chill brightness that had lit the city from the hill-top was gone. Perhaps it would rain later on. He shivered and returned to the more sheltered street before climbing to the top of the Round Tower and looking out once more over Spithead and then at the jumble of buildings edging the narrow lanes of that part of the old city. As he watched, ferries passed each other in the sea-lanes but Linus had no idea whether they were going to and from France or merely the Isle of Wight. There were seats up here and in summer they were probably crowded but now it was too chilly to want to linger and he made his way back to the street and the sign pointing to the Camber.

This small natural harbour came as something of a surprise. It was of the same scale as the streets and houses around – and, although many modern buildings discreetly filled the gaps left by the war's bombardment, the street plan and the scale of the houses was much as it must have been in the seventeenth century – but in a city whose harbour could accommodate the biggest aircraft carriers in the world, it seemed peculiarly old-fashioned. Linus felt as if he had wandered into a Rip van Winkle world where nothing had changed for two hundred years. An angry shout behind him from a man driving a fork-lift truck laden with cases of whisky quickly annihilated this temporary nostalgia and he jumped out of the way. The Camber was very much a working wharf.

A smallish ship in battleship grey with a large F37 on its side looked incongruously out of place, as if it would have been more at home in the dockyard, while a three-masted sailing vessel that seemed to Linus's untutored eye as if it were big enough to take part in the Tall Ships' Race, rode snugly on its cables at the quayside. It appeared to be deserted. Round the corner, Linus found what he sought: the fish-packing factory, except that 'factory' was rather a grand word for this modest enterprise. He could see how easy it would have been for Lewdown to slip in accidentally. There was water all over the place and every now and then a pile of ice chippings that had overflowed from the wooden boxes in which the fish were packed. Linus himself found one piece under his foot and only a hand hastily outstretched against the wall stopped him falling.

'Watch it, mate,' one of the packers called out. 'We've had one chap in the drink this week. Don't want another. They might start asking questions.'

His companions laughed at this sally and Linus smiled with them.

'What happened?' he asked. 'Did he fall or was he pushed?'

'They reckon he did what you've just done – slipped on the ice, though we can't see how he did.'

'Why not? You've just seen me do it.'

'Ah, but that's now. There's always ice around when we're working. When we shut up shop for the night, we sweep it all into the Camber. Unless the temperature dropped during the night, there'd be nothing to slip on, and that's what we told them.'

'And did they believe you?'

The man shrugged. 'Who can tell what the police believe? They know it didn't freeze that night. It's my belief he was three sheets to the wind but it's no good trying to tell that to the coppers, is it? Besides, these days they've got all these tests and things they can do.'

Linus looked about him. 'It's not a place I'd choose to come on my own when I'd had a few,' he admitted. 'Was he on his own, this chap?'

'No idea. Not at night, anyway. He certainly was during the day, though.'

'Oh, I see. He'd been hanging around, had he?'

The man looked at him suspiciously and Linus suddenly became aware that the tool of his trade consisted of a large and vicious-looking knife. 'Who are you, then, taking all this interest?' the man asked. 'You don't look like police.'

'I'm not,' Linus told him. 'I'm a vet. As far as this is concerned, I'm just a curious tourist.'

'You don't look like a vet, either,' the man commented. 'Don't expect them to have a beard. Not a little one like that, anyway. Round here beards is mostly a full set. Ever thought of doing it properly?'

'Can't see myself looking like a sailor,' Linus said. 'Was this chap who drowned a seaman?'

'Back to him, are we? No. Didn't look like one. Wasn't a tourist, either. He was hoping to cadge a lift to France. We told the police.'

'Sounds as if he didn't get one,' Linus commented.

'He didn't. He was offering too much. People reckoned he was too keen to get out. The skipper of that little barque out there directed him to the ferry. Didn't seem very pleased. Said if he'd wanted the ferry, he could find it for himself. We wondered if he came back hoping to stow away during the night. If he did, it backfired on him.'

'You certainly see life round here,' Linus said.

The man pulled a face. 'We get them all: seamen, weekend sailors, tourists, ghouls. You name it, sooner or later we get it.'

Correctly guessing that he ranked with both tourists and

ghouls, Linus took his leave. He had found out quite a lot, though what he was going to do with the information he had no idea, and he saw no reason to begrudge the source of his information an entirely reasonable insult. In normal circumstances he, too, would have deplored someone who wanted to know all about the death of a complete stranger.

He recalled that the man who discovered Lewdown's body had been walking his dog. That suggested it was certainly before midnight, quite possibly around closing-time. Linus knew that Clarissa had been here and had been seen in Lewdown's company, though whether he knew her or not, it was hard to guess: Clarissa was very good at getting to know complete strangers, as he had found out himself. She had been at the Dolphin at about six o'clock because that was when she had received the phone call and she must have left Portsmouth virtually straight away or she would never have been back in Oxford in time to keep their date. He should have asked the fishpacker what time they finished work. That had been a stupid oversight. Still, common sense said it was likely to be five o'clock, possibly as late as half past and there was always the possibility, with a job like that, that they simply packed up when they'd finished. One thing was certain. Whenever Lewdown had fallen in the Camber, and whether it had been an accident or not, it must have happened when there was no one about, and if it had been an accident, it was reasonable to assume it must have been fairly dark. He decided to go back there at about five and see just how empty the place was. In the meantime, he would time the walk back to the Dolphin. It might be necessary to know whether Clarissa could have been back there by six if she hadn't been able to leave the Camber until it was relatively dark. He didn't think it could possibly take longer than ten minutes, but assumptions were not good enough.

He realized as he strolled back to his hotel that he was beginning to think that perhaps it was Clarissa who had given Lewdown that fatal shove but he knew this was little more than a feeling, for such 'evidence' as he had accumulated was entirely circumstantial. He didn't even know for sure that Lewdown *had* been pushed. Maybe thinking like this was his way of getting some small revenge on her for the way in which she had used him. Was he trying to turn his thoughts into facts? Was that why he had come here – to turn Clarissa into a murderer just because she had made a fool of him? He would be better advised to forget all about it, to be conent with what he had found out so far and not bother to go back to the Camber tonight.

He did, though, and found no solution. By the time the place was deserted – and it emptied very quickly – it was darkening fast. Lewdown might easily have fallen in. Equally easily, someone could have pushed him in without the slightest chance of being seen. It was not a comforting realization and Linus found himself looking over his shoulder for no good reason. A quiet drink and dinner suddenly became irresistibly attractive.

Chapter Nine

A good meal and a night on his own in a comfortable but unfamiliar bed served to crystallize his intentions. He wanted to pay Clarissa back for the way she had used him. Just passing on to the police any information he gleaned was a sneaky, unsatisfying way of doing it, like a schoolboy 'ratting' to a teacher. He also wanted to have a personal hand in taking up the cudgels on behalf of the dogs because they couldn't do so on their own account. He wanted to nail whoever was behind this gross maltreatment of dogs, and he wanted to do it personally.

His resolve was still there before breakfast. As soon as he was up and dressed, Linus strolled along the High Street until he found a little newsagent's. He bought a copy of that week's *Exchange and Mart* and went in to breakfast with that to read instead of the *Guardian*. Fred had been quite right. There were a lot of adverts for Pit Bulls. Like most of that paper's advertisements, they gave telephone numbers rather than addresses and the numbers for Pit Bulls ranged pretty widely over the country. He only recognized the better-known codes, but there were certainly dogs on offer in Manchester, Birmingham, Coventry and London. He would limit himself to the London adverts: there were more of them, for a start; London was nearer; the address 'C. Pensilva' had given the Dolphin was there. Such a felicitous conjunction of signs must augur well.

Newcomen Road proved to be a busy little through road in Soho and No. 57 was a betting-shop. Linus was somewhat taken aback by this. He hadn't speculated at all on the possible nature of 57 Newcomen Road because he had assumed it would either house Clarissa's office – whether the import/export one she had claimed or the one she used as a solicitor – or else it would be where she lived. An old house divided into flats, perhaps. He certainly wasn't expecting a betting-shop. Above the door was its telephone number. Linus memorized this and sought out a telephone box. The first one he found had uselessly dangling wires and the second had been used as a public urinal, but its apparatus worked. He dialled the number over the shop.

The phone was picked up almost immediately and an uninformative man's voice said simply, 'Hello?'

Linus's hesitation was momentary. 'Good morning,' he said. 'Could I speak to Miss Calshot, please?'

Such a long silence ensued that Linus wondered if they'd been cut off.

'Who?' the unidentified voice asked.

'Miss Calshot. Miss Mary Calshot.'

The next silence was even longer. Then, 'Sorry, mate. You've got a wrong number.' The speaker hung up without waiting for a response.

Linus wondered if he should have asked for Miss Pensilva. Too late now, anyway. The man would recognize his voice. He put the hand-set back and left the malodorous cubicle. He made his way back to Newcomen Road and found a small café diagonally opposite the betting-shop. He bought a cup of coffee and a soggy jam doughnut and seated himself at a plastic-topped table in the window from where he had a good view of the betting-shop. He wasn't sure what to do next and had some vague idea that if he sat here long enough, something would happen that would give him an idea. He opened *Exchange and Mart* partly for something to spin out the cup of coffee and partly to refresh his memory. He had already ringed those Pit Bull advertisements that gave a London telephone number and now he looked them over, wondering how widely scattered they might be.

One of them took his eye. It seemed familiar. Linus looked up from the paper and across the road. That was it. The numbers were the same. The betting-shop was advertising Pit Bulls. Now he knew what to do. He did not have to ring various advertisers at random, hoping sooner or later to establish a link with the dogs in the Highnoon kennels. He had the connection handed to him as neatly as if it had been gift-wrapped.

This fortuitous circumstance had no sooner delighted him than he realized that he couldn't use it – not yet. It was barely ten minutes since he had rung that number asking for Jones-Drybeck's solicitor. If he rang again now, there was a good chance the same person would answer and he could hardly fail to recognize Linus's voice. Linus considered disguising it but abandoned the idea very quickly. It wasn't the sort of thing he was any good at and his problems would only be magnified if the man at the other end realized that the person who had asked for Miss Calshot was now asking for Pit Bulls in a phoney voice.

If, on the other hand, he left it till evening, it might be someone else who answered and even if it wasn't, there would be less chance of being recognized, partly because there would have been time for the first call to have been forgotten and partly because this time he would be asking about dogs and the fact that the content of the call was different would throw them off the track.

He studied the first floor above the betting-shop. There were net curtains at the windows but they were full and clean, quite a contrast to the skimpy, unwashed ones above several of the shop-fronts opposite. They looked as if there might be living quarters behind them that were in regular occupation. That would mean that a phone-call made some time after the betting-shop had closed was likely to be answered – unless the flat had a separate phone. Linus had a hunch that a bookmaker would be very selective in his choice of tenant. He suspected that it was more than likely that whoever lived over the shop was connected with it and might therefore very well use the same phone. It was a chance he would take. Now he needed an hotel.

Linus booked himself into a small hotel just off the Bayswater Road. He felt it was wiser not to be too close to Soho: if he had to meet anyone, it looked more genuine. The hotel was clean and it seemed perfectly respectable – just the sort of place someone from the provinces might be expected to choose. He went out for some lunch and when he came back, settled down with *Exchange and Mart* and an outside line to make some more calls.

If he was going to answer the betting-shop's advertisement for Pit Bulls, it made sense to find out first what sort of line produced the best results. The first call he made was typical. It was a Coventry number.

Like the man in the betting-shop, the one who answered gave no number and no name, simply, 'Hallo?'

'Good afternoon,' Linus said. 'I've just seen your advert in *Exchange and Mart*.'

'Oh yes?'

'About Pit Bulls,' Linus persisted. 'It says you have puppies for sale. I'd be interested in a bitch.'

'Why?'

It seemed an odd question for a seller to ask.

'I'm told they're nicer than the dogs,' Linus said.

The man snorted. 'I mean why do you want one at all?'

'I saw them in the States when I was there,' Linus lied. 'Thought they looked rather interesting. I could have bought one then but I didn't fancy all the business of quarantine. Six months is a long time. The dog would lose its spirit, don't you think?'

The man appeared to be digesting this remark. 'They can be pricey,' he said at last.

'Don't mind paying,' Linus told him. 'Not if it means I get something good.'

'I might know of something that could be what you want. It depends whether you want one for working or breeding.'

'Does it make a difference?' Linus asked.

'It makes one hell of a difference to the price. I know of a proven brood they want to get rid of. Nothing wrong with her, but they're a bit overstocked. She's producing first-class workers. She'll set you back about £1500 but you'll get two, possibly three, more litters from her. A bitch puppy of working stock will set you back about £450.'

'Have you got such a puppy right now or would I have to wait?'

'I can get hold of a couple for you to choose from,' the man said.

'Great,' Linus said. 'Let me have your address and I'll pop up to see them.'

There was a brief hesitation. 'Best not,' the man said. 'The wife's been ill. Tell you what: I'll meet you at the Watford Gap service station on the M1. It's a good place to do business, is that.'

'OK,' Linus agreed. 'This evening? About half seven? Who do I look for? What's the registration number?'

The man hung up.

The next man hung up on being asked what sort of work the dogs did and the third was not prepared to say whether he would accept a cheque.

Linus learnt a lot. Not one of the people he called admitted either to owning a Pit Bull or to having bred any of the puppies offered. The numbers he rang were in different

142

parts of the country but the prices he was quoted seemed to be standard. No one to whom he spoke was prepared to give a name, an address, a vehicle registration number or any means of identification. Nor did any of them ask for any such details from Linus. Each had volunteered an assignation at a named pub or a service station. Had Linus seriously intended to buy a Pit Bull, he had no idea how he would actually have made contact with the sellers.

When he rang the betting-shop in the evening, he felt a lot more confident of his ability to present a convincing front and his confidence was boosted when the person who answered the phone proved not to be the one to whom he had spoken earlier. This time he was speaking to an American and, from the sound of him, a young American, although Linus reminded himself that disembodied telephone voices can be deceptive.

'I've just seen your advert for Pit Bulls,' Linus began.

'And?'

'I'm looking for a bitch. Preferably young but not necessarily a puppy. Can you help?'

'Any particular reason you want a bitch?'

'I've got a dog and I want to breed good working pups.'

There was a pause on the line while the man absorbed this. 'Does the dog work?' he asked at last.

Linus hesitated carefully. He mustn't seem too keen to volunteer information. 'He has done,' he said guardedly.

'Any good?'

'Not bad. I'd like to get something from him before I push him, though.'

'Makes sense. You know things are a bit difficult right now?'

'I heard a rumour,' Linus said cautiously.

'Most good bitches are imported but it looks like there aren't going to be any more of those for a while. It's just possible there may be a good English-bred one available.'

Linus said he wasn't too bothered about its background.

'OK,' the American said. 'Are you looking for a proven brood or will you take a pup?'

143

Linus appeared to hesitate again. This was ground he thought they had covered. Was the man trying to catch him out? 'Like I said, I'd like her young but not necessarily a pup. Of course, if there's no choice, I'll make do with a pup but I don't really want my dog out of action for too long. A proven brood would be just about perfect.'

'It'll set you back a tidy packet.'

'I thought about $1500, maybe a bit more. Something like that,' Linus offered.

'About £500 more, I'd say,' the American commented but Linus had the feeling he had relaxed a bit, as if he had decided that Linus was genuine and knew what he was talking about. 'Are you ringing from London?' the American went on.

Linus felt it advisable to hesitate again. 'That's right,' he said.

'There's a pub called the Talbot in Wessex Street. D'you know it?'

'No, but I can find it.'

'OK. Be there tomorrow lunch-time. Take a table and put *Exchange and Mart* flat on the table beside you, front page up. Any problems?'

'None at all. I'll be there.'

Linus had no difficulty finding Wessex Street and was curiously reassured to discover it to be an eminently respectable, well-cared-for little backwater. The Talbot was a small turreted Victorian pub with a façade of glazed bricks that had somehow escaped the enthusiastic modernizing hand of its brewery's designer. It still boasted its engraved glass windows and the inside exactly matched the exterior. The pump-handles were patterned china and gleamed twice, once on their own account and once in the reflection of the highly polished bar counter. The predominating smell was beer and tobacco but underneath was the hint of wax polish. It was the sort of pub that made one feel warm and expansive the moment one stepped in the door. It was a pub that was much loved by both landlord and customers, and it showed.

144

Linus bought a pint and went over to a highly-polished table under one of the windows and sat down. He put the weekly paper flat on the table beside him as if he intended to read it once he had slaked his immediate thirst.

He had no idea what sort of person would be contacting him but it seemed a reasonable assumption, given the secrecy that surrounded Pit Bull matters, that it would not be the young American with whom he had conversed. He was therefore quite surprised to observe the entrance of a tall young man whose fair hair was covered by a very American good-ol'-boy baseball cap. Linus studied the new arrival, who made no attempt to come across. He had the open face of the all-American college-boy film hero with the frank, widely spaced blue eyes and corn-fed jaw of his type. Jeans and a checked shirt accentuated the American image and Linus suspected that, had he been able to see the newcomer's footwear, it would prove to be cowboy boots worn under the trouser-legs. From this distance and in the subdued light of the bar, Linus judged him to be in his late twenties and he behaved with that indefinable air of being at home that identifies the regular in any given pub. Eventually he moved over to Linus's table.

'May I join you?' he asked.

'Of course,' Linus replied, moving the paper to one side. He decided he had underestimated the man's age by some ten years. 'Nice pub.'

'I like it – been coming here for years now. It's my local. The name's Hank.'

If Hank lived over the betting-shop, he had a strange concept of what constituted a local, Linus thought. Still, maybe this was a different American. Linus never had been able to correlate telephone voices and the real thing. He held out his hand. 'Rodney,' he lied.

'Pleased to meet you, Rod,' the American said, shaking it. 'One of the guys at the bar was saying you're an animal lover.'

Since Linus knew that no one in the pub had ever seen him before and since Hank must know perfectly well no

145

such comment could have been made, Linus assumed this was the equivalent of a password. 'I've got a dog,' he admitted.

'Me, too,' Hank admitted. 'A fawn-coloured bitch. What's yours?'

'A brindle dog,' Linus said. 'Big brute but devoted to me. Not very nice with other dogs, though. I have to watch him. Funnily enough – you being an American, and all – he's from the States, too.'

The American smiled but it was a guarded smile and Linus realized that his smiles, which were frequent, never reached his eyes. 'That so? There's a coincidence. Where's he from?'

Linus did a quick think and recalled something he had read in one of the canine magazines. 'New Mexico,' he said. 'They passed some daft legislation stopping people keeping them, or something. Never did work out the ins and outs. Ishmael was going to be put down.'

'You were over there, I take it?'

Linus knew he could never sustain a bluff which involved him in visits to the States. 'No,' he said. 'My brother knew I was interested and got him for me. It cost me a tidy packet in quarantine fees, but it was worth every penny.'

'Where did you quarantine him?' It was a perfectly natural question.

Linus named a kennel in Scotland that, so far as he knew, had never had a Pit Bull through its hands in all its years of operation. 'I was working up there at the time,' he added.

'What line are you in?' Again, the question was a natural one.

'On the periphery of the oil business,' Linus told him. 'It's all to do with supplying the rigs. Nothing glamorous. Just chandling on a bigger scale.' He got the impression that Hank was not entirely familiar with the word 'chandling'.

'And you're down here now?' Hank went on.

'There's belt-tightening going on up there,' Linus told

him, with the authority of one who reads his newspapers thoroughly. 'I'd some leave due. Thought I'd see what prospects there were down south.'

'Any luck?'

'Too soon to say for sure. I'm putting this and that together: a contact here, another one there. What about you? You're obviously not local.'

The sally was not well received. 'I just like it here,' Hank said; deliberately vague. 'I made a packet in the music business so now I can please myself.'

'Lucky you.' Linus wondered just what it was Hank had done in the music business but he had an idea that it was as usefully uncheckable an occupation as being on the periphery of the oil business. There would be little point in asking.

'Got any papers on your dog?' Hank asked suddenly.

Linus shook his head. 'I was told the Kennel Club wasn't interested and it didn't much matter to me, anyway. Never could see what difference all that paperwork made.'

'It doesn't. Either the dog's good or it's not. That's all there is to it. There is another registering body, of course, and they'll do the breeds that the British Kennel Club doesn't want to know about, so you can always get the documentation if you need it. You said this dog of yours used to work?'

The direct question took Linus off-guard. It was one he should have anticipated but he hadn't and once again he was aware of the danger of trying to bluff his way through.

'That's what I was told,' he said cautiously. 'What I mean is, I gather from my brother that he used to but I've never worked him. Not sure how to go about it, for one thing. I've often thought it was a waste of a good dog, sitting around in front of the fire. That's why I decided to get hold of a bitch if I could. I can make use of the dog and, who knows? I might be able to make the sort of contacts that can help me get him back doing what he's good at.'

Hank nodded. 'More than likely. I've been asking around since you rang and I reckon we may be able to help you.'

Linus noted the 'we' and wondered whether it had slipped out deliberately or accidentally, or whether it was no more significant than the royal We. He said nothing but gave a good impression of a man whose interest had just quickened.

'Where can I reach you?' Hank went on.

Linus tore a corner from *Exchange and Mart* and scribbled the hotel telephone number on it. He handed it to Hank. 'That's where I'm staying.'

Hank took a wallet out of his hip pocket and put the little piece of paper carefully in it. 'OK, Rod, I'll be in touch. Nice meeting you. So long.'

The next day began tediously and got steadily worse. Linus dared not leave the hotel in case he missed the phone call. It came just before lunch and, as a consequence, he knew he could then relax for a few hours, have something to eat and go for a walk.

The rush-hour traffic was just beginning to build up when he collected his car from the underground car park and followed Hank's instructions through the steadily increasing traffic. He thought Hank had underestimated the delay he would experience and was surprised to reach the appointed lay-by at almost precisely the time the American had indicated.

The location made him uneasy. He could see the roofs of a large housing estate but no houses overlooked this stretch of road and behind him on the opposite side, this lay-by's twin was occupied by travellers. The washing strung between two trees, a pile of rusting metal, the lurcher tied to a caravan's towbar, all indicated a semi-permanent camp-site. Not the best place to leave a car unattended for any length of time.

Hank's directions had been specific and, since he had been so accurate in his estimate of the time it would take Linus to get here, perhaps he had also taken into account the presence of these other road-users. Linus leant over and checked that the passenger door was locked before getting out of the car and locking the driver's. He checked the other two doors and the hatchback and then, finally satisfied that the car was secure, walked along the verge away from his vehicle and the travellers' encampment. After twenty minutes of fairly brisk walking, he came to the junction he was expecting and there he stopped. Several cars sped past on the main road and one turned into the lane but none was interested in him. Linus glanced at his watch. Perhaps he had walked a shade too briskly. He stamped his feet on grass that was just too damp to make for comfortable standing around and wondered if this was going to turn into a wild goose chase. It occurred to him that anything that required such elaborately structured stratagems was either a hoax from start to finish or very dangerous indeed and he had a nasty feeling it might prove to be the latter. It was also entirely possible that all this business was simply a means of testing him out before deciding whether to let him have a bitch. He glanced at his watch again. He looked at the road. How long should he give it before going back to his car?

He had barely had time to formulate the question before an old, rusty and exceedingly tatty van that might once have been red, pulled up alongside him. Almost before it had completely stopped, a burly man unfolded himself from the passenger seat and ran round to open the door in the back of the van.

'Hop in,' he said to Linus, jerking his head towards the door.

Linus did as he was told with barely time to realize that there was no one – no nearby house, no passing motorist – to see him disappear inside the van. The door was closed and he heard the key turn. Then the burly man resumed his place beside the driver. Both men were in their middle twenties and looked as if they could give a good account of themselves in a scrap but any verbal description of either of them could have fitted about half the male population. Linus was beginning to feel a healthy respect for Hank's powers of organization.

The van moved slowly down the lane until the driver found an allotment entrance in which he could back the van and, as he reversed, the first man turned to Linus.

'Move over here, mate,' he said and Linus obediently came closer to the seat. 'Turn round.'

Linus did so and the man fastened a large, soft piece of folded fabric over his eyes, tying the blindfold very securely.

'Sorry about this, mate, but orders is orders. It's only because you're so new and all. Nothing personal.' He sounded genuinely apologetic.

'Glad to hear it,' Linus said drily. 'It's not going to increase the comfort of the ride, is it?'

'It'll be easiest if you lie down,' the man told him.

Linus thought he was probably right but it would also make it even more difficult to estimate their speed or direction. He was surprised that they had left his hands free. He could perfectly easily release the blindfold and he found it hard to imagine that they had overlooked so important a detail. Then he realized that they had no need to bind his hands. If he was genuine, he would be perfectly content to be transported in this manner to his first assignation – quite probably to his first two or three, until they were sure of him. If he were not genuine and tried to remove or rearrange the blindfold, the two men would have no difficulty overpowering him and leaving him in some wayside ditch. Dead, he could tell nothing and alive, very little more: a decrepit red van of whose registration number he now realized he had taken no note, containing two nondescript men of the labouring sort, one somewhat larger than the other. No, it didn't really matter to his companions whether his hands were free or not.

He did know that they had arrived almost precisely on time and estimated that it had taken no more than five minutes before he was blindfolded and the van had left the little access-path. He would be able to look at his watch when he arrived at wherever they were going. Whether he could form a reliable estimate of their speed between now and then remained to be seen. An uncomfortable vehicle always seemed to be travelling faster than it was, just as a luxury one seemed to be going more slowly.

They spent some considerable time twisting and turning into what must have been a succession of minor roads but then the van levelled out and speeded up and they travelled for so long in what felt like a straight line that Linus knew they must be on a motorway. It was quite impossible to estimate either time or speed and he finally stopped trying but when at last they swung off to the right, Linus realized they could not still have been on a motorway at that juncture and the succession of turns and bends that followed told him they were either on an estate or on very minor roads indeed. Eventually the van turned left on to what could only have been a farm track. It pitched and bucketed along this for some way before it finally pulled over and stopped. Linus heard both men get out of the van and one of them opened up the back.

'Come here,' he said and Linus groped his way towards the voice.

The man removed the blindfold and extended a hand to help Linus out of the van. It took him a few moments to get his bearings. Having been without vision and with the impaired balance of one who doesn't know which way he's facing, he was unsteady when he first set foot on the churned-up surface of a large farmyard. All around them were other vehicles, varying from old bangers and well-used Land-Rovers to a couple of Mercedes, some Range-Rovers and even a Roller tucked away under the cover of an old cart shed. In front of them loomed a massive barn of the sort that would net someone a small fortune if it were sold for conversion to three or four dwellings. Behind it, Linus could just make out the smaller bulk of the farmhouse but whether it was deserted or simply shuttered against intrusion, he had no idea.

The night was clear and there was a waxing moon. There was no other light at all, not the smallest chink to indicate where the owners of all these vehicles might be. Linus's eyes ranged further afield, thinking he might catch sight of the moving beams that would indicate the presence of a road. Nothing. That bumpy track must have taken them further than he had thought, unless the nearest road was screened by thick hedges.

One of his companions nudged him. 'Come on,' he said.

They made their way over to the barn not, as Linus had expected, heading for the huge central doors, but for one of the wings that jutted out towards them at either end. Here there was a smaller door and the smaller of Linus's escorts knocked on this. There was a pause and then the shuffling sound of someone walking through scattered straw. The door was opened and Linus was nudged over the threshold. For the first time he caught the glow of artificial light which seeped dimly round the edges of a huge partition of straw separating this wing of the building from its main bulk.

A tarpaulin hung down in one place and one of Linus's companions lifted this and pushed him through into the central area. So unused had he become to light that Linus was momentarily blinded by the glare that suddenly struck him. The sensation was short-lived because the light was, in fact, relatively dim, emanating from a number of hurricane lamps hung around the building from its supporting timbers. Now Linus was able to take a quick glance at his watch. The journey had taken something under an hour and a half, much of it on a motorway. Bearing in mind that he had no idea what sort of speed the van had been able to make, he nevertheless estimated that he must be seventy or eighty miles from London. He looked about him. The barn bore that out. It was built of Cotswold stone and, peering up between the rafters, Linus was almost sure he could make out the underside of a Stonesfield slate roof. If that was so, then he was only a few miles from home.

The irony of this was soon superseded by a very healthy fear. His face was well-known to farmers in the area and they would be very surprised to discover that his name was Rodney and he was in business on the periphery of the oil game. Whether he would be able to bluff his way through recognition by saying he had given a false identification because of the nature of the enterprise was arguable. For most people it would have been a plausible excuse, but for a MAFF vet already involved in Pit Bulls and related illegalities but from the other side, it would carry little weight. He cast his eyes around the assembly with seeming indifference but very real interest. It would be best to know straight away where danger was likely to come from.

There were a lot of people. At a rough guess there must be at least two for every vehicle. Linus estimated there might have been as many as thirty or forty standing around the barn. He was relieved to note that he was personally acquainted with none of them.

That did not mean they were all unknown to him. Most were complete strangers and they seemed to come from all walks of life with perhaps a preponderance of the flat-cap-and-green-wellie brigade, but two of the faces he knew. One was a someone whom he had seen once or twice on TV. Not a household face and Linus racked his brain to recall his name and failed but he rather thought he held some sort of minor official post, though he could not recall in what capacity. The other familiar face was Sir Giles Frinton, a prominent local businessman with a finger in most pies, both national and international, that were worth having a finger in. A devout self-publicist, Sir Giles's views on everything from the state of the economy to the morality of the lower orders were well known and scarcely a week went by without his face appearing on the screen pontificating on some aspect of current life. Linus wondered at his presence here. It betokened hypocrisy on quite a substantial scale and even if Sir Giles considered himself to be beyond the standards he expected of others, it should have occurred to him that news of his involvement in anything so unpalatable as dog-fighting would finish him if it got into the papers. Except, he supposed, that someone

153

as influential as Sir Giles could probably control what appeared in the Press when it was in his interest to do so.

Having ascertained as well as he could that there was no one present who knew Linus Rintoul, he turned his attention to the barn itself and the arrangements that had been made to accommodate the evening's entertainment. The 'pit' itself was an enclosure made entirely of bales of straw. These had been placed broad side down, presumably for stability, and had been bonded, like bricks, three high. Tarpaulins covered this improvised ring and Linus assumed their function was to take the blood. It would be a lot easier to dispose of a blood-soaked tarpaulin than several bales of blood-bespattered straw. The floor encircled by this wall of bales had been swept clean. It looked like dusty concrete but Linus knew it was the same impacted earth that had constituted the floor of the barn for the past three or even four hundred years. Everywhere else that he could see was carpeted with straw and more bales lined the walls, keeping the light in and the draughts out. Even the pigeonholes in the gable-end had been blocked with straw. No light would escape that way.

In the dim recess of the barn away from the illuminated area, Linus could hear scrabblings and the occasional bark which, while it could hardly have been called muffled, certainly seemed remarkably unpenetrating. Then he realized that another effect of all this carefully arranged straw was to deaden the acoustics. The barn was as well insulated for sound as any carpeted and curtained sitting-room. He tapped one of his escorts on the shoulder and nodded his head in the direction of the barking.

'Is that where the dogs are kept?' he asked.

'That's right. They're crated, of course, and surrounded by bales of straw. They can hear each other and smell each other but they can't see anything much until they get into the pit. No, don't go and have a look. You don't want to be accused of interfering with any of the contestants, now do you?'

Linus thought of the possible consequences of such a

misunderstanding and found nothing to quarrel with in the man's assessment of the situation. He stayed where he was.

It was a very well-behaved group of people. They shuffled in the straw and chatted quietly and, although there was an air of suppressed excitement, it was an excitement well held in check. In so far as there was any direction in the movement, it circulated around one particular man whom Linus took to be a bookmaker. He knew he was right when his burly companion jerked his head in that general direction.

'Want a flutter on this one?' he asked.

Linus could think of few things he wanted less but he appeared to give it his consideration. 'No, thanks,' he said. 'Not just yet. Think I'll watch it a few times first.'

The man shrugged. 'As you like. Adds a bit of spice, though, that's all.'

Linus was indifferent to the prospect of a little spice. He was going to have some difficulty stomaching ungarnished meat.

As if there had been a signal, the assembled men – Linus noticed there were no women among them – gravitated towards the 'pit' and Linus found himself pushed well to the fore.

'You wouldn't want to miss anything, would you?' one of his companions said. 'Not the first time out.'

A man with a black-and-white Staffordshire Bull Terrier came into the ring first and went across to the other side. A few minutes later another man, this time with a small fawn Pit Bull, followed him and stood at the opposite side. The dogs were held by their collars and, as dogs held like that will do, they hurled abuse at each other, rearing up on their hind legs and doing their utmost to twist out of the grip holding them.

'Two untried youngsters,' Linus's mentor told him. 'Complete gamble, this match.'

They might have been untried, but they certainly weren't untrained. Although neither dog was fully mature, each bulged with hard, solid muscle and no one could doubt their will to fight. Their lips were drawn back over gleamingly healthy young teeth and when the signal was given for their release, they sprang forward the instant they felt themselves free.

Most dogs, when restrained by a chain or a fence, will hurl themselves at any passing dog but if that restraint is suddenly removed, their behaviour changes. They rush just so far towards the strange dog and then both animals circle each other stiff-legged and wary and the only circumstances in which a fight will ensue are if both dogs are so evenly matched, not so much in size but in lack of fear and a desire to be 'top' dog, that a fight is the only way of establishing superiority. Fighting breeds take less time to make up their minds and the secret of training a successful fighter is to eliminate that assessment time altogether so that the dog pitches straight in without asking questions.

These youngsters were not yet quite that sharp, though the Pit Bull had a slight edge on the Staffordshire. They'd probably had plenty of practice on Jack Russells and other breeds game enough to be interesting but not large enough to do much damage. After their initial rush at each other, they pulled up short and began to circle but their training and the shouts of encouragement from the ringside soon overcame their inhibitions and the Pit Bull suddenly charged in. The initial onslaught of both dogs was directed at the head, neck and front legs. In a very short time the Staffordshire's white markings were pink and the Pit Bull's fawn was similarly discoloured. Linus knew that a relatively small puncture could produce the most impressively misleading quantity of blood and so far he could see no injuries at all. He guessed a tongue had been bitten. That would fling the available blood around very effectively.

Once the dogs began to be aware of experiencing pain, the intensity of the fight increased and Linus saw that each of the owners was now circling the dogs with a stout stick in his hands. Did this mean the dog could expect a beating? It was a prospect that made him feel sick. Wasn't the fight enough?

It is a characteristic of bull breeds not to let go and it was a characteristic these specimens exhibited well. The Pit Bull had hold of the Staffordshire's cheek and he pulled. He braced his four feet well apart and tore at the other dog's face while the Staffordshire tried desperately both to wrench free and dive in himself under his opponent to do some damage on his own account. Neither dog intended to submit and if either had exhibited signs of doing so, no amount of uging from the crowd would have prevented the time-honoured conclusion to the fight taking place.

Linus could see that real damage was now being done. A flap of skin had been torn from the Staffordshire's face, revealing the thin layer of muscle that overlay the bone. If there was a way of stopping the fight now, the flap could be sewn back on but once it was totally severed, the chances of doing that successfully were virtually nil and the dog's chances of survival similarly small.

Now Linus learnt the purpose of the sticks. The dogs' owners were obviously as fully aware as Linus of the danger to the Staffordshire and they moved in not, as Linus had assumed, to beat the dogs apart, but to lever them away from each other. Each man forced his stick between the teeth of his dog so that the gripping jaw was transferred from the opponent to the breaking-stick. That accomplished and the dogs separated, each man led his dog out, the Pit Bull still clasping the stick, to the amusement of the onlookers. Linus saw the Staffordshire's face as it passed him and wondered where they were going to get it stitched up. It needed to be done within the hour and most vets would ask awkward questions.

He suddenly realized that ethically, for the sake of the dog, he ought to offer to do it and he was ashamed of his fear of revealing that he had an expertise which was not one usually associated with people in the oil business. He turned to his escort.

'That dog looked bad,' he said. 'Will they be able to get it treated?'

'Par for the course in a first fight,' he was told. 'The

handler's pretty good with a needle. They have to be. It's the anaesthetics and antibiotics that pose the problems but there's usually ways and means of getting hold of them. That dog'll be back in the ring in a few months. Mind you, the Pit Bull's the better of the two.'

The Pit Bull was declared the winner and Linus was interested to observe the very considerable amounts of money changing hands.

There was quite a long interval before the next match and he wondered what precautions had been taken against anyone stumbling on this enterprise. He had not been aware of any lookouts when he came in but then, he had been too preoccupied with what he could see easily to think about the more subtle arrangements the organizers must have made. He pondered what might happen if the police suddenly descended on this barn. Even assuming an advance warning was given, it would be very difficult to disperse a crowd of this size, not to mention their cars and all the incriminating evidence of bloodstained tarpaulins and injured dogs. He had thought dog-fighting was a sordid little so-called sport involving some half-dozen people at a time in some deserted spot where it would be easy to fade into the landscape the moment intruders were sighted. Well, it was certainly sordid enough but the participants must be very sure of themselves to be able to operate on this scale. Did that mean they had good reason to know the police posed no threat? It was a question Linus would dearly have liked the answer to but not one he could safely ask.

The dogs in the next two matches were experienced fighters and the betting was much heavier. Since he wasn't betting himself, it was difficult for Linus to exhibit too overt an interest in the sums being bandied about but he kept his eyes open and strained his ears and came to the conclusion that bets of several hundreds were normal and those running into four figures were not unusual. Either way, it was out of his league.

Having seen one fight, any residual academic interest

Linus might have had in the proceedings was extinguished and he regretted the necessity of staying to watch the remaining fights. They lasted longer and were more determinedly savage but the pattern remained the same. Dogs fight to certain quite specific rituals which have nothing to do with training or any form of human intervention. It follows therefore that one fight is much like another, differing only in the degree of injury inflicted by one party on another and by its length. In this respect a dog-fight and a boxing-match are very similar and Linus enjoyed neither. He found himself watching the faces of the onlookers rather than events in the pit and he found them illuminating.

The expressions were not dissimilar to those at boxing-matches. It was a vicarious thrill at seeing others hurt and the greater the hurt, the greater the thrill. Linus had once, against his better judgement, gone to a colleague's party at which blue movies had been part of the evening's entertainment. He had seen the same expressions on that audience's face, too. He imagined that the faces on the audience in the Colosseum when the gladiators fought and when Christians were thrown to the lions could not have been very different. Not much progress had been made in two thousand years. The ghoulish interest in the proceedings even extended to the taking of photographs. More than once the sudden blinding flash of a camera stabbed the dimness between the hurricane lamps, though whether there was one photographer or several, Linus was unsure.

'Enjoy yourself?' one of his escorts said as the audience dispersed and they returned to the van.

'It was certainly interesting,' Linus told him and the man seemed satisfied, obviously equating interest with enjoyment.

Back at the van, the burly man apologized for the fact that he must again blindfold Linus. 'Sorry, mate, but orders is orders,' he said. 'I'm afraid this is the routine until we know you a bit better. Never do for you to know where we are, would it?'

'You've succeeded in disguising it so far,' Linus said. 'All

I know is that it's one hell of a long way from Town.' There was no reason for anyone to assume that someone in the oil business would recognize Cotswold stone or, more esoterically, Stonesfield slate, and Linus was happy to endorse that assumption.

'Matches are always a long way from where people live: we don't advise anyone, however genuine, of matches in their vicinity. No one you saw there tonight was local.'

That explained the absence of anyone who might have known Linus. It didn't quite fit Sir Giles Frinton, however, and it suddenly struck Linus that the venue had most likely been one of Sir Giles's properties. He wondered what his chances were of identifying it from an Ordnance Survey map and thought they might be quite high. At least he now had one big name involved in the game. The sensible thing to do would be to take that name to Inspector Lacock and let his people dig deeper. Then he remembered his suspicion that the police, if not actively involved, were at least turning a blind eye to what went on in their area. He couldn't imagine Lacock being implicated but then, who would have thought Sir Giles Frinton would have been involved? No, even if it were time to hand the matter over to someone else, he must first be sure where their loyalty lay. He needed to have a far more detailed knowledge of the whole set-up. Right now, he had two choices: either Rodney, the oilman, disappeared and let the whole thing drop, or he pursued it through to the end.

He thought of Ishmael and knew which course he would take.

Chapter Ten

Linus fell into bed that night in a state of total exhaustion, not all of it physical. He slept far into the next day and didn't wake up until a chambermaid came in to clean up on the assumption that the room was empty.

The hotel was no longer serving breakfast so he walked up to the Victory Services Club and had a fry-up there. With that inside him, he felt at peace with the world and disinclined to think about dog-fighting, drugs, or anything unpleasant at all. He bought a paper and strolled back through Hyde Park.

When he finally returned to the hotel, it was to learn that there had been a phone call for him but that the caller – an American, the receptionist volunteered – would ring back. Accordingly, Linus abandoned any plans he might have to go out again and settled himself down in his room with the paper.

Hank's call when it came was brief.

'I gather you enjoyed yourself last night,' he began.

For the second time Linus equivocated that it had been interesting and noticed once more that his listener took that to be confirmation of his assumption.

'I think I may have something for you,' Hank went on. 'Can you be ready at very short notice?'

'Whenever you like,' Linus told him. 'This isn't the most exciting place in the world to have to hang around but I suppose it's all in a good cause.'

Hank laughed shortly. 'I can save you some of your misery, then,' he said. 'I won't be in touch before tomorrow. OK?'

'Fine,' Linus said and put the phone down.

Linus was not entirely pleased that Hank had already found him a bitch. The search for a bitch had been nothing more than the tool that would get him into the game more quickly. The last thing he had envisaged was being faced with one, or maybe two, such animals and having to decide which to buy, but that was exactly what Hank's phone call seemed to imply. On the other hand, it did look as if he had been completely accepted. That realization helped to untie the knots in his stomach and he acknowledged for the first time just how frightened he had been.

He rang Thelwall. 'How's Ishmael?' he asked.

'Fine. He's thriving. How's the week's leave?'

It was surprisingly reassuring to hear a familiar voice, even though his acquaintance with Thelwall was recent. Linus realized that he regarded the younger vet as a friend, a possible consequence of the cooperative effect they had made to deal with the succession of recent crises.

'Tedious, most of the time. I spent a lot of it just hanging around. I've made some progress, though. I'm on to something which is right up Ishmael's street, if you take my meaning.' Linus was disinclined to be too specific on the telephone.

Thelwall sounded concerned. 'So that's what you're up to! Take care. There's been a number of calls here asking what's going to happen to the Pit Bulls now that Jones-Drybeck has been charged. As if they didn't all have owners! It's been in the papers, by the way. Some of them even claim to be the owners, though, if they are, each Pit Bull must belong to a consortium. Others are offering "good homes". Funny thing – no one has rung up to offer any of the other dogs a good home. Must mean something!'

'Did any of them give names?'

'What do you think? No, of course not, unless people called Smith, Brown and Jones have a monopoly of offering Pit Bulls good homes. Some of them sounded pretty rough characters. Your RSPCA friend was round here the other day. Wanted to have a look at that section. I know it's not customary to let anyone but the owner see a dog but I thought in the circumstances I might stretch a point. He said he'd been making a few inquiries of a general sort and had come to the conclusion it was something *not* to get involved with. He was talking generally, of course. Neither of us thought you'd be daft enough to do just that.'

'Don't worry. I've not roused any suspicions. Besides,' Linus added in an unsuccessful attempt at levity, 'time was hanging heavily.'

'I should think it must have been,' Thelwall retorted.

'I'll have to go – someone coming. What is it they say? "Have a nice day."'

'Thank you very much,' Linus said sarcastically but Thelwall's phone had been replaced before he finished.

Time hung heavily and as it dragged itself along, his confidence gradually ebbed. Not only was he on his own but he was also an amateur among professionals. A woman had hurt his pride and the abuse of a dog had offended his professional principles and what had he done? He had taken it upon himself to put that little bit of the world to rights, regardless of his fitness or suitability for the task. None of his acquaintance knew where he was, and if anything happened to him, no one would start wondering about it until he failed to return to work. He ought to tell someone but he had become paranoid about the whole business. Lacock, for instance. The policeman was probably as upright as they come but what if he dropped a word unwittingly in the wrong ear? Trevarrick, too. What was it those posters had said in the war? 'Careless talk costs lives.' No, he was safest if no one knew anything. The thought didn't make him feel comfortable but at least it made him feel sane. Scared, but sane.

The next day – the last of his leave entitlement – began like its predecessors and the monotony continued till midday. The call came just as Linus was deciding whether to eat in the hotel or risk going out and missing the call. Part of him wanted to miss it – it would give him an easy get-out without losing face – but he also wanted to finish what he had started.

'It's all set up for you,' Hank told him. 'You'll need to leave now. OK?'

'No problem,' Linus said. 'Where do I go?'

Briefly, Hank gave him explicit directions. 'It'll take you about an hour,' he went on. 'You'll put your car in the multi-storey and a man called Ralph will meet you. You can trust him implicitly. Go with him. Do whatever he says.'

'He has the bitch, has he?' Linus asked.

There was a momentary hesitation the other end. 'Not personally, no, but he'll take you to the right place. Don't worry. They're expecting you.'

It sounded all very cryptic, but then it would, Linus supposed. As for trusting Ralph implicitly, that was something he was extremely disinclined to do. Doubtless Ralph would take him to wherever he had been told to. Thus far would Linus trust him.

Linus collected his car and headed south, over the river, on to the A3 and southwards still, past – the ultimate irony this, he thought – the Ministry's headquarters at Tolworth. He found the multi-storey car park without difficulty and drove up to the third level in accordance with his instructions. He got out, locked his car and stood looking about him.

There were very few people about. One or two housewives laden with supermarket boxes or pestered with small children too young to be at school. An older woman who hastened her pace when she saw a solitary man standing by his car, looking about him. She would be the one who might remember him, he thought.

A white Saab came down from the level above and the driver slowed down as he came abreast of Linus. 'Rod?' he asked.

It took a moment's reflection before Linus recalled his pseudonym. He hoped the hesitation would be taken for a healthy wariness.

'Ralph?' he replied.

The passenger door opened. 'Hop in.'

Ralph was not what Linus had expected. In his mid-thirties he looked sleek and prosperous and Linus couldn't imagine him in any milieu except the City. He wore a black jacket and the traditional pin-striped morning trousers while on the back seat the ubiquitous bowler rested on top of the briefcase with its companion umbrella beside it. Ralph was almost a caricature of the City gent but in some indefinable way Linus knew he was the real thing.

'Stockbroking?' he asked.

Ralph shook his head. 'Banking,' he said. 'And you?'

'Oil. Well, chandling for the rigs.'

'Interesting?'

'Not bad.'

'Profitable?'

'It has been. Less so now. Everyone's pulling in their horns.'

'Same story everywhere, if you ask me.'

The conversation was so normal it was almost surreal and Linus didn't like it for that very reason. They were speeding south. 'No blindfold?' he asked.

Ralph grinned. 'No need.'

Linus felt a tinge of uneasiness. Did that indeed mean they were satisfied he was genuine? Would they really make up their minds that quickly? Had he done anything, said anything, to arouse their suspicions? He couldn't think of anything, but that did nothing to reassure him. Why should he be allowed to see exactly where he was going? Two reasons occurred to him. The first was that he would not be coming back, but that could only apply if he had given them cause to suspect him. More probably – he hoped – it was because it was daylight, which must make it inadvisable to blindfold a passenger. It was the sort of thing which could be expected to attract undesirable attention from the occupants of other cars – at traffic lights, for instance. It was the sort of thing they would remember even if they did nothing about it at the time. That must be the explanation. He felt very slightly easier.

The unease returned as the road signs suggested they were going to Portsmouth. Lewdown had gone there – and Lewdown had died. Had he gone because there were dog-fighting connections in the city or simply because it was the port closest to home? Linus had no idea but he wished they were making for somewhere else. He was happier when Ralph swung off that road and began to head more directly south and into Sussex, obviously knowing his way very well indeed, taking a cross-country route and navigating the twisting country roads with the expertise of long acquaintance.

Finally, and when Linus was least expecting it, he turned off a single-track lane that was bordered by a high flint-faced wall and in through high wrought-iron gates. They sped down a drive between manicured verges lined with beeches and Linus saw before them a large country house in the mock-Gothic style with a crenellated roof and a disproportionately large porte-cochère. Like its boundary wall, the whole building was faced with flint. Linus thought he had seen a picture of this house somewhere but it wasn't one of the better known stately homes. It didn't have the look of a place that the public could see upon production of a pound or two. He tried to put a name to it and failed, and although he knew so much flint must indicate they were still in Sussex, he realized that somewhere on their twisting drive through narrow lanes he had stopped taking note of the unfamiliar names of the villages through which they had passed. You fool! he thought. No wonder they didn't need to blindfold you! They know you better than you know yourself.

The Saab didn't pull up at the door but swept on past and turned into the former stable yard before slowing down and pulling up at the kitchen entrance. Linus supposed it was to be expected that puppies would be here rather than in the house and felt a decided twinge of regret: it was the sort of house where one might reasonably expect to see some good pictures. It appeared that that was a privilege to be denied him.

'This way,' Ralph said, guiding him towards the kitchen door.

The room was obviously a working kitchen in general use but right now it was completely empty. Something simmered on a hot-plate, vegetables lay on a chopping-board half way through their preparation. The room had an air of the *Marie Celeste* about it, as if the staff had simply downed tools and disappeared. He shivered slightly.

'This way,' Ralph said again, leading him through the

166

kitchen into the butler's pantry. This room, too, looked as if it were still used by some modern major domo, a concept Linus found hard to accept though he supposed there must still be people outside Buckingham Palace who actually rose to the heights of a butler. Ralph opened a door in this room and switched on a light. 'Down here,' he said.

Linus peered down. The door opened on to some steps leading down to a wine cellar. His feeling of unease returned, magnified. He looked questioningly at Ralph. 'Funny place to put puppies,' he said.

Ralph smiled. 'Good place to put anything you don't want found. Go on. You'll find they're waiting for you.'

That, Linus had plenty of time to reflect later, was the moment when he should have shoved Ralph over and made a run for it. Unfortunately, Linus was a well-behaved, cooperative and conscientious member of society who said 'Excuse me' when he bumped into people and held doors open for women and the elderly. He didn't use buses but if he had done, Linus would have been the person who gave up his seat to someone less well able to stand than he was. He valued these little courtesies and knew he was regarded as old-fashioned for observing them. That didn't bother him but it equipped him ill for the sort of situation where a quick shove or a sudden thump was called for. So he obeyed Ralph's instruction and went into the cellar.

Half way down the steps he realized that Ralph was not following him. He turned. The immaculate morning trousers were still at the top of the steps. 'Aren't you coming?' Linus asked.

'My job was to deliver you,' Ralph said. 'I'm off now. Hope it all goes according to plan.' He closed the cellar door and Linus heard the key turn, a sound which did nothing to increase his confidence.

It was the first cellar of such magnitude Linus had ever seen and he doubted whether there could be many like it in private hands. He walked down the narrow aisle between the ranks of dusty bottles whose labels meant little to him even though some, like Château Mouton

167

Rothschild, had attained the status of legends known by reputation to all and by taste to very few. Another aisle crossed the one he was in and as he drew level with it, two men emerged, one from either side. They were his escort of a few nights ago.

'Nice to see you . . . Rodney,' one of them said. Linus decided later that that pause was the moment when he knew there would be no puppies.

They steered him into the new aisle, each of them holding an arm in a way that might have looked friendly to a casual observer, had there been one, but which was so firm as to allow no latitude at all.

There was a small open space at the end of the aisle with a chair in it. A perfectly ordinary dining-room chair with a slatted back, a padded seat and no arms. When they stood just in front of it, Linus's escorts turned him round and pushed him down until he was sitting on it. One of them tied his arms firmly behind the back of the chair and then tied his ankles together. Linus wriggled and flexed his wrists and concluded that they had done their job well. He wasn't going to be able to do a Richard Hannay.

One of his escorts stayed with him while the other disappeared between the racks of wine and Linus heard his footsteps heading towards the door. Then he heard the rap of knuckles on wood. Two short followed by two long. A pre-arranged signal. This suspicion was vindicated when the raps were followed by the sound of the key turning and then several sets of footsteps approached through the cellar. Four newcomers finally stood before him. One was Hank. One was the politician Linus had seen at the dog-fight and been unable to put a name to. One was a complete stranger whose clothes proclaimed him a foreigner. The fourth was Clarissa.

The politician produced a snapshot from his pocket and he and the foreigner looked from it to Linus and back. Linus recalled the flash-bulbs at the fight. His stomach lurched. Fool! Why hadn't it occurred to him that it might not be the dogs who were being photographed?

'He was at the match,' the politician stated positively. 'No doubt at all.'

'He's the one I met in the pub. The one who wanted a bitch. Rodney,' Hank confirmed.

The politician turned to Clarissa. 'Mary?'

'Rintoul. Linus Rintoul, MRCVS,' she said. 'MAFF Veterinary Officer based in Oxford. The man who upset our Highnoon operation.'

'Not so,' Linus interrupted. 'The lid was blown off that little stew when a pet dog developed rabies and bit a kennelmaid. Even then, if Jones-Drybeck and her tame vet had only followed the rules, nothing would have come to light. Her explanation of the Pit Bulls' scars would have been accepted and she'd have been there to receive the crash survivor. In fact, it was that dog's survival that really blew the whole thing wide open.'

The foreigner nodded. 'The guy's right,' he said. 'Someone ballsed that up. I only hope for his sake he can explain how come the dog, of all things, survived. A passenger wouldn't have mattered, but the dog – !' He rolled his eyes upward in a classic Latin expression and Linus suddenly knew who he was. The gravelly voice had been familiar from radio or television. Associated with so potently Italian an expression, Linus guessed him to be Frank Teramo. For the moment, however, he was more interested in what the man was saying than in who he was.

'So it was a bomb on that plane,' he said.

'Right,' Teramo grinned. 'But the authorities will never know why.'

'Seems a pity to take so much effort only to find that the one thing you needed to destroy was the one thing to survive,' Linus said drily.

The American scowled. 'You've got too much to say for yourself. I don't like lip.'

The politician laid a hand on the American's vicuna sleeve. 'Forget it, Frank. Mouth is all he's got. No need to let it rile you.'

Linus turned his attention back to Clarissa. The imperfect light down here threw her features into unusual relief. The stoat-like sharpness was more noticeable, the resemblance to the Leonardo more pronounced. 'Clarissa Pensilva or Mary Calshot?' he asked.

'So you got on to that, did you? Mary Calshot. The other sounds better, though, don't you think?'

Linus wouldn't be drawn on that. 'Why use Pensilva in Portsmouth?' he asked. 'Lewdown must have known who you were.'

Her eyes widened with surprise. 'My, you have been putting two and two together. Lewdown didn't know me, full stop. He might have recognized my real name, though.'

'But you sat and chatted to him,' Linus exclaimed. 'He must have known you!'

She laughed indulgently. 'Middle-aged men are always happy to chat to an attractive woman, I find. Perfectly happy to meet them for a little tête-à-tête in some lonely spot, too.'

'Like the Camber when everyone's gone home?'

'Exactly like that.'

Linus sighed. 'So it was you who pushed him. Another illusion shattered. Even though I knew it must have been you, I didn't really want it to be.'

'I'm a survivor, you see. You'd be amazed what one can do when it's a matter of survival. I'm sorry you've turned out to be so inquisitive: I quite liked you. If only you'd stuck to the job you're paid for, but no, you have to poke your nose in and ferret around, and this is where you end up. Pity, but there's nothing I can do about it now.' She turned to the politician. 'May I go?'

'Go straight back to Town. No need to hang around here.'

'I won't.' She turned to Linus. 'Goodbye,' she said. 'Sorry I shan't see you again.'

Nobody spoke until they heard the door close behind her. Then the two men who had tied Linus up moved menacingly close to him.

170

'Right,' said the politician. 'Now we are quite sure who you are, we can get down to business. Why are you here?'

'Would you believe to buy a Pit Bull bitch?' Linus asked.

'No.'

'It's not so far off,' Linus told him. 'I wanted to find out what sort of people could misuse dogs the way you've been doing.'

The man shifted impatiently. 'We've no time to play games,' he said. 'You're working for the police or Customs and we want to know which.'

'Does it matter?' Linus asked.

'It matters. We have more influence with one than with the other.'

'Then I'm afraid you're going to be disappointed. I work for neither.'

'Not in the normal course of events. We know that. Which are you working for now?'

'Neither.'

The blow to his solar plexus left him doubled up and gasping. He heard Hank's voice through his attempts to breathe again. 'Come on. What do you take us for? It has to be one or the other.'

'I told you. I don't like dogs being treated like that,' Linus gasped. 'I suppose I might have gone to the police eventually, when I'd found out more about it, but I wasn't working for them.'

'The man's a fool,' Teramo growled angrily. 'What's worse, he's taking us for fools, too. Do him over good, boys. He won't hold out for long. He's not the type.'

'Hold on, there,' the politician interrupted. 'You could be wrong, Frank. He's just the sort who would get involved for some crackpot reason like that. This is England, remember. Sometimes people here do things for altruistic reasons. Besides, if they beat him up too thoroughly, he'll be no use to us.'

Linus might have wondered what use they had in mind if one or two things hadn't clicked neatly into place just then. Lord Sangobeg. That's who the politician was. Something at the Home Office. He remembered it now. There'd been some fuss about this Frank Teramo. He'd been declared an undesirable visitor because of his connections with organized crime. No, it wasn't quite that. There had been a Press campaign to get him banned and it had failed. It had been Sangobeg who had said there was no proof. No wonder they could claim influence with one of the law and order agencies – they already had someone at the Home Office. The police was by far the most likely bet, though Linus didn't doubt that someone at that level might also be able to put the occasional pressure on Customs, too. He began to feel his reluctance to confide in Lacock had been vindicated.

Teramo looked at Linus derisively. 'You think we've got the material for a real match?' he asked scornfully.

Sangobeg seemed unconcerned by the implicit criticism. 'I think so,' he said. 'We've some very good dogs just now. Very good indeed.'

Teramo snorted. 'I suppose you're sure you can keep him?' he asked.

'Oh, we'll be able to keep him. Won't we, Hank?'

Hank grinned. 'I don't think that'll be a problem, sir. We've never lost one yet.'

'How soon?' the other American asked.

'Tomorrow, I should think. You can set it up by then, Hank, can't you?'

'No reason why not. After all, a few phone calls is all it takes.'

Sangobeg looked at Linus. 'I'm afraid you're going to be rather uncomfortable for a while,' he said. 'However, it will be temporary. We shall meet again – in more salubrious circumstances, I assure you. In the meantime, I must ask you to excuse me: one does have other concerns, you know.'

Sangobeg and the two Americans departed, leaving Linus with his guards. The one who had punched him smiled apologetically. 'Sorry about that, mate,' he said. 'Just doin' my job. No hard feelings, I hope?'

172

Linus assured him there were none and was amused that the man seemed pleased. The bizarre nature of his question, in the circumstances, did not appear to have struck him and Linus realized that the man had spoken no more than the truth: he had simply been doing his job and bore Linus no more animosity than a boxer bears a punch-bag.

'What's this match they're on about?' he asked. 'It sounds as if it's something special.'

'You could say that.'

'Pity I'm tied up here,' Linus went on. 'I'd have liked to see it.'

'Oh, you will,' the man said, surprised. 'They don't intend to keep you here, you know.'

Linus didn't know and such was the general drift of the conversation that he suspected ignorance might indeed be bliss. He still wanted to find out what was in store for him, though, and he was uncertain how much he could get out of either of these two men. He was sure they knew what was going on but they weren't exactly bright. 'What will they do with me, then?' he asked.

He discovered that neither man was quite that stupid. 'Not for us to say,' one of them replied. 'His lordship'll let you know whatever he wants you to know. We just look after you.'

With his hands tied behind him, Linus had no idea how much time passed, only that it seemed interminable and, although both men had watches which they consulted with increasing frequency as time went by, neither would tell him what time it was.

'Sorry, mate,' they said, genuinely apologetic. 'More than our job's worth.'

Linus knew there was never an answer to that argument.

At last the time they had been waiting for came. One of them released Linus's hands from the back of the chair though they remained tied together behind his back. Then his feet were freed.

'Bit stiff, are we?' one of them said. 'Better wriggle about a bit to get the blood moving again. Take your time. There's no mad rush.'

Linus took full advantage of this considerate advice and his feet felt almost normal as he went with his escort up the cellar steps and into the pantry. Sounds from the kitchen indicated that it was no longer empty and the smells that emanated from it made him realize just how very hungry he was.

His companions guided him through the baize door and across a huge hall which boasted a massive mock-Gothic fireplace in which a fire blazed, consuming the better part of what seemed to be a whole tree. So vast was this atrium that Linus counted no fewer than six sofas which he loosely classified as William-and-Mary, as well as too many arm-chairs for him to count as he was led across to a room on the other side. One of his escorts reached forward past Linus and opened the door, then stood aside to let him enter.

The dining-room was considerably smaller than the hall but was by no means a small room. The Gothic element had been drawn with a lighter touch here and the strangest aspect of the room was that the table was in the middle of a shallow sunken square in the centre of the room. It was probably no more than a foot or a foot and a half below the surrounding floor but it looked more because the sides were stepped for their entire length.

The table was laid with two covers and Lord Sangobeg sat behind one of them. The centrepiece was a huge architectural salt – silver-gilt, Linus guessed – that bore a striking resemblance to St Pancras Station. Side tables on the raised surround bore silver serving dishes on very modern hotplates, but the thing that took Linus's eye and quite diverted his attention was a painting on the wall opposite the door. Oblivious both of his host and his peculiar circumstances, Linus walked straight round to look at it. It was not a large picture and its frame was of plainly carved ebony. A window at one side of the composition flooded with light a simple domestic scene: a young mother dandled a baby on her knee while a doting, and much older, father looked on. Linus had never seen anything so beautiful in his life.

'Very nice,' he said and turned to Lord Sangobeg. 'Vermeer?'

His host left his seat and came over to join him. 'One of the very few in private hands. I'm surprised you recognized it. I didn't think it had ever been reproduced.'

'I didn't,' Linus told him. 'That's to say, I've never seen a print of it. That light, though – and the blue of her gown. That can only be Vermeer. You're a lucky man.'

'And you're a discriminating one. I wish we'd met in different circumstances.'

'Have you any more of this calibre?'

'Nothing to stand comparison with a Vermeer. One or two worth looking at, though. After dinner, perhaps?'

He led the way back to the table and beckoned one of Linus's guards forward to untie his hands. 'I'm afraid your companions will have to stay,' Lord Sangobeg said apologetically. 'A safety measure, you appreciate. The secret is to pretend they're not here, rather as the Japanese can admire a landscape without seeing the litter. It's a mental technique, that's all.'

His host was quite possibly right, but Linus found it a difficult technique to acquire. It also struck him as rather unfair that he and Lord Sangobeg should be tucking into a lavish repast while the two guards, who had been without food for at least as long as Linus had, should be obliged to stand and watch them eat it. Despite the formality of the table-setting and the undoubted wealth of the host, the meal itself was incongruously informal. No one came to serve them and Lord Sangobeg indicated that they should serve themselves, buffet-style, from the side-tables.

'Please don't stint yourself,' he told Linus. 'You will get a breakfast tomorrow but nothing after that. Make the most of this. The quails' eggs in aspic are particularly fine. I don't know what Jean-Paul adds to them but the result is a masterpiece.'

175

Linus obediently helped himself to quails' eggs. 'You make it sound like the condemned man's hearty breakfast – or dinner, in this case.'

Lord Sangobeg beamed at him. 'Precisely,' he said. 'I couldn't have put it better myself. What do you think of the quails' eggs?'

'They're everything you said they were,' Linus said politely. It was true enough but his host's other comments had somehow not increased his feeling of well-being.

'I have had a turbot *à la reine* sent up, too,' his lordship went on. 'Not everyone's cup of tea, perhaps, but one of my favourites. Then there is a very simple, very plain, haunch of venison. One needs at least one unadorned, straightforward course that speaks for itself, don't you think? Then I'm afraid I had a problem. I wasn't at all sure what your taste in puddings might be so I've been rather vulgar and had the cook send up what they call a sweet trolley. The strawberry malakoff is really rather splendid, if you like cream. Or you may fancy the simple astringency of oranges in Cointreau.'

Linus found the urbanity of Lord Sangobeg's manner and conversation-matter bizarre, if not, in the circumstances, positively macabre, yet he found it impossible to inject a note of more urgent realism. To his host, the meal was the only thing of any importance and it seemed genuinely to matter to him that his guest should both enjoy and appreciate it. Linus expressed himself well pleased with the turbot.

It was indeed a superb meal, one which Linus would remember for a long time – always supposing he had the opportunity, which some of Lord Sangobeg's comments implied would not be the case. He suspected that the wines served with it were classic vintages. Linus had long ago moved beyond the stage of buying the house plonk but his modest government salary obliged him to stay near the bottom of the wine list. Now, for the first time, he realized the delight of a first-rate vintage and began to see why those who could afford twenty, thirty, forty pounds a bottle, did so. He savoured every mouthful, a fact which did not escape his host.

'You obviously enjoy good wine as much as you enjoy good pictures,' he said. 'One would not wish to be impertinent, but one must confess to a little surprise that a civil servant can afford to indulge in such luxuries.'

'A civil servant can't,' Linus told him. 'Good paintings can be appreciated free by anyone who chooses to set foot in a public gallery. As for good wines, well, I freely admit I've never before had the opportunity of tasting anything so excellent as this.'

His host beamed. 'I am delighted, Mr Rintoul. Nothing pleases me so much as bringing pleasure into someone's life.'

The odd thing was, Linus was sure he meant every word of it. He was very tempted to remark that he would gain greater pleasure from a cheap wine and the knowledge that he would live than from an expensive one that was to be followed by death, a condition he was increasingly certain lay in store for him. It was a temptation he resisted because his instinct told him not to upset Lord Sangobeg's mood. He was beginning to doubt whether the man was entirely sane – yet surely he must be? Surely he would be removed from any official post if his irrationality was apparent? Linus ventured a more topical question.

'Your American friend – Frank, I think you called him – he doesn't join us?'

Lord Sangobeg frowned. 'Hardly a friend. A business associate, and a much valued one, but not the sort of person one invites to share one's board.'

It was a sentiment with which Linus heartily concurred and not entirely for cultural reasons. 'Conversation with him would be difficult,' he agreed.

'Impossible. He can talk, of course. Does little else, in fact, and mostly about money. So tedious. But conversation . . . ! A barren field to Mr Teramo, I'm afraid.'

Linus was smugly satisfied to have the man's identity so thoroughly confirmed, even if that confirmation only underlined his own probable fate. He recognized that fear now lay permanently in the pit of his stomach but overlaying it and still capable of disguising it was an almost objective curiosity. There was a lot more he wanted to find out but he would have to play Lord Sangobeg on a very careful line. He decided on the strawberry malakoff.

'I normally avoid cream if I can,' he confided, patting his midriff. 'Cholesterol and all that. But I really think I can afford to indulge myself this evening, don't you?'

Sangobeg smiled benignly. 'I certainly don't think you need worry too much about a heart attack,' he said.

The coffee was made to perfection and the accompanying brandy slid down like liquid silk. Linus decided that if there were other good pictures in the house, he might as well see them. Quite apart from his genuine interest, he could hardly fail to learn something of the layout of the house and that might well come in useful. He drained his balloon. 'You said there were other pictures,' he suggested.

'Of course. I was forgetting. How remiss of me. One or two worthy of small note.'

Sangobeg put his own glass down and stood up. 'No time like the present, as they say. Perhaps you will forgive me if I lead the way? I'm afraid our friends here will have to come too.'

'Naturally.' Linus was disappointed but not surprised.

Among the one or two pictures worthy of small note were a Goya, a Van Gogh, a small Caravaggio, two Claudes and no fewer than four Renoirs, one of them a delightful nude of exceptional luminosity. In one room a Landseer hung opposite a Sartorius and a Ben Marshall, while in another it was clear that an earlier Lord Sangobeg had been an ardent patron of Sargent. Nowhere in the house did Linus see anything painted since the First World War. It was an interesting omission.

'I'm surprised you don't have this in the dining-room,' Linus commented as they stood in front of the Landseer. It was a vast canvas of skilfully painted dead game, the sort of picture that was customarily hung in the dining-room of great houses.

Lord Sangobeg wrinkled his nose. 'It used to be there but I found it rather . . . distasteful. The Vermeer is a far more satisfying accompaniment to good food, I find.'

'I shouldn't have thought the subject-matter would bother you, given your hobby,' Linus said cautiously, but his host was unperturbed.

'I know what you mean, Mr Rintoul, but there is a place for everything and one really prefers not to be reminded, as one eats, what the contents of one's plate used to look like.'

Linus was rather disturbed to find himself once more in complete agreement with his host and to realize that, if he had met him in different circumstances, they might well have struck up a small friendship. He wondered how unwise it would be to bring up the topic rather closer to his immediate concern than his host's choice of pictures. Probably very, but he had little to lose and, if they intended him to die, at least he wouldn't do so in ignorance.

'Has it ever struck you,' he began, 'how very closely Miss Pensilva – Miss Calshot, I mean – resembles a Leonardo?'

Lord Sangobeg looked startled. He considered the remark and finally smiled. 'Do you know, it hadn't but you're absolutely right. How very observant of you.'

'It struck me straight away,' Linus told him. 'Right from the first time I saw her. It took a little longer to pin down the exact picture.'

His host considered the matter. 'Which one did you decide it was?'

Linus told him.

Lord Sangobeg thought about it and the smile spread slowly across his face. 'You're absolutely right,' he said again. 'I do wish I'd noticed it for myself. Still, every time I see her now I shall think about it. Such a beautiful woman. Not at all what one expects in a solicitor.'

Linus was not sure why a solicitor should be expected

to be plain, but that was not the argument he wished to pursue. 'How did you come across her?' he said.

'Very odd, that. I had an elderly relative. Ridiculously wealthy and quite dotty. She held the oddest notions. One of them was that the State should provide. She could never get it into her head that supermarkets and department stores did not belong to the State, so "shopping" for Aunt Augusta meant helping herself to whatever she needed. She always paid for the luxury items, but the necessities she took as being her due from the State. They call it shoplifting, of course, and it finally got so out of hand that the shops insisted on prosecuting instead of letting the family pay for what she had taken. Miss Calshot was recommended and, amazingly, she got Aunt Augusta acquitted at magistrate level. What's more, she somehow managed to prevent any publicity. We were very grateful.'

'I can imagine,' Linus said truthfully. 'So she's been handling your business ever since?'

'Good gracious, no! We have a very good firm of City solicitors who have been dealing with the family's normal legal affairs for generations. Miss Calshot handles the more . . . unorthodox matters.'

'Like Mrs Jones-Drybeck.'

'Dreadful woman – or so I'm told. I'm happy to say I've never met her. She was one of Teramo's discoveries. She'd been a very successful madam in the Virgin Islands, of all places, and mixed that with organizing some of Teramo's other business. She wanted to retire and open a boarding-kennel. Grew up with dogs, it seems, and wanted to get back to it. Teramo suggested a more profitable variation to her. I was at MAFF at the time and I knew there was no check on the criminal records of people applying for quarantine licences, so that was all right.'

'Even if there had been, convictions in the Virgin Islands wouldn't have shown up,' Linus pointed out.

'Ah, but she'd had a bit of bother before that. Something to do with procuring. Under a different name, of course.'

'Teramo's scheme couldn't work without a vet willing to

cooperate,' Linus persisted. Lord Sangobeg seemed perfectly willing to answer his questions, so he might as well see just how much he could find out. He might never be able to use it but at least he would know. 'Who discovered James Erbistock?'

'I have to claim credit for that,' Sangobeg said modestly. 'A very foolish young man. I did mention I had been at MAFF?'

Linus nodded. He knew now that that was probably why his host's face had seemed familiar at the fight. He had assumed he had seen it on television but that might not be the full story. His face must have appeared in various agricultural publications during his time at that Ministry and the residual memory had stayed with Linus.

'It was drawn to my attention that this young vet – who, to be fair to him, had been under some strain at the time – had been issuing health certificates without actually going to the trouble of examining the animals concerned. As you will appreciate better than most, that's enough to get any vet struck off. I had a chat with him and found out what had led to it and was able to put a suggestion to him which would render it unnecessary for the Royal College to be told.'

'In other words, you blackmailed him?' Linus said bluntly.

Sangobeg frowned. 'An unexpectedly crude phraseology from a man of your taste. I prefer to say that a mutually acceptable arrangement was entered into.'

'Aren't you afraid of what he will say now that the police have him?' Linus asked, intrigued.

'Not at all. I'm at the Home Office now. It isn't easy to arrange matters with the police: one has to be so careful with whom one makes contact, but I am entirely confident that anything young Erbistock says will be in the right ears, and of course, although we may not be able to keep him at liberty, we shall see to it that he is handsomely recompensed for his discretion.'

'I hope for your sakes he knows that,' Linus said drily.

'Why else do you imagine Miss Calshot is his lawyer?'

'Of course,' Linus admitted. 'How foolish of me.'

His host turned to the two guards who had accompanied them silently on the tour of the pictures and Linus wondered just how sure Lord Sangobeg must be of their loyalty and dependability. He supposed it operated on the same basis as Erbistock's: generous rewards for their discretion. All the same, it must be hazardous to talk quite so freely in front of minions. On the other hand, it was even more hazardous to talk so freely to Linus who was hardly a sympathizer. What if Linus got away? Obviously Lord Sangobeg had ruled that possibility out of court. It was not a consoling thought and Linus knew the fear was now beginning to supersede the curiosity.

'Take Mr Rintoul to the room that's been prepared for him,' Lord Sangobeg said. He turned to Linus. 'I hope you will have a comfortable night. We shan't meet again – not directly, at any rate – but I would like you to know how much I have enjoyed our discussion this evening.' He held out his hand. 'Goodbye, Mr Rintoul.'

Linus's escort led him up several flights of deeply carpeted stairs to the third floor and showed him into an attic room that had quite clearly once been the nursery. Like all good nurseries, an iron grille prevented any over-adventurous child from falling out of the window on to the drive beneath. It also prevented any captive from escaping. The room was pleasantly decorated and the bed extremely comfortable but the door was locked once Linus was inside and he knew his companions would be on guard outside. He hoped someone would bring them a meal. There was nothing Linus could do except go to bed and try to sleep.

The first was easy, the second impossible and he wondered whether that was why a varied selection of books had been placed on the bedside table. He found none of them as enthralling as contemplating his unenviable position.

Thanks to his interest in paintings, he had a good idea of the general layout of the house but he could see no possibility of its being the slightest use to him. He opened the windows and examined the grille. A three-year-old couldn't have squeezed between the bars, let alone a middle-aged vet who was rather more substantial for his height than he should have been.

He went over to the door and tried the handle.

'Are you all right, Mr Rintoul? Anything you need?' one of the men asked.

A key, he thought, and a fat lot of good it will do me to say so.

A lifetime of books, films and television told him that in this situation a real man would get out. He might have to use improbable and dangerous methods but it could be done. Richard Hannay, the hero of his youth, was a case in point. It was a matter of honour for any red-blooded male to escape from the sort of situation in which Linus found himself. OK, he thought. How?

The window was no good and neither was the door. What else was there? He looked round the room. The chimney. This was an old house and old houses once had their chimneys swept by little boys. Linus got out of bed again and went over to the fireplace. He knelt down and peered up the chimney. Then he withdrew his head. It wasn't that sort of chimney and his girth was definitely greater than that of some half-starved nineteenth-century parish orphan.

He thought again. If he piled things against the door and then set light to them, he could, like his hero, burst out when the door was well alight or when the guards opened it to see why there was smoke seeping underneath. This was pure Buchan and, in the days when heroes smoked, would have been quite simple to organize. Linus didn't smoke. Nor did he have a magnifying-glass through which to focus the sun's rays – his sight wasn't that bad yet. In any case, it was dark and he'd never heard of anyone using the moon's light to start a fire. Furthermore, his inconsiderate host had left nothing that could conceivably be used to that end. The ceiling had no trapdoor through which he might escape into the vast expanse of roof and he was of the opinion that it would be a complete and utter waste of time hunting for the concealed entrance to some secret passage. He would be better advised conserving his energy by sleeping so that, in the unlikely event of a means of escape presenting itself next day, he would at least be physically fit enough to take advantage of it. If not, well, he supposed his body would turn up in some future archaeological dig in the foundations of a motorway bridge. It was a form of posterity he could do without.

He went back to bed and started counting sheep to no avail but then discovered that it was far more soporific to recall all the places on the motorway system where repairs were currently being carried out.

Chapter Eleven

Full English breakfast woke him up. It arrived on a brass-handled rosewood tray with legs and included a damask napkin and a single carnation in a tall, narrow, crystal vase. One of his guards was carrying the tray. The other stood warily at the door.

'Good God,' Linus said. 'What's the carnation for?'

'His lordship likes things done right,' the man said reprovingly.

Linus sat up and made himself comfortable. 'I'm not at all sure I want anything to eat,' he said.

'I would if I were you, sir,' the man told him. 'It's the last you'll be offered and it's got to last you till this evening.'

Linus noticed with some amusement that he had risen – or dropped – from 'mate' to 'sir'. He also noted that his guard seemed very well informed about the day's programme. 'What happens this evening?' he asked.

The guard was not so easily caught out. 'Now you know I can't tell you that, sir,' the man said, much as one chides a child who asks what Father Christmas is going to bring him.

The answer had been inevitable but it didn't lead Linus to anticipate the day ahead with any pleasure. 'I hope you two have had something to eat,' he said, changing the subject. 'You had to watch us feed our faces last night and I suppose you've been on guard all night long.'

'It's very kind of you to think of us, sir, in the circumstances. But don't worry. We've been very well looked after. Just give us a knock when you've finished and Bill here will come in and shave you.'

'I have a beard,' Linus pointed out, fingering it.

'Indeed you have, sir, but it's not what you might call a full set, is it? No doubt you will want it tidied up. You strike me as a gentleman who likes to look his best. Just knock, sir. By the way, the housekeeper said to tell you there's a new toothbrush in the drawer.'

The transformation from polite ruffian to archetypal gentleman's gentleman was complete and Linus almost wondered if it was only in his imagination that this man had punched him so resoundingly in his diaphragm the previous day.

When Linus had breakfasted, he washed and did what he could to make himself look presentable, helped by Bill's efficient 'tidying up' of his beard. Clearly Lord Sangobeg was not letting his guest loose with either razor or scissors. Then, satisfied that their charge had no further requirements, Linus's minders escorted him downstairs, along the corridor, across the hall and back into the cellar. They put him back on his chair and tied him to it in the same manner as before. This time, though, as if in witness to the fact that this was going to be an extended sojourn, they each had a stool which they placed either side of a small card table.

'Fancy a game of chess?' Bill asked Linus. 'You look like a chess bloke.'

'I am,' Linus said, thinking that at last his luck had

changed and opportunity was offering itself. 'I'm no Grand Master but I like a game. Do you have a set?'

Bill produced one from a bag which, Linus could see, also contained a pack of cards, Scrabble and other things which he couldn't immediately identify, and carefully laid it out on the table.

'You'd better undo my hands,' Linus suggested.

The other man laughed, but not nastily. 'Good try, sir, but you won't need your hands. Just tell me the moves you want to make. I'll shift the pieces.'

Another idea bites the dust, Linus thought gloomily. Ah well, at least it would pass the time.

David Thelwall looked at his watch. Ten o'clock. Rintoul ought to be in his office by now, unless he had gone straight out to the stockyards or something. That was unlikely on his first day back at work. Anyway, it was worth a try. One of the Pit Bulls was due to leave today and he had an idea Linus might like to be around when the owners called for him. He was put through to Trevarrick. He recognized the older man's West Country burr.

'Trevarrick? Sorry – I didn't mean to bother you. I wanted to speak to Rintoul if he's not tied up.'

'That makes two of us. Thelwall, isn't it? Thought I recognized your voice. Our mutual friend was due back from leave today and there's plenty of work piled up here. My secretary has rung his home but there's no answer. He's normally pretty punctilious so I suppose the car's broken down somewhere. Still, it's annoying. Can I help you?'

'Not really. There's no problems this end. It's just something I thought he'd like to be reminded of but if he's not there, there's no point.' He hesitated. 'You've tried his home, you say?'

'About half an hour ago.'

'Do you know what he was doing on this leave?'

Trevarrick sounded surprised. 'No. I assumed he felt he needed a rest after all that rabies business, especially in view of his son's involvement. Why? Is it relevant?'

'I think so.' Briefly, Thelwall told him the gist of his recent conversation with Linus.

Trevarrick heard him through without interruption. 'Bloody fool,' he said at last when the other man had finished. 'Leave it with me, Thelwall. I know how to deal with this. I'm glad you rang.'

When the line was clear, Trevarrick rang Thames Valley Police Headquarters.

'Get me Inspector Lacock,' he said.

Chess or no chess, it was a long, slow day. Linus became increasingly hungry and neither of his companions would tell him the time. Eventually, however, the waiting seemed to be over when they untied his feet and released him from the chair.

'This way,' one of them said.

The remark was superfluous: there was only one way out of the cellar. Once again Linus went through the kitchen and into the yard outside. This time the car standing there was a hard-topped Land-Rover.

'I'm afraid we're going to have to tie you up,' Bill said. 'Get in.'

Linus did so. 'Do I get blindfolded as well?' he asked.

'No need. It's dark. You're not going far.'

It felt far. The back of a Land-Rover was a lot more uncomfortable than the van had been but at least he didn't feel so completely disoriented this time. They sped down the drive, through the gates and then twisted and turned through country lanes until finally they turned on to a very long, very straight and exceedingly bumpy cart track which led relentlessly uphill. Trees loomed in front of them at the top of the climb and the Land-Rover turned off into them. It wasn't the only vehicle there. Linus could make out about half a dozen cars among the trees. They were all expensive, top-of-the-market cars. Three of them were Rollers and he thought he could make out a Daimler. There was also, as incongruous as the Land-Rover in this company, a big Transit van. There was a building of some sort in front of them, too, but Linus, still in the back of the vehicle, couldn't quite make out what it was. Some sort of barn, he supposed but, from what little he could see, it couldn't be a very large one.

Bill came round to the back of the Land-Rover and untied Linus's feet. 'You'd better come out and walk about a bit. Get the circulation going again,' he said. 'Don't think you can try anything, though. It may be dark but we're not stupid. We're not alone, either.'

He jerked his head in the direction of the Transit and Linus could see the heads of two men behind the windscreen. All the same, this was likely to be the best chance he would get. Another man came out of the trees, a German Shepherd at his side. So much for the best chance, Linus thought, his spirits sinking even further and an unexpected feeling of panic beginning to creep into his mind. I might be able to evade the men. I'll never get away from the dog.

Now that he was standing on the ground and able to look around, he could see that the building in front of him was no barn. It was built of brick and here and there patches of flint cladding showed that it had once been entirely faced with these local stones. So far as he could tell in the moonlight, it was quite one of the most extraordinary buildings he had ever seen and a description of it in the right ears – always assuming he ever had the opportunity to give one, which was not something on which he would be prepared to bet right now – would bring instant identification. The first two floors seemed to be triangular with a circular tower at each angle. Darker recesses in both flat walls and towers indicated boarded- or bricked-up windows. Above these floors and situated over the centre of the triangle soared a single round tower, stabbing the night sky like a pointing finger. It was neither roofed nor shuttered and the clouds drifted past three storeys of empty window-sockets.

On the ground floor a door opened. Linus heard nothing but he saw the faint glow of flickering light from inside the tower and it silhouetted a beckoning figure. It would have been a spine-chilling scene had the figure not been wearing a baseball cap. Linus assumed it was Hank.

Bill pushed him towards the door which had been closed again. 'This way,' he said.

There was a slight slope towards the foot of the building and Linus realized that the door was quite a way up the wall and there were some makeshift brick steps leading up to it. He climbed them and when Bill tapped twice on the wooden door it was opened once more. Bill pushed him through and stepped back. The door was fastened.

Linus looked about him, his curiosity mingled with apprehension. He stood in a circular arena some twenty-four or -five feet across. The round tower obviously went down to the ground inside the building and the triangular appearance of the outside must be just a façade to accommodate the three corner towers which here led more or less directly off the central space. Two of them had metal grilles across. The third had a door which at present stood open and revealed the bottom of a spiral staircase which ascended in the corner tower to the next floor. This was not a complete floor but a narrow mezzanine running right round the building. Above it, the tower was completely roofed over which explained why no light from the first two floors escaped through the gaping eyes in the tower above. Illumination was provided only on the ground floor but in this building it did not come from hurricane lamps. Iron brackets were fastened to the walls, one between each corner tower, and these held what Linus could only think of as cressets: torches of burning pitch that flared and guttered, unevenly lighting the arena below. It was, Linus realized, the perfect arena for a dog-fight, though why Lord Sangobeg should want him to witness another was a subtlety that escaped him.

He was not alone. Hank had closed and barred the door behind him and was now untying his hands. Above him, on the mezzanine, several faces peered over, the flickering torchlight casting their features into grotesquely distorted relief. There were, Linus supposed, seven or eight of them. Sangobeg and Teramo he recognized but he could not see Sir Giles Frinton. The others were strangers. He could not recollect having seen them at the previous fight.

Linus was puzzled. He knew that Sangobeg and Teramo could not afford to let him go. The sensible thing for them to do was to get someone to bump him off quickly and dispose of the body. Yet they were apparently staging another fight for him. It didn't add up unless, he thought suddenly, they thought it would be a nicely intellectual sadistic touch to make him watch something he so strongly disapproved of. It was a subtlety beyond Frank Teramo but not beyond Lord Sangobeg. Well, that would not present too great a problem. He would steel himself not to betray his revulsion. That would deprive them of the satisfaction of seeing how he felt. He supposed this would have to be a fight to the death in order to have the maximum effect on this involuntary spectator. He could cope with that. It was the fear of the unknown, of what came after, that he was having difficulty dealing with. He felt no alarm when Hank said, 'Wait here,' and disappeared through the doorway leading to the staircase.

Alarm, and the terrifying feeling that he had guessed wrong, struck him when the door to the staircase was closed and bolted from the other side. He heard Hank's footsteps running up to the next floor and saw his tall figure appear on the mezzanine with the others. Sangobeg leant over, something in his hand.

'Stand back, Mr Rintoul,' he called out. 'I wouldn't want this to hit you. It's quite heavy.'

Linus stepped back under the overhang of the floor above and a pickaxe handle thudded to the ground beside him.

'Pick it up,' Sangobeg called down. 'That's your weapon. We thought you'd like to see a real fight.' He laughed. 'Not so much "see", I suppose, as "experience". This is the real combat, Mr Rintoul. A return to gladiatorial values. Sadly, in these unenlightened days, there is little opportunity to stage a real challenge, but every so often we have a situation where it becomes possible. You, Mr Rintoul, have presented us with such a situation.'

Linus began to understand. Intellectual sadism was not in Lord Sangobeg's mind. And he had credited him with subtlety! He had anticipated a bullet, maybe even a heavy blow on the back of the skull. A quick end. Lord Sangobeg and his cronies had very different plans. He picked up the handle and balanced it in his hand. 'You'd better explain the ground rules,' he said.

He heard Teramo's gravelly laugh. 'He's real cool, Sangobeg,' he said.

That wasn't how Linus felt but he wasn't about to disillusion his audience. He needed to know what chance there was of survival. Not much, he guessed. 'The rules, Sangobeg,' he called out.

'The dogs will come at you in threes,' his host replied. 'If you lay one out, another will take its place. It's as simple as that.'

'I've been handling Pit Bulls lately, Sangobeg. They don't go for people.'

'Who said anything about Pit Bulls? This is the *real* sport, Rintoul. The one where the real money changes hands. The one that sorts out the real men.'

'And if I win? Do I get presented with the dogs' ears, or something? What's my reward?'

'A nice touch, that. It's an idea we hadn't thought of. Thank you. Maybe it will be incorporated another time. You won't win. To be frank, you haven't the gladiator's muscle. But in the improbable event of your doing so, I'm afraid your reward won't be freedom. You know too much.'

'Then why go to all this bother? Why not just dispose of me?'

'You've missed the point, Rintoul. One way or another we are going to dispose of you. Be under no illusions about that. We want to precede it with a little excitement — excitement of a sort we get very little opportunity for.'

191

'Then my best way of thwarting you is just to sit here and let the dogs kill me,' Linus said.

'You won't,' Sangobeg said confidently. 'Self-preservation is a stronger instinct than you realize.'

He pulled his head back and Linus knew the conversation was over. He saw Hank move to one side of the mezzanine, by one of the corner towers which, on Linus's floor, was closed off by a grille. There was a rasping sound as the cover to a pop-hole slid up allowing three dogs to enter the small circular enclosure behind the grille. It was not easy to make out what they were in the peculiar light of the arena, a difficulty accentuated by the fact that the dogs were predominantly black with tan flashings. Rottweilers, he thought, or maybe Dobermans. Somehow, even in the relatively dim light, he knew they were neither but something in between. Possibly a cross or maybe they had a dash of one of the lesser-known continental attack breeds. Whatever their pedigrees, they were nasty-looking individuals and Linus's hand tightened on his stave. Sangobeg was right. Self-preservation was a powerful instinct.

He could hear bets being laid, not on whether he survived but for how long. He thought rapidly, pushing the rising tide of fear back with one part of his mind while he forced another to calculate the odds. He would never be faced with more than three at a time but he wasn't particularly fit. He had no idea how many dogs they had available but it couldn't be an unlimited supply. If the dogs had been in the Transit van, presumably in crates, there couldn't be much more than half a dozen. Which was half a dozen too many. His only chance of survival was to lam into each dog as fast as possible and lay them out before he tired because he would tire before any dog did. He refused to consider the purpose of surviving the dogs since he knew there was no question of his being set free. He would deal with that problem – if he was lucky – later.

The bottom section of the grille lifted like a portcullis and the dogs slipped out one after the other. Linus kept his eye on the foremost one as a cricketer watches the ball and, as it sprang at him, he wheeled round and the pickaxe handle smashed into its skull with a thud that would have been sickening if Linus had had time to think about it.

He had time to think about nothing but survival. The other two dogs were already on him, tearing at his arms and hindering his ability to swing his only weapon. He could hear another dog being bundled into the holding tower. One of his attackers, having grabbed more sleeve than arm, found the material insufficient to support his weight. The sleeve ripped off and the dog dropped to the ground.

With a tremendous wrench – because the other dog was still hanging on to one arm – Linus managed to swing his club round. He aimed for the dog's head and missed as the animal sprang for him again but he caught it in the ribs. The dog squealed in pain. Its impetus was lost and Linus brought his foot up sharply under its jaw as it tried to hurl itself at him once more. He heard its jaws click together but he had no time to assess how badly incapacitated it was. The new dog had been released into the arena, fresh and keen.

Already Linus was tiring. The new dog hurled himself straight at Linus's back and, as a replacement for the second dog bounded into the fray, Linus by some fluke of balance was able to twist so that the dog on his back somersaulted off and his spine smashed on the hard floor. He knew his arm was bleeding from the relentless onslaught of the dog that had never given up on it but he had no time to think about that for this new dog made straight for his face. Linus felt the skin give but there was miraculously no pain. Was this how Pit Bulls could come back again and again for such punishment? He pushed the incongruity of thought from his mind. At least the dog had missed his throat. He must get rid of one of these before the next replacement came in.

The pickaxe handle was getting heavier by the minute and slippery with the blood running down his arm. He could no longer swing it but he managed to drive the end of the handle vertically upwards under the dog's jaw as it renewed its attack on his face. It caught the dog in the throat and temporarily stopped its breath. It dropped to the ground to catch its breath and Linus suddenly realized that no more replacement dogs had been sent in.

The realization lent him an unexpected surge of strength. His arms were free because the dog that had been so assiduously hanging on to one or other of them was itself tiring and had transferred its attention and its teeth to his leg. With a tremendous effort, he swung the pickaxe handle up over his head and brought it down hard on the black head of the still-gasping dog. It gurgled and lay still. The handle slipped from his bloodied hands and spun across the floor.

There was one opponent left and it was nearly as exhausted as Linus, but there was no sign of exhaustion dampening the dog's determination. Warm, wet blood had seeped into Linus's shoes from the innumerable punctures and gashes and he knew it was only a matter of time before the dog succeeded in ripping a muscle and crippling him. He tried to grab one of its ears, intending to wrench its face away from his leg and realized for the first time that its ears had been cropped so short that there was virtually nothing to seize. He found himself incongruously indignant that someone had performed an illegal operation and then self-preservation supervened. He needed a weapon.

The pickaxe handle was only a few feet away – out of reach but not impossibly so. He lunged towards it, the dog a heavy weight on his leg. The lunge was just enough. He bent down and his fingers fastened round the shaft.

Bending down was a mistake. The dog, sensing his quarry was off-balance, let go of his leg and threw himself at the man's throat. Linus lost his balance and went down under the dog's renewed onslaught. Now it was the dog who experienced an unexpected surge of strength and Linus heard the cheer that went up from the spectators as they, too, realized what had happened.

Desperation is a master-teacher. Linus fastened his

bloody hands round the dog's throat. His thumbs, with the unerring accuracy of the professional, found the larynx and pressed. He knew there was no more strength in his arms yet he found some, pressing the larynx against the animal's windpipe until no vestige of air could get past it. When the dog's body went limp, so did Linus. He lacked even the strength to push it off.

There was silence. Then Sangobeg's voice floated down.

'Quite a turn-up for the books, gentlemen. Hank, go and check.'

Linus heard the words but they didn't register. In the same way he knew Hank was bending over him. He heard him call up. 'He's not dead.'

'You want I should shoot him?' It was the unmistakable voice of Teramo.

'Certainly not – not on my property, at all events. Will he recover, Hank?'

'I doubt it. He's pretty badly mauled about. If he gets no treatment, shock will do for him. Mr Teramo's right, though. Put him out of his misery and get rid of the carcase.'

'Open the door and let our friends go,' Lord Sangobeg said. 'No need for them to know what we decide to do. I'm sorry about this, gentlemen, but rest assured everything will be tidied up as efficiently as usual.'

When the visitors had gone, the two men from the Transit came in and looked at the dogs. 'What do we do with these, my lord?' one of them asked.

'The dogs don't matter. They can be buried up here. Just make sure they're buried good and deep. Pity we've no longer got the quarantine kennel's incinerator, but it can't be helped. Get them out quickly. We've more important things to attend to here.'

The men got the bloodsoaked carcases out of the building without further delay while the other three men, Hank, Teramo and Sangobeg, stood round Linus's inert body.

'Damn that Jones-Drybeck woman,' Sangobeg said. 'This is the body we need to get rid of.' He looked at Linus with distaste. 'I didn't expect to have to deal with such unpleasant details.'

'You should have thought of it before,' Hank said bluntly. 'You insisted on setting up this match knowing full well we didn't have the incinerator. What did you expect to do with the corpse?'

'It never crossed my mind he'd dispose of the dogs,' Sangobeg protested. 'I thought they'd be glad to solve the problem for us.'

'I never took you for a fool before,' Hank said scornfully. 'It would take a big cat to get rid of bones this size.'

The ensuing silence was suddenly broken by Lord Sangobeg. 'That's it! Big cats!' he exclaimed.

'You have some?' Teramo asked.

'No, but I know where there are some. Hank, you say he won't last long? Presumably if he's left in the cold that will hasten the inevitable?'

'I reckon so. Shock followed by exposure – not to mention infected wounds – that's a combination you don't have to be a doctor to guess is guaranteed fatal.'

'Right. What we've got to avoid is anything to link him with us and if we can prevent it looking as if he's been killed by human hand, so much the better. When the body's found, it will look as if it's been mauled by some animal for the very good reason that it has been. There's a little zoo not far from here. We take him there. Leave him in some woods. When he's found, they'll think something escaped. Of course, it will start a scare like the Surrey puma but that's all to the good, don't you think?'

'I think it's the biggest damnfool idea I've ever heard,' Teramo said. 'Someone told me you were crazy. Now I believe them.'

'Hang on,' Hank interrupted. 'It's not so crazy. Not big cats, though: forensic would soon identify the wounds as being caused by a dog. We take him, the pickaxe handle and two of the dogs. We leave them well away from here in woodland where, with any luck, they won't be found for a long, long time. If they are, well, he was attacked by dogs – no one will admit to owning them, so that's all right – he killed them but was so badly injured he didn't make it himself. The teeth will fit, the pickaxe handle will fit. No problem.'

'It might work,' Teramo said grudgingly.

'It's brilliant,' Lord Sangobeg corrected him.

'Mr Teramo's right,' Hank said. 'It may work and it may not. I can't see we've much choice. We can't stage another contest like that until we've got an incinerator again, no matter how tempting the circumstances – and first we lie low and make sure we're safely out of this one. OK?'

Chapter Twelve

White. Everything was white. Snow? No. Snow didn't form itself into neat right-angled corners. What did? Ceilings did, that's what. Ceilings and walls. Rooms. Indoors, then.

Linus's eyelids flickered again. White walls were not a good background for paintings. It wasn't home. A face loomed over him. A familiar face. Pity he couldn't recall the name.

'Dad? Dad, are you awake?'

He knew the voice, too. A bell rang somewhere. Footsteps in a hurry.

'He's come to, Nurse. I think he's conscious,' the voice said. Sean, that's who it was. Sean. What was his son doing in hospital? It must be hospital. He'd said 'nurse'. Gail was dead. Sean should have gone home. Sean's face disappeared and another one took its place. A girl. Young and therefore pretty.

'You're in hospital, Mr Rintoul.' She spoke slowly, enunciating carefully, the way some people spoke to foreigners. 'You're going to be all right. Can you hear me, Mr Rintoul? They got you here in time.'

A third voice murmured something he couldn't make out. The nurse's answer was clear enough.

'Not till the doctor's seen him, Constable. He's on his way. You're just going to have to wait.'

During the doctor's visit, Linus realized that moving hurt. It hurt a lot. He also realized that he was attached to assorted tubes. Maybe that was what hurt. He tried to smile but one side of his face wouldn't move.

'I wouldn't try to do that yet awhile,' the doctor said. 'The stitches won't let you smile comfortably for some time. Take it easy.'

When the doctor had gone, the nurse and Sean returned. 'There's a policeman to see you,' the nurse said. 'He won't stay long. Doctor's orders. You don't have to speak to him but it would help if you do. OK?'

She didn't wait for any answer but she didn't leave while the man was there. He didn't look much older than Sean. Young, pink-faced, eager. 'We need to know what happened, Mr Rintoul,' he said. 'We know you were attacked by dogs but the hospital tells us there are signs you had been tied up. Can you give us a name?'

Linus nodded imperceptibly and opened his mouth. He heard his voice come out loud and clear. It was odd that his throat hurt so much. 'Sangobeg,' he said.

The young constable heard only a rasping whisper. 'Saint what?' he asked.

Linus repeated it, louder. 'Sangobeg.'

'Saint Gilbert?' He looked across at Sean. 'What's that when it's at home?'

Sean shook his head. Linus closed his eyes. That was enough. It was more of a strain than he'd thought, talking.

'I'm sorry,' he heard the nurse say. 'He needs to sleep. You'll just have to come back later.'

Linus had no idea how long he slept. He only knew he felt marginally better next time he woke up. It still hurt to move his head but it wasn't so stiff and there didn't seem to be all those tubes now. Inspector Lacock had replaced Sean at his bedside.

'How're you feeling?'

Linus considered the question. Better, but not good. 'Bloody,' he whispered.

'Never mind. If the gamekeeper's dog hadn't found you, you'd be dead by now.'

Linus frowned. It hurt less than smiling, he discovered. 'Gamekeeper? Whose?'

'Marlborough's. You were on the Blenheim estate. Who's this Saint Gilbert you told my constable about?'

Linus shook his head. 'Don't know,' he said.

Inspector Lacock was not happy. The doctors had said Rintoul might not be able to think straight for a time. It looked as if they had been right. 'I'd better fill you in, Rintoul. You were found in some woods on the Blenheim estate. There were two dead dogs there. Nasty-looking brutes. One of our dog-handlers says they look like a cross between Rottweilers and Dobermans. Nasty combination. Also a pickaxe handle. Your wounds are commensurate with being attacked by the dogs and theirs tie in with the pickaxe handle. That leads one to suppose they sprang at you for whatever reason; that you beat them off but were too badly wounded to get help. Shock and exposure nearly killed you. Fortunately for you, one of His Grace's Labradors found you. Simple enough story – apart from one or two details. First, your wrists show rope burns. Not nasty ones, but rope burns for all that. Secondly, why should anyone go for a walk in the woods carrying a pickaxe handle? Thirdly, footprints. There were three sets of them round where you were found. One set belonged to the gamekeeper. None of them were yours. There you must have been, flailing about with that confounded handle, in a state of levitation. Unless it all happened somewhere else and you were brought there.'

Linus nodded. Lacock recorded that fact in his notebook.

'Now we get to the tricky bit. This is what my constable was trying to establish. We need a name. If you can put a name to whoever was responsible, we'll pull him in. We'll get him anyway but a name would cut down the work no end. Do you know who it was, Rintoul?'

Linus thought about it and discovered that thinking was almost as painful as moving. He forced himself to make the effort. He would tell Lacock and then Lacock would deal with Sangobeg. Always assuming Lacock was straight. Whether he could make anything stick, especially where a man of Sangobeg's wealth and influence was concerned, was something else. Or he could *not* tell Lacock. Then it wouldn't matter whether Lacock was straight. Sangobeg would carry on as if nothing had happened until he, Linus, was in a position to bring him to book himself. Yes, that was it. He wanted the satisfaction of dealing with it himself.

Inspector Lacock repeated his question.

Linus nodded. 'Teramo. Frank Teramo,' he said. He couldn't hope to deal with him as well. Besides, it was Sangobeg he owed.

'The Mafia man?' Lacock asked.

Linus nodded again.

'He's left the country. Doubt if we could extradite him anyway but at least we can make sure he doesn't come back next time he wants to. Is that all? No one else?'

Linus turned his head away. He didn't want to tell a direct lie, not to the police. He wasn't brought up that way. The nurse interrupted the Inspector's next question.

'I'm sorry, Inspector. I do realize this is important but so is Mr Rintoul's sleep. You've kept him awake quite long enough.'

Sean came to see his father next day and gave him a bottle of whisky from Trevarrick. 'He says he knows you can't drink it yet but perhaps the expectation will spur your recovery.'

Linus managed a twisted, painful grin. 'He doesn't like the way the work's piling up, that's all,' he said. He felt easier today. He still ached but it was more manageable.

He dozed again after Sean had gone. He could see the head of a young policeman outside his door and supposed he was waiting for him to be well enough to give a fuller account of recent events. Then, since Teramo was gone, they would be able to close the case. He tried to marshal the amended sequence of events into some sort of order in his mind. He failed, but the effort sent him soundly to sleep.

When he awoke, the young policeman had gone. Linus frowned. That must mean Lacock believed his statement that Teramo's was the only name he could give him. If Teramo was no longer in Britain and out of reach of the British authorities, there couldn't be any rush to get his statement. That must surely exonerate Lacock from any involvement because anyone involved would know there were other big names. Or was Lacock being remarkably devious? If he was, Linus's mind was in no condition to unravel the complexities. He slept again.

When he was not asleep, Linus laid his own plans with a fair amount of deviousness on his own part. He learnt that the clothes he had been wearing when he was found had been destroyed.

'Your son told us to go ahead,' the nurse told him. 'You wouldn't have had any use for them, not the state they were in – not unless you wanted to go to a fancy dress party as a scarecrow.'

Sean could see no reason why his father was so insistent on a new set of clothes being brought in, especially since it would be some days before the hospital would be prepared to release him but, since their absence seemed to agitate him, the Sister recommended that he do so.

He could walk unaided to the lavatory now, and to the shower, but getting into and out of a bath without assistance was still excruciatingly difficult. There were no mirrors and the nurse refused to bring him one.

'Wait till the stitches are out,' she told him. 'The bruising will be less and you'll be almost back to normal.'

'Except for the scars,' he suggested. His fingers told him they were extensive.

'Well, yes, but they probably feel a lot worse than they look.'

'Then bring me a glass.'

But she didn't.

Linus knew what he was going to do. Sean had brought him some money. Not much, but enough. It couldn't be much because the only reason he could give for needing it at all was to enable him to buy a paper each day. He reckoned it would get him to Sangobeg Hall. Getting back was something he'd work out later. He'd slip out of the hospital during the mid-morning lull, when the nurses would be enjoying a well-earned cup of coffee. However much it hurt, he would have to walk out of the hospital as if he were perfectly fit – as if he were a visitor, not a patient. That way he ought to escape challenge.

He had managed to get into everything but his jacket when the door of his individual ward – they had not yet suggested he might like to go into the main ward, though he no longer needed the sort of treatment that made a single ward necessary – opened. Linus heard it and cursed. When the nurse saw him there was bound to be a scene and, although he had a perfect right to discharge himself, he would have preferred to be able to do so without a fuss. The door of the small wardrobe hid both himself and the top half of the bed from anyone until they were well inside the room. The concealment could last only a matter of seconds, but those seconds were sufficient for the door of the room to be closed behind the new arrival. Linus heard it close before he removed his jacket from its hanger and shut the wardrobe.

Clarissa Pensilva was at least as surprised as Linus Rintoul.

Linus frowned. The gladiatorial combat and its consequences had pushed the score he had to settle with Clarissa out of his mind, perhaps because it wasn't such a big one, anyway. She'd made a fool of him, a complete fool, but he wasn't the first man who would have to admit to that and he wouldn't be the last. He felt his heart beating abnormally fast and he knew that its driving force was fear, not desire.

'What are you doing here?' he asked, knowing that the inevitability of an untruthful answer rendered the question futile as well as trite.

'I didn't expect to see you up and about,' she said, fumbling in her handbag.

'I don't suppose you did,' he said, and reminded himself that the woman with whom he was exchanging these civilized banalities had murdered Henry Lewdown. He backed away and was brought up short by the edge of his bed.

'You look a sight,' she went on.

'Hardly surprising,' Linus commented. She was still trying to find something in her handbag and his instinct was to keep one eye on that fumbling hand. A gun was the most likely weapon but surely she would have found a gun by now? Guns, even small ones, were substantial objects, especially in relation to a woman's handbag.

His stomach turned over when she withdrew, not a gun, but a pencil-slim hypodermic. 1 ml, his professional eye noted automatically. Not very much. Must be powerful stuff.

'What is it?' he asked.

'Poetic justice, I suppose,' she said, smiling. 'Only you were supposed to be asleep.'

'I'm sorry to be disobliging.' He reckoned his best bet was to get out of the door. She would hardly risk drawing attention to herself by chasing him down the corridor, waving a syringe. He wasn't sure that he had the strength to overcome her.

She moved between him and the door. Some involuntary movement must have given his intention away. 'No, you don't,' she said. 'I came here with a job to do and I've every intention of doing it.'

'What kind of poetic justice?' Linus asked, his eye fixed on that little plastic cylinder.

She laughed. 'Immobilon. Appropriate, don't you think?'

'Dangerous stuff. I hope you've got the antidote. An

accident could be nasty.' The drug was an anaesthetic. At least one vet had used it to kill himself. Death took – how long? One minute? One minute to inject the antidote. No vet prepared a syringe of Immobilon without filling another with Narcan and having it handy, just in case. If an animal moved unexpectedly, an accident was all too easy.

'There's not going to be an accident,' she told him, 'and I've not gone to all this trouble in order to give you any antidote.'

She moved towards him and the space between the bed and the wall was too small for him to hope to get past her. If he'd been fitter he could have jumped over the bed. Maybe. It would be beyond him now. His only chance was to force it out of her hand. That wouldn't normally have been too difficult, but his muscles no longer worked as well as they should. Several strips of surgical embroidery had seen to that. Still, there wasn't much choice. He moved towards her.

He watched the uncovered needle. If she'd been carrying it like that in her bag, she had run a more serious risk than she probably knew, fumbling for it like that. If this was the sort used for large animals, he rather thought one drop was all it would take to kill a person. It didn't much matter where it went in, either.

Linus kept his eye on that needle and slipped his jacket on. The cloth would afford a little extra protection. Not much but enough to make it worth the agony of getting the jacket on.

He hoped the action had distracted her – a man facing death did not usually pause to finish dressing, he was sure. He winced as his second arm went into the sleeve and again when he shrugged it over his shoulders. Then he lunged towards her and grabbed her wrist. His fingers fastened round it but they lacked their normal strength. He had the slight advantage of surprise and he must use it now, quickly, before she robbed him of it.

He attempted to flick the hand that held the syringe in the hope that that would make her drop it but Clarissa had guessed his intent and countered by pushing against his hold so that the steel tip headed dangerously close to his arm. He dared not let go. If he did, she would be free to inject it at random, yet already he could feel his strength fading.

He exerted what counter-pressure he could and suddenly realized that, in the effort to get the needle ever closer to his arm, Clarissa was very slightly off-balance. In desperation, he summoned both speed and strength. He side-stepped and at the same time twisted her wrist round, expecting her grip to loosen and the syringe to clatter to the floor.

Instead, she stumbled and overbalanced forwards. Her arm twisted out of Linus's grasp and she fell on it, collapsing almost instantly in an untidy heap by the bed. She had not let go of the syringe.

Appalled, Linus bent over her and raised her, hoping to find it lying harmlessly beneath her. It wasn't. It had penetrated the hollow of her shoulder and, worse, the pressure of her fall had forced the plunger in.

He removed it and let the body slump. Then he snatched her handbag and emptied in on the bed. Surely she hadn't been foolish enough to come out without the antidote? But there was no phial and no other syringe. She had been that confident – or someone had failed to point out the risks. Linus sighed with exasperation. Now he would have to make statements to the police and he could ill afford the time, especially now that he knew they were not going to let him get on with his life. He glanced down at Clarissa. There was nothing anyone could do for her now. At least it had been a far tidier and less painful death than her employers had set up for him in that macabre arena.

His hand closed on something beside him on the bed. He glanced down. Car keys. Of course! She must have driven here. He glanced at the rest of her handbag's contents. A wallet. He opened it. Credit cards. A chequebook. Cash. With only a moment's hesitation, Linus took the cash. He didn't bother to count it but estimated there must be something like a hundred pounds there. Very handy. He'd pay it back to the estate later, he thought punctiliously. All he had to do now was to get out of here quickly and find her car. He'd never seen her car but the key-fob was for a BMW. That should cut the odds down a bit.

He slipped the keys into his pocket and opened the door. No one about. Good. Getting out of this ward was going to be the biggest problem. His luck held. Everyone was taking a well-deserved break. He went through the double doors at the end and let his breath out. The fingers of both hands were firmly crossed, he noticed. He uncrossed them and smiled to himself. Fool!

He thought rapidly as he made his way as fast as he could without attracting undue attention towards the main exit. He hadn't seen Clarissa's car but the BMW fob rang a bell. Someone, somewhere, had referred to it. Then he remembered. The Dolphin. The receptionist had said something. Yes, that was it. 'A black BMW – very elegant.' That was it.

What's more, by an exceptional stroke of luck, it was parked right by the entrance. Obviously Clarissa had felt the double yellow lines were a risk worth taking in the interests of a quick getaway. Linus blessed her forethought and wasted no time heading out of the car park and the city and south towards the sea.

Linus knew that the house where he had been kept must be Sangobeg Hall and he knew it must be in Sussex but he had only the vaguest idea whereabouts in that county to start looking and when he summarized what he knew, it boiled down to 'west of Brighton', a location which was somewhat less than precise. He knew, too, that since the discovery of Clarissa's body would take place within about half an hour of her death and quite probably within a few minutes of it, it could not be long before the police started searching for her car. The absence of any keys might throw them off the track for a while but someone would be sure to have noticed the black BMW parked on the double yellow lines just outside the hospital's main entrance. The search would start in the Thames Valley area but it could only be a matter of hours before it was extended nationwide. He had to find Sangobeg quickly. Then he would return and face the music which, he thought dispassionately, was likely to be cacophonic.

The car was a joy to drive despite the fact that every move he made, however slight, was pure agony. His mind was working steadily as he drove, trying to recall places he had passed through with Ralph. It was a pity his present journey had started from Oxford. Had he been able to set out from London, there would have been a greater likelihood of passing memory-jogging signposts. There was a book of road maps in the glove compartment and under it, interestingly, an OS map. Not something one necessarily expected to find in a car. He fished it out and when he saw the area it covered, he pulled over into the first lay-by he came to and spread it out. His hopes rose when he saw that something had been circled in ballpoint. They sank again when he saw it had nothing to do with Sangobeg Hall. The object ringed was Notcar Folly. No help to Linus at all. He didn't give up at once, though: an OS map, unlike a road map, would certainly identify a single house if it was as important as the one he sought. Maybe he should take some precious time to search the map grid by grid and just hope the police were not yet hunting for Clarissa's car.

When his eye happened to fall once more on the encircled area, he noticed that the road – no, lane – to Notcar Folly was long, straight and uphill. Just like the track to that weird tower. What's more, Notcar Folly was a ruin, too. He changed his technique. A series of concentric circles centred on the Folly should give him Sangobeg Hall. It hadn't been all that far, as well as he could recall.

It wasn't. It wouldn't have surprised him at all to learn that the Folly stood on Sangobeg's estate, if not in the immediate vicinity of the Hall. He put the map away and the car into gear.

Linus recognized the gates when he reached them. He drove up the long drive and pulled in under the vast porte-cochère with an irrelevant feeling of satisfaction. Part of him – the vulgar part, he admitted ruefully – had always wanted to arrive in a car like this at just such an entrance. He slipped the keys into his pocket. Who knows? Maybe he'd need the car again. He rang the bell.

He thought afterwards that that was an incongruously civilized thing to do and very probably ill-advised. Unfortunately, it was done and the door opened almost immediately, in time for him to have realized his folly but not to have vanished round the corner. He wasn't at all sure which of the two of them was the more surprised at seeing the other, for the man who faced him was the smaller of his two guards, the one who had stepped so easily into the role of gentleman's gentleman. It looked as if that was exactly what he was – most of the time.

'Mr Rintoul! Not a visitor we were expecting! You don't look at all well, sir, if you'll forgive me mentioning it.'

'Not at all,' Linus said politely. 'I imagine I look much as I feel. Is Lord Sangobeg at home?'

'Well, he is and he isn't, as it were,' the man said apologetically. 'That's to say he's not actually in the house or grounds just now. He went over to the old folly. Thinking of doing it up as a summerhouse, or something. You'll know the place, of course.'

'It rings certain bells,' Linus said grimly. 'Would that be the place the map calls Notcar Folly?'

'It would, sir. Would you like me to direct you by the shortest route?'

'Why should you do that?' Linus asked suspiciously.

'I'm a practical man, sir. I observe that you are not in the best of moods and that you have arrived in what looks suspiciously like Miss Calshot's car, from which I deduce that Miss Calshot is in no position to be needing it herself.

I happen to know that his lordship is alone at the folly, a situation ideally suited to the settling of old scores. If he wins, I shall know nothing of your presence in Sussex. If he doesn't, I am anxious that there shall be no hard feelings between us.'

'You were only doing your job,' Linus said with heavy irony.

The man beamed. 'Precisely, sir. Lord Sangobeg does pay exceedingly well, you know, even though he has some funny little ways.'

'Or quite possibly because of them,' Linus remarked. He looked at the man thoughtfully. Oddly enough, he was inclined to believe him. 'Very well,' he said. 'If no one tips his lordship off and if I come out on top, I shall have no idea of the identity of my guards. Will that suit you?'

'Admirably, sir.'

Linus followed the man's instructions implicitly and soon found himself driving up that long, straight track. In daylight he realized that anyone on top of the tower would have views across the downs to the sea. As a summerhouse, it would be superb. He also realized that anyone in the tower would see the car coming up the track. That didn't much matter, he decided. It was Clarissa's car – Mary Calshot's, he corrected – so it didn't matter if Sangobeg recognized it. He would probably assume she was returning to report on the success of her mission. At this angle, no one at the folly would be able to see that a man was driving.

Trees and bushy shrubs surrounded the building, much as he remembered. Only where the track passed it was the boundary clear. Linus, knowing his approach must have been observed, pulled up just past this clear section. By doing so, he eliminated any sense of stealth which might serve to warn Lord Sangobeg that everything was not entirely normal. At the same time, it meant he had some cover during those vulnerable moments when he got out of the car.

Getting out of the car was not easy. His aching muscles

had settled themselves into their new shape while he drove and now they were being asked to unshape themselves again. They didn't like it. He would have liked to walk upright and with dignity, to prove himself undamaged – apart from a few external marks – by recent events. He was obliged to limp, and to hunch over until his back had sorted itself out.

He saw no one, but that meant nothing. As he approached the door he was irresistibly reminded of a poem from his childhood. The tower wasn't moonlit and he had no horse but he had to fight the urge to call out, 'Is there anybody there?'

Instead, he lifted the latch and the door swung open on oiled hinges. He left it open. With blocked-up windows and a roof, the first two floors were in darkness. He had forgotten they would be and that error of calculation disconcerted him. He heard a movement above. Then sunlight flooded down the spiral staircase. There must be a trapdoor leading above the mezzanine floor. He heard steps as if to confirm this and then a pale moon of a face leant over as it had done on a previous occasion, before the contest started.

'I think it would be fair to say that you are about the last visitor I was expecting,' Lord Sangobeg said. 'My plans appear to have gone somewhat awry.'

'Somewhat,' Linus agreed.

'And Miss Calshot? I see you are driving her car.'

'I'm afraid Miss Calshot had a slight accident. Someone omitted to explain to her the importance of Narcan to the veterinary profession.'

'How did you find this place? My house, I could understand. Not the folly.'

Linus remembered his deal with the gentleman's gentleman. 'Miss Calshot left a map in the car on which this was clearly marked. I thought I'd like to see over it in daylight before tackling you. Your presence is a useful bonus.'

'Then you'd better come up. I see no reason why we shouldn't discuss this little awkwardness like civilized

210

people, and I found you a man of taste and discrimination. Your opinion of the potential of this building in relation to its views will be one I value.'

And then what? Linus thought. Teramo would have shot him. Hank would beat him up and then toss him from the top. He knew what Clarissa could do. None of that was quite Sangobeg's style. He might order others to do it. He wouldn't do it himself. Not unless pushed, and if it came to that, Sangobeg had the advantage of being fit and fresh. Linus was horribly aware that he was neither.

Despite his estimate of Sangobeg's fastidiousness, Linus guessed he must have something in mind for his unexpected visitor and he was in two minds whether he wanted to find out what it was. There was also the question of just what Linus intended to do by way of revenge and he suddenly realized that his plans in that respect were so vague as to be unworthy of the name. He was a great deal less capable of physical violence than Sangobeg even though he had the slight advantage that Sangobeg didn't know that Clarissa's death had been entirely accidental. Now that he was actually faced by the object of his revenge, Linus supposed he would probably do nothing stronger than forcibly escort Lord Sangobeg to the local police station. It seemed a pathetically inadequate sort of revenge and he couldn't quite see how it was to be accomplished, but nor could he see any alternative. In the meantime, conversation across the storeys was physically difficult so he might as well accept the invitation.

'Stand well back,' he called out. 'I've no wish to be kicked down the staircase.'

Sangobeg raised both arms in a gesture of mock-surrender. 'You do me an injustice, Mr Rintoul. I'll move to the far end. You'll be safe enough.'

Linus went over to the stair-tower, his limp less pronounced now that his body was getting used to all this activity. He came safely out on to the mezzanine floor and faced Lord Sangobeg along the balcony.

'The real view begins on the next floor,' Sangobeg told him. 'Do you want to go first or shall I?'

That was a tricky one, Linus thought, his suspicions instantly aroused by any suggestion from his host. If he went first, he risked Sangobeg's operating some device which could isolate him on the tower. If Sangobeg went first, he could beat Linus's head with a brick as it emerged from the narrow shaft. This might not be Sangobeg's style but it was marginally the more likely of the two eventualities: Linus could think of no reason why the stairs should have been constructed in the first place with a device for marooning someone at the top. He went first and Sangobeg followed him. On the next level, scaffolding, planks and a guard rail was all there was inside the tower, and Sangobeg exhorted him to go on up to the top.

'There's the width of the tower and a low parapet up there,' he called out. 'We can look over the countryside and back down into the folly. Much the best place. How's your head for heights?'

'Fine,' Linus called back. He had the uneasy recollection that characters on television who climbed *up* tall edifices invariably got into difficulties. They also, he reminded himself unconvincingly, got out of their difficulties by the end of the programme.

The view was spectacular. As he had suspected, it reached across the edge of the downs to the sea while in all the other directions it looked out over woods and pastures, farms and hamlets. A room up here, circular and equipped with a telescope, now that was something worthy of consideration. He said as much to Sangobeg.

'My idea precisely,' that gentleman beamed. 'I knew we'd see eye to eye over that. A living-room up here and the master bedroom on the floor beneath, I thought. Bathrooms, kitchen, dining-room – they don't need the views. They can go downstairs. The corner towers are my uncertainty. Take the ground floor. If the central area were for dining, one could have a kitchen in one tower, a utility room in another and the third would be the hall. What do you think?'

Linus nodded. 'That would be one solution,' he agreed. 'You've decided to abandon its gladiatorial use, I take it?'

Sangobeg grimaced. 'It seems wisest. I think that sport may have to be transferred abroad for the time being. To somewhere less squeamish where the authorities are more persuadable. Fortunately, it's a rich man's sport and the people who want to watch are well able to travel for the purpose.'

'It's not as widespread as the dog-fighting?' Linus asked.

'Goodness me, no! Far more select! We have to be *very* sure of our spectators. Attendance is by invitation only, you know. We really do have to be most awfully careful.'

'I can imagine,' Linus said drily. 'It must help to have the occasional policeman on your side.' It was a shot in the dark but if Sangobeg was in one of his expansive moods, it might be productive.

'A policeman? Oh, you're thinking of Denbigh. He's only of use where our drugs operation is concerned. He knows nothing about this.'

So Lacock was straight. Linus was glad. He said, 'Presumably he must know about the dog-fighting, then?'

'That I couldn't say, though I imagine he may well have put two and two together. He's no fool, after all. He knows his interests are best served by the development of a blind eye.' He looked speculatively at Linus. 'Sergeant Denbigh should be a relatively wealthy man,' he went on.

'Should be?'

Sangobeg shrugged. 'He's one of these people who spends money like water – and not on the sort of thing you or I would spend it on. I don't imagine you set much store by fast cars, for example.'

Linus conceded that that was true enough.

'Exactly. Let me guess what you'd do with a sizeable sum – not a huge one, but well into four figures, shall we say, and liable to replenishment from time to time. I think you'd buy the occasional painting, perhaps branch into sculpture. No one would notice – or think anything of it if they did – because they know you always have spent your money like that and because they really haven't the slightest idea what any given painting might cost. Am I right?'

Linus thought about it. 'I suppose you are,' he said, 'but since I'm not in that happy position, I can see little point in thinking about it.'

'Come, come, Mr Rintoul. You're not that obtuse. Here we are, two men with similarly civilized tastes and in need of the wherewithal to indulge them.'

'I don't regard dog-fighting as civilized and I certainly don't regard what took place here in that light,' Linus said angrily.

'So our tastes diverge in some respects,' Lord Sangobeg said, unperturbed. 'Do I have to spell it out?'

He didn't, but Linus was determined to make him, knowing that Sangobeg would prefer to convey such nastinesses as bribery by innuendo and what he would doubtless describe as 'mutual understanding'.

'I'm afraid you do,' Linus said. 'You seem to have overestimated my acuity.'

'Very well. In return for your silence about what happened to you (I'm sure the trauma could have caused amnesia, aren't you?) and my involvement with anything relating to Pit Bull Terriers, I will ensure that an arrangement such as we have been considering comes into effect. Ten thousand forthwith would be reasonable, don't you think? To compensate for your pain and suffering, you understand. Subsequent amounts would be rather smaller. One would not wish to alert your bank manager into asking questions. These sums would arrive irregularly and could be passed off as your winnings. Do you play the ponies, Mr Rintoul? No, I was afraid not. Never mind. You'll be able to think of something.'

'The newspapers would have a field day with a story of a politician who operates on a basis of bribery,' Linus pointed out.

'Indeed they would, but the line between bribery and

214

payment for services rendered is a very fine one. Would you prefer me to retain your services as a veterinary surgeon?'

'I thought you had one in James Erbistock?'

Lord Sangobeg snorted. 'He's going to be unavailable for several years, I fancy, and one would wish to avoid any overt association with him when he comes out. A replacement will be needed, sooner or later, and a man of your integrity would be infinitely preferable to that spine-less young man.'

Linus felt himself go very still. He found it difficult to keep his voice steady. 'You intend to continue smuggling drugs inside fighting dogs?'

Sangobeg looked surprised. 'Of course! Those kennels belong to me. Oh, my name doesn't appear on the deeds, but if you knew how to dig far enough back and far enough down, you'd find me. As an investment, it's just about paid for itself. I want to see it go well into profit before I consider pulling out.'

'The Ministry intends to withdraw the licence and close it down.'

'I know, but they can be persuaded to change their minds. Especially if one of their own vets takes it over.'

'And you think I'll overcome my detestation of what goes on there for the sort of money we're talking about?'

'You'd be a fool not to.'

Pure anger, white and searing, swept over Linus, drowning the pain of his aching body and his awareness of where he was. He could see only two things. In his mind, Ishmael's trusting brown eyes; in front of him the smug smirk on Sangobeg's face. It was a smirk that needed to be destroyed. His fist lashed out and caught Sangobeg on the chin, knocking his head sideways and temporarily unbalancing him.

He staggered and recovered. Linus saw the smirk had vanished, to be replaced first by a look of understandable surprise and then by one, not of anger, but of vicious cunning. It was, he realized suddenly, Sangobeg's true face.

For the first time, it occurred to Linus that the top of a high tower on a ledge three feet wide with a sheer drop inwards and only an eighteen-inch high parapet between you and the drop outwards was not the ideal spot to start a fight. Not unless you could be sure of winning. He had no time for further contemplation of his stupidity.

Sangobeg's fist struck out towards his jaw. Linus twisted his top half sideways and the blow, its force diminished, made contact with his shoulder. He smashed back a blow to his opponent's chest and heard the grunt as the air was forced out. If I fall inwards, Linus thought suddenly, the plywood roof over the arena will break my fall.

Sangobeg's fists were no longer clenched. He'll grab me and get me off-balance, Linus knew. He stepped backwards carefully. If he could find the staircase, maybe he could lure the other man down. Sangobeg followed him, taking his apparent retreat as an advantage to be pressed home. He came fast enough to be able to make a lunge at Linus's arm. He grabbed it and twisted and Linus felt himself scream as the stitches holding it together under his sleeve were torn apart.

But the lunge had left Sangobeg momentarily unbalanced and when the fist on the end of Linus's other arm smashed into his diaphragm he both doubled over and turned. His foot struck the parapet, forcing him across it and when his arms, seeking instinctively to redress his balance, flung themselves in the air, that act shifted his centre of gravity and Linus, aghast, saw him toppling over.

It could have been only a split second yet it happened excruciatingly slowly, like an action reply on television or a Peckinpah movie. Linus's reaction was excruciatingly slow, too. He reached across to grab the man's ankle. Caught it – and felt it slip through his grasp with the impetus of the fall.

There was a long silence. A dull thud. The speed of life returned to normal.

Linus sank to his knees and clutched weakly at the parapet, hardly daring to look over. From this height there was no detectable sign of movement from the body below, its limbs at unnatural angles. Linus dared not stand up. He doubted he had the strength to, anyway. He crawled to the steps and then crawled backwards down them, like a child who can't trust his legs. I must get him an ambulance, he found himself thinking. How far will it be to a phone?

When he reached the bottom and stumbled out, he knew there was no great rush. No one in that position with that much blood could possibly be alive. All the same, he went over to it. He must be quite sure. The pulse in the neck would be the best place. One glance at Sangobeg's head told him there could be no pulse. A wave of nausea swept over him and he turned to the bushes and vomited. Then, without looking round, he made his way painfully back to Clarissa's car.

Linus woke up and lay still for a long time, flat on his back, staring up at the white ceiling. He'd been back at the John Radcliffe for some days now – well, two, or maybe three. His memory of the days immediately before that was hazy. He'd managed to drive somewhere – a pub, though he couldn't remember what it was called. They'd taken one look at him and sent for the police – and an ambulance. After that it had been questions. Lots of them, one after another and then another questioning face going through it all again. They were interested – intrigued, even – with his story but when it implicated another policeman, even one from another force, they became distinctly hostile. Lacock had sorted that out. It seemed there had been one or two unspoken questions in people's minds about Denbigh for some time. It was Lacock who got him moved back to Oxford with the hardly sympathetic comment that he'd not travel with him because he wasn't too keen on the limited life expectancy of those who associated with Mr Rintoul. It gave, he said, a whole new interpretation of the phrase 'accident prone'.

The doctors had looked disapprovingly at his arm and admonished him for his foolishness in the patronizing way some people admonish small children. Then they sewed it up again. The nurses at the JR had been a great deal more forthright and earthy about it. Linus preferred the nurses' technique.

The door of the individual ward opened and one of them came in, kidney dish in hand. Linus remembered. The stitches that hadn't had to be re-done were due to come out today.

'Ready to lose the embroidery?' she asked.

'All of it?'

'Afraid it will hurt?' she said sympathetically. 'It shouldn't. All the same, I'm only going to do your face today: it should help the bruising go down more quickly. We'll do the rest of you – the bits that are ready – tomorrow.'

Linus nerved himself against expected pain and she chided him. 'Come on, Mr Rintoul. You're a vet. Surely you know stitches can come out without hurting?'

'I know it right enough, but you don't have to be as careful as a vet.'

'That's an insult,' she said indignantly. 'I'd like to hear you justify it.'

'You would? Tell me this: how many of your patients are likely to turn round and bite you?'

She laughed. 'You'd be surprised. Still, it's a good sign when a patient can make jokes about it.'

'Dog bites are no joke,' Linus said with feeling.

Despite her contention that it wouldn't hurt, she kept his attention on other matters, asking him about his visitors. 'There was another vet who came,' she said. 'He told me he's looking after your dog. What sort of dog is it?'

Linus told her and she admitted the name of the breed meant nothing to her. 'What's his name?' she went on, taking out the last stitch as she spoke.

'Ishmael,' Linus said.

She picked up a mirror. 'Ishmael? Funny name for a dog. There you are, Mr Rintoul. All gone.'

It was the first time he had seen himself since before

that contest and he studied his reflection with a mixture of dismay and distaste. 'Ishmael was an outcast. In a sense, that's what all Pit Bulls are.' He turned his head from side to side, studying the angry red line of the various joins in his skin, each bordered with two neat rows of regular dots where the stitches had been. 'He'll be in good company, won't he?' he said bitterly.

'You can grow your beard again,' she said helpfully. 'You could make it a bigger one next time. The other was more distinguished, I suppose, but it didn't cover up as much.'

'Nothing will cover up all this.'

'It won't always be so livid. You should know that.'

'But it will always be there. Maybe it's just as well I've got the dog. At least he'll be company.'

The nurse's heart went out to him. The surgeon had done what he could but there was no denying the dogs had made a pretty good mess of what had been a very pleasant face. Still, it was no part of her job to encourage patients into a deep melancholia.

'My, we are feeling sorry for ourselves, aren't we?' she said briskly. 'I'll have you know, Mr Rintoul, that those scars give you a distinctly raffish look – and there are a lot of women who are irresistibly drawn to raffish-looking men.'

Linus laughed in spite of himself. 'Good try, Nurse, but I'll not hold my breath waiting for one to come along.'

'You won't have to,' she replied and planted an unprofessional kiss firmly on his scars. 'I'd make a dead set at you myself, only my husband wouldn't like it,' and she whisked herself and her kidney dish of dead stitches out of the room before he had time to think of a reply.

Linus snorted disbelievingly and once more traced the course of the livid scars with the aid of the mirror. Perhaps when they faded, 'raffish' wouldn't be so far off the mark. Perhaps there were women who wouldn't mind. Perhaps . . .

COLLINS CRIME

Funnelweb

Charles West

A bizarre and brutal killing in lonely Australian bush country
. . . a body, hidden for seven years, uncovered by an
accidental rock-fall . . . and 600 miles away, in a popular
beach resort, a young prostitute found dead from a drugs
overdose.

No one even suspects there is any link between these
incidents – until film actor Tom Grant stumbles across the
thread that binds them together in a vicious web of deceit,
trickery and murder.

What Tom does *not* discover until too late is that guarding
the secrets of this web of crime is a swift, deadly and
merciless killer – Funnelweb.

COLLINS CRIME

A Certain Blindness

Roy Lewis
The first Eric Ward novel

In the eyes of solicitor Eric Ward there was something odd about Arthur Egan's life and death. But Ward was a former police inspector, and trained to be suspicious.

Egan's estate comprised a large sum, to go to an heir no-one knew he had. Ward made no progress tracing the dead man's offspring, but he did discover Egan had served a term for manslaughter, and that the evidence against him may have been planted. Why had he accepted his fate so meekly?

Despite warnings that he was wasting the firm's time, Ward persisted in his investigations – which soon led to murder. And by the time he realized why, he learned his life and career were both at risk.

'A thorough, unpretentious and immensely solid piece of work with an interesting and likeable hero' *The Times Literary Supplement*

'Believes in keeping his readers on their toes with plenty of twists and surprises. He writes well, too . . .' *Daily Telegraph*

'Strongly recommended'   H.R.F. Keating

COLLINS CRIME

Death Swap

Marian Babson

To the Harper family from New England – academic Arnold, Nancy and the twins – the prospect of a summer in Rosemary Blake's house in England seemed idyllic.

It wasn't quite like that.

Miserable weather, unpalatable food, a nerve-racking day trip to Boulogne, they could just about cope with. But there was also the behaviour of English hire cars and football hooligans – both of which they could have done without.

More sinister was the fear that these two represented organized attempts to kill Arnold. A third attempt left them in no doubt. But why one earth should anyone want Arnold dead? And what was the macabre connection that seemed to exist between the Harpers and the Blakes?

'An expert practitioner of the traditional murder story' William Weaver, *Financial Times*

Fontana Paperbacks: Fiction

Fontana is a leading paperback publisher of fiction. Below are some recent titles.

- ☐ JUSTICE Ian St James £4.50
- ☐ FIRST STRIKE Douglas Terman £3.99
- ☐ NOW AND THEN, AMEN Jon Cleary £3.50
- ☐ THE SHEIKH AND THE DUSTBIN
  George MacDonald Fraser £2.95
- ☐ FLASHMAN AT THE CHARGE
  George MacDonald Fraser £3.50
- ☐ BLACK WIDOW Bart Davis £3.50
- ☐ PAPER DOLL Jim Shephard £2.95
- ☐ TRAPP AND WORLD WAR III Brian Callison £2.95
- ☐ THE LAZARUS FILE Stuart Prebble £2.95

You can buy Fontana paperbacks at your local bookshop or newsagent. Or you can order them from Fontana Paperbacks, Cash Sales Department, Box 29, Douglas, Isle of Man. Please send a cheque, postal or money order (not currency) worth the purchase price plus 22p per book for postage (maximum postage required is £3.00 for orders within the UK).

NAME (Block letters)_____

ADDRESS_____

_____